W9-AUT-463

THE SHEPHERD OF THE HILLS

Harold Bell Wright

Published by
McCORMICK-ARMSTRONG CO., INCORPORATED
Publishing Division

Distributed by
SHEPHERD OF THE HILLS HISTORICAL SOCIETY
HCR1 Box 770, Branson, MO 65616

"That all with one consent praise new-born gawds,
  Tho they are made and moulded of things past,
  And give to dust that is a little gilt
  More laud than gilt o'er-dusted."
                    Troilus and Cressida. Act 3, Sc. 3

TO FRANCES, MY WIFE

IN MEMORY OF THAT BEAUTIFUL SUMMER
IN THE OZARK HILLS, WHEN, SO OFTEN,
WE FOLLOWED THE OLD TRAIL AROUND
THE RIM OF MUTTON HOLLOW—THE TRAIL
THAT IS NOBODY KNOWS HOW OLD—AND
FROM SAMMY'S LOOKOUT WATCHED THE
DAY GO OVER THE WESTERN RIDGES

Contents

CONTENTS

THE SHEPHERD
OF THE HILLS

Introductory

The Two Trails

This, my story, is a very old story.

In the hills of life there are two trails. One lies along the higher sunlit fields where those who journey see afar, and the light lingers even when the sun is down; and one leads to the lower ground, where those who travel, as they go, look always over their shoulders with eyes of dread, and gloomy shadows gather long before the day is done.

This, my story, is the story of a man who took the trail that leads to the lower ground, and of a woman, and how she found her way to the higher sunlit fields.

In the story, it all happened in the Ozark Mountains, many miles from what we of the city call civilization. In life, it has all happened, many, many times before, in many, many places. The two trails lead afar. The story, so very old, is still in the telling.

"Preachin' Bill" who runs the ferry says, "When God looked upon th' work of his hands an' called hit good, he war sure a-lookin' at this here Ozark country. Rough? Law yes! Hit war made that a-way on purpose. Ain't nothin' to a flat country nohow. A man jes naturally wear hisself plumb out a-walkin' on a level 'thout ary downhill t' spell him. An' then look how much more there is of hit! Take forty acres o' *flat* now an' hit's jest a forty, but you take forty acres o' this here Ozark country an' God 'lmighty only knows how much 'twould be if hit war rolled out flat.

1

'Tain't no wonder 't all, God rested when he made these here hills; he jes naturally *had* t' quit, fer he done his beatenest an' war plumb gin out."

Of all the country Bill had seen, "from Ant Creek Head t' the mouth of James an' plumb to Pilot Knob," he " 'lowed the Mutton Hollow neighborhood was the prettiest."

From the Matthews place on the ridge that shuts in the valley on the north and east, there is an Old Trail leading down the mountain. Two hundred yards below the log barn, the narrow path finds a bench on the steep slope of the hillside, and, at that level, follows around the rim of the Hollow. Dipping a little at the head of the ravine east of the spring, then lifting itself over a low, heavily timbered spur of one of the higher hills, it comes out again into the open. Following a rocky ledge, the way, farther on, leads through a clump of sumac bushes, and past the deer lick in the big low gaps, then around the base of Boulder Bald, along another ledge, and out on the bare shoulder of Dewey Bald, which partly shuts in the little valley on the south.

From the big rock that Sammy Lane calls her Lookout, the Old Trail leaves the rim of Mutton Hollow and slips easily down into the lower valleys; down past the little cabin on the southern slope of the mountain where Sammy lived with her father; down to the banks of Fall Creek and to the distant river bottom. Here the threadlike path finds a wider way, leading, somehow, out of the wilderness to the great world that lies miles and miles beyond the farthest blue line of hills; the world that Sammy said "seemed mighty find to them that knowed nothin' about it."

No one seems to know how long that narrow path has lain along the mountain; but it must be very long for it is deeply worn at places.

Often, in the years of our story, swift leaping deer would cross the ridge at the low gap and follow along the benches to the spring. And sometimes a lithe-bodied panther, in the belt of timber, watched hungrily for their coming, or a huge-pawed catamount, on some overhanging rock, would lie in wait for fawn or doe. Or perhaps a gaunt timber wolf would sniff the trail, and with wild echoing howls call his comrades to the chase.

Jim Lane, young then, followed that winding way from the distant river, and from nobody knows where beyond, when he came to build his lonely hunter's shack by the spring on the southern slope of Dewey. And later, when the shack in the timber was replaced by a more substantial settler's cabin, Jim led Sammy's mother along the same old way. Then came the giant Grant Matthews with Aunt Mollie and their little family. They followed the path three miles farther and built their home where the trail climbs over the ridge.

When Grant Matthews, Jr., was eighteen, his father mortgaged the hard-won homestead to purchase the sheep ranch in Mutton Hollow. Then it was that another path was made, branching off in the belt of timber from the Old Trail and following the spur down into the little valley where the corral was snugly sheltered from the winter winds.

So the Lane cabin, the Matthews homestead, and the sheep ranch in Mutton Hollow were all connected by well-marked paths; but it is the trail that leads from Sammy Lane's home to the big log house where young Matthews lives, that is, nobody knows, how old.

3

1

The Stranger

It was corn-planting time, when the stranger followed the Old Trail into the Mutton Hollow neighborhood. All day a fine rain had fallen steadily, and the mists hung heavy over the valley. The lower hills were wrapped as in a winding sheet; dank and cold. The trees were dripping with moisture. The stranger looked tired and wet.

By his dress, the man was from the world beyond the ridges and his carefully tailored clothing looked strangely out of place in the mountain wilderness. His form stooped a little in the shoulders, perhaps with weariness, but he carried himself with the unconscious air of one long used to a position of conspicuous power and influence; and, while his well-kept hair and beard were strongly touched with white, the brown, clear lighted eyes, that looked from under their shaggy brows, told of an intellect unclouded by the shadows of many years. It was a face marked deeply by pride; pride of birth, of intellect, of culture; the face of a scholar and poet; but it was more—it was the countenance of one fairly staggering under a burden of disappointment and grief.

As the stranger walked, he looked searchingly into the mists on every hand, and paused frequently as if questioning the proper course. Suddenly he stepped quickly forward. His ear had caught the sharp ring of a horse's shoe on a flint rock somewhere in the mists on the mountainside

4

above. It was Jed Holland coming down the trail with a week's supply of corn meal in a sack across his horse's back.

As the figure of the traveler emerged from the mists, the native checked his horse to greet the newcomer with the customery salutation of the backwoods: "Howdy."

The man returned Jed's greeting cordially, and, resting his satchel on a rock beside the narrow path, added, "I am very glad to meet you. I fear that I am lost."

The voice was marvelously pure, deep, and musical, and, like the brown eyes, betrayed the real strength of the man, denied by his gray hair and bent form. The tones were as different from the high keyed, slurring speech of the backwoods, as the gentleman himself was unlike any man Jed had ever met. The boy looked at the speaker in wide-eyed wonder; he had a queer feeling that he was in the presence of a superior being.

Throwing one thin leg over the old mare's neck and waving a long arm up the hill and to the left, Jed drawled, "That thar's Dewey Bal'; down yonder's Mutton Holler." Then turning a little to the right and pointing into the mist with the other hand, he continued, "Compton Ridge is over thar. Whar was you tryin' to git to, mister?"

"Where am I trying to get to?" As the man repeated Jed's question, he drew his hand wearily across his brow. "I—I—it doesn't much matter, boy. I suppose I must find some place where I can stay tonight. Do you live near here?"

"Nope," Jed answered. "Hit's a right smart piece to whar I live. This here's grindin' day, an' I've been t' mill over on Fall Creek; the Matthews mill hit is. Hit'll be plumb dark 'gin I git home. I 'lowed you was a stranger in these parts soon's I ketched sight of you. What might yer name be, mister?"

The other, looking back over the way he had come, seemed not to hear Jed's question, and the native continued, "Mine's Holland. Pap an' Mam they come from Tennessee.

5

"Jim Lane lives up the trail 'bout half a quarter. Ever hear tell o' Jim?"

Pap he's down in th' back now, an' ain't right peart, but he'll be 'round in a little, I reckon. Preachin' Bill he 'lows hit's good for a feller t' be down in the' back onct in a while; says if hit warn't fer that we'd git to standin' so durned proud an' straight we'd go plumb over backwards."

A bitter smile crossed the face of the older man. He evidently applied the native's philosophy in a way unguessed by Jed. "Very true, very true indeed," he mused. Then he turned to Jed, and asked, "Is there a house near here?"

"Jim Lane lives up the trail 'bout half a quarter. Ever hear tell o' Jim?"

"No, I have never been in these mountains before."

"I 'lowed maybe you'd heard tell o' Jim or Sammy. There's them that 'lows Jim knows a heap more 'bout old man Dewey's cave than he lets on; his place bein' so nigh. Reckon you know 'bout Colonel Dewey, him th' Bal' up thar's named fer? Maybe you come t' look for the big mine they say's in th' cave? I'll hep you hunt hit, if you want me to, mister."

"No," said the other, "I am not looking for mines of lead or zinc; there is greater wealth in these hills and forests, young man."

"Law, you don't say! Jim Wilson allus 'lowed thar must be gold in these here mountains, 'cause they're so dadburned rough. Lemme hep you, mister. I'd like mighty well t' git some clothes like them."

"I do not speak of gold, my boy," the stranger answered kindly. "But I must not keep you longer, or darkness will overtake us. Do you think this Mr. Lane would entertain me?"

Jed pushed a hand up under his tattered old hat, and scratched awhile before he answered, "Don't know 'bout th' entertainin', mister, but 'most anybody would take you in." He turned and looked thoughtfully up the trail. "I don't guess Jim's to home though; 'cause I see'd Sammy a fixin' t' go over t' th' Matthews when I come past. You know the Matthews, I reckon?"

7

There was a hint of impatience now in the deep voice. "No, I told you that I had never been in these mountains before. Will Mr. Matthews keep me, do you think?"

Jed, who was still looking up the trail, suddenly leaned forward, and, pointing into the timber to the left of the path, said in an exciting whisper, "Look at that, mister; yonder thar by that big rock."

The stranger, looking, thought he saw a form, weird and ghostlike in the mist, flitting from tree to tree, but, even as he looked, it vanished among the hundreds of fantastic shapes in the gray forest. "What is it?" he asked.

The native shook his head. "Durned if I know, mister. You can't tell. There's mighty strange things stirrin' on this here mountain, an' in the Holler down yonder. Say, mister, did you ever see a hant?"

The gentleman did not understand.

"A hant, a ghost, some calls 'em," explained Jed. "Bud Wilson he sure seed old Matt's—"

The other interrupted. "Really, young man, I must go. It is already late, and you know I have yet to find a place to stay for the night."

"Law, that's all right, mister!" replied Jed. "Ain't no call t' worry. Stay anywhere. Whar do you live when you're to home?"

Again Jed's question was ignored. "You think then that Mr. Matthews will keep me?"

"Law, yes! They'll take anybody in. I know they're to home 'cause they was a fixin' t' leave the mill when I left 'bout an hour ago. Was the river up much when you come acrost? As the native spoke he was still peering uneasily into the woods.

"I did not cross the river. How far is it to this Matthews place, and how do I go?"

"Jest foller this Old Trail. Hit'll take you right thar. Good road all th' way. 'Bout three mile, I'd say. Did you come from Springfield or St. Louis, maybe?

The man lifted his satchel from the rock as he answered:

8

"No, I do not live in either Springfield or St. Louis. Thank you, very much, for your assistance. I will go on, now, for I must hurry, or night will overtake me, and I shall not be able to find the path."

"Oh, hit's a heap lighter when you git up on th' hill 'bove th' fog," said Jed, lowering his leg from the horse's neck, and settling the meal sack, preparatory to moving. "But I'd a heap rather hit was you than me a-goin' up on Dewey t'night." He was still looking up the trail. "Reckon you must be from Kansas City or Chicago? I heard tell they're mighty big towns."

The stranger's only answer was a curt "Good-by," as his form vanished in the mist.

Jed turned and dug his heels vigorously in the old mare's flanks, as he ejaculated softly, "Well, I'll be dod durned! Must be from New York, sure!"

Slowly the old man toiled up the mountain; up from the mists of the lower ground to the ridge above; and, as he climbed, unseen by him, a shadowy form flitted from tree to tree in the dim, dripping forest.

As the stranger came in sight of the Lane cabin, a young woman on a brown pony rode out of the gate and up the trail before him; and when the man reached the open ground on the mountain above, and rounded the shoulder of the hill, he saw the pony, far ahead, loping easily along the little path. A moment he watched, and horse and rider passed from sight.

The clouds were drifting far away. The western sky was clear with the sun still above the hills. In an old tree that leaned far out over the valley, a crow shook the wet from his plumage and dried himself in the warm light; while far below the mists rolled, and on the surface of that gray sea, the traveler saw a company of buzzards, wheeling and circling above some dead thing hidden in its depth.

Wearily the man followed the Old Trail toward the Matthews place, and always, as he went, in the edge of the gloomy forest, flitted that shadowy form.

9

2

Sammy Lane

Preachin' Bill says, "Hit's a plumb shame there ain't more men in th' world built like old man Matthews and that thar boy o' his'n. Men like them ought t' be as common as th' other kind, an' would be, too, if folks cared half as much 'bout breeding folks as they do 'bout raising hogs an' horses."

Mr. Matthews was a giant. Fully six feet four inches in height, with big bones, broad shoulders, and mighty muscles. At log rollings and chopping bees, in the field or at the mill, or in any of the games in which the backwoodsman tries his strength, no one had ever successfully contested his place as the strongest man in the hills. And still, throughout the countryside, the old folks tell with pride tales of the marvelous feats of strength performed in the days when "Old Matt" was young.

Of the son, "Young Matt," the people called him, it is enough to say that he seemed made of the same metal and cast in the same mold as the father; a mighty frame, softened yet by young manhood's grace; a powerful neck and well-poised head with wavy-red-brown hair; and blue eyes that had in them the calm of summer skies or the glint of battle steel. It was a countenance fearless and frank, but gentle and kind, and the eyes were honest eyes.

Anyone meeting the pair, as they walked with the long swinging stride of the mountaineer up the steep mill road that gray afternoon, would have turned for a second look; such men are seldom seen.

When they reached the big log house that looks down upon the Hollow, the boy went at once with his axe to the woodpile, while the older man busied himself with the milking an other chores about the barn.

Young Matt had not been chopping long when he heard, coming up the hill, the sound of a horse's feet on the Old Trail. The horse stopped at the house and a voice, that stirred the blood in the young man's veins, called, "Howdy, Aunt Mollie."

Mrs. Matthews appeared in the doorway; by her frank countenance and kindly look anyone would have known her at a glance as the boy's mother. "Land sakes, if it ain't Sammy Lane! How are you, honey?"

"I am all right," answered the voice. "I've come over t' stop with you tonight; Dad's away again; Mandy Ford stayed with me last night, but she had to go home this evenin'." The big fellow at the woodpile drove his axe deeper into the log.

"It's about time you was comin' over," replied the woman in the doorway. "I was a-tellin' the menfolks this mornin' that you hadn't been nigh the whole blessed week. Mr. Matthews 'lowed maybe you was sick."

The other returned with a gay laugh, "I was never sick a minute in my life that anybody ever heard tell. I'm powerful hungry, though. You'd better put in another pan of cornbread." She turned her pony's head toward the barn.

"Seems like you are always hungry," laughed the older woman, in return. "Well, just go on out to the barn, and the men will take your horse; then come right in and I'll mighty soon have something to fill you up."

Operations at the woodpile suddenly ceased, and Young Matt was first at the barnyard gate.

Miss Sammy Lane was one of those rare young women whose appearance is not to be described. One can, of course, put it down that she was tall; beautifully tall, with the trimness of a young pine, deep bosomed, with limbs full-rounded, fairly tingling with the life and strength of perfect womanhood; and it may be said that her face was a face to go with one through the years, and to live still in one's dreams when the sap of life is gone, and, withered and old, one sits shaking before the fire; a generous, loving mouth, red-lipped, full-arched, with the corners tucked in and perfect teeth between; a womanly chin and nose, with character enough to save them from being pretty; hair dark, showing a touch of gold with umber in the shadows; a brow, full broad, set over brown eyes that had never been taught to hide behind their fringed veils, but looked always square out at you with a healthy look of good comradeship, a gleam of mirth, or a sudden, wide, questioning gaze that revealed depth of soul within.

But what is the use? When all this is written, those who knew Sammy will say, " 'Tis but a poor picture, for she is something more than all this." Uncle Ike, the postmaster at the Forks, did it much better when he said to "Preachin' Bill," the night of the "Doin's" at the Cove School, "Ba Thundas! That gal o' Jim Lane's jest plumb fills th' whole house. What! An' when she comes a-ridin' up t' th' office on that brown pony o'hern, I'll be dad-burned if she don't pretty nigh fill th' whole outdoors, ba thundas! What!" And the little shrivelled-up old hillsman, who keeps the ferry, removed his cob pipe long enough to reply, with all the emphasis possible to his squeaky voice, "She sure do, Ike. She sure do. I've often thought hit didn't look jest fair for God 'lmighty t' make sech a woman 'thout ary man t' match her. Makes me feel plumb 'shamed o' myself t' stand 'round in th' same county with her. Hit sure do, Ike."

Greeting the girl the young man opened the gate for her to pass.

"I've been a-lookin' for you over," said Sammy, a teasing light in her eyes. "Didn't you know that Mandy was stoppin' with me? She's been a-dyin' to see you."

"I'm mighty sorry," he replied, fastening the gate and

"I've been a-lookin' for you over."

coming to the pony's side. "Why didn't you tell me before? I reckon she'll get over it all right, though," he added with a smile, as he raised his arms to assist the girl to dismount.

The teasing light vanished as the young woman placed her hands on the powerful shoulders of the giant, and as she felt the play of the swelling muscles that swung her to the ground so easily, her face flushed with admiration. For the fraction of a minute she stood facing him, her hands still on his arms, her lips parted as if to speak; then she turned quickly away, and without a word walked toward the house, while the boy, pretending to busy himself with the pony's bridle, watched her as she went.

When the girl was gone, the big fellow led the horse away to the stable, where he crossed his arms upon the saddle and hid his face from the light. Mr. Matthews coming quietly to the door a few minutes later, saw the boy standing there, and the rugged face of the big mountaineer softened at the sight. Quietly he withdrew to the other side of the barn, to return later when the saddle and bridle had been removed, and the young man stood stroking the pony, as the little horse munched his generous feed of corn.

The elder man laid his hand on the broad shoulder of the lad so like him, and looked full into the clear eyes. "Is it all right, son?" he asked gruffly; and the boy answered, as he returned his father's look, "It's all right, Dad."

"Then let's go to the house. Mother called supper some time ago."

Just as the little company were seating themselves at the table, the dog in the yard barked loudly. Young Matt went to the door. The stranger, whom Jed had met on the Old Trail, stood at the gate.

14

3

The Voice from Out the Mists

While Young Matt was gone to the corral in the valley to see that the sheep were safely folded for the night, and the two women were busy in the house with their after-supper work, Mr. Matthews and his guest sat on the front porch.

"My name is Howitt, Daniel Howitt," the man said in answer to the host's question. But, as he spoke, there was in his manner a touch of embarrassment, and he continued quickly as if to prevent further question, "You have two remarkable children, sir. That boy is the finest specimen of manhood I have ever seen, and the girl is remarkable—remarkable, sir. You will pardon me, I am sure, but I am an enthusiastic lover of my kind, and I certainly have never seen such a pair."

The grim face of the elder Matthews showed both pleasure and amusement. "You're mistaken, mister; the boy's mine all right, an' he's all that you say, an' more, I reckon. I doubt if there's a man in the hills can match him today; not excepting Wash Gibbs; an' he's a mighty good boy, too. But the girl is a daughter of a neighbor, and no kin at all."

"Indeed!" exclaimed the other. "You have only one child then?"

The amused smile left the face of the old mountaineer, as he answered slowly, "There was six boys, sir. This one, Grant, is the youngest. The others lie over there." He

15

pointed with his pipe to where a clump of pines, not far from the house, showed dark and tall, against the last red glow in the sky.

The stranger glanced at the big man's face in quick sympathy. "I had only two; a boy and a girl," he said softly. "The girl and her mother have been gone these twenty years. The boy grew to be a man, and now he has left me." The deep voice faltered. "Pardon me, sir, for speaking of this, but my lad was so like your boy there. He was all I had, and now—now—I am very lonely, sir."

There is a bond of fellowship in sorrow that knows no conventionalities. As the two men sat in the hush of the coming night, their faces turned toward the somber group of trees, they felt strongly drawn to one another.

The mountaineer's companion spoke again half to himself. "I wish that my dear ones had a resting place like that. In the crowded city cemetery the ground is always shaken by the trampling of funeral processions." He buried his face in his hands.

For some time the stranger sat thus, while his host spoke no word. Then lifting his head, the man looked away over the ridges just touched with the lingering light, and the valley below wrapped in the shadowy mists. "I came away from it all because they said I must, and because I was hungry for this." He waved his hand toward the glowing sky and the forest-clad hills. "This is good for me; it somehow seems to help me know how big God is. One could find peace here surely, sir, one could find it here—peace and strength."

The mountaineer puffed hard at his pipe for a while, then said gruffly, "Seems that way, mister, to them that don't know. But many's the time I've wished to God I'd never seen these here Ozarks. I used to feel like you do, but I can't no more. They 'mind me now of him that blackened my life; he used to take on powerful about the beauty of the country and all the time he was a-turnin' it into a hell for them that had to stay here after he was

16

gone."

As he spoke, anger and hatred grew dark in the giant's face, and the stranger saw the big hands clench and the huge frame grow tense with passion. Then, as if striving to be not ungracious, the woodsman said in a somewhat softer tone, "You can't see much of it, this evening, though, 'count of the mists. It'll fair up by morning, I reckon. You can see a long way from here, of a clear day, mister."

"Yes, indeed," replied Mr. Howitt, in an odd tone. "One could see far from here, I am sure. We who live in the cities see but a little farther than across the street. We spend our days looking at the work of our own and our neighbors' hands. Small wonder our lives have so little of God in them, when we come in touch with so little that God has made."

"You live in the city, then, when you are at home?" asked Mr. Matthews, looking curiously at his guest.

"I did, when I had a home. I cannot say that I live anywhere now."

Old Matt leaned forward in his chair as if to speak again, then paused; someone was coming up the hill; and soon they distinguished the stalwart form of the son. Sammy coming from the house with an empty bucket met the young man at the gate, and the two went toward the spring together.

In silence the men on the porch watched the moon as she slowly pushed her way up through the leafy screen on the mountain wall. Higher and higher she climbed until her rays fell into the valley below, and the drifting mists from ridge to ridge became a sea of ghostly light. It was a weird scene, almost supernatural in its beauty.

Then from down at the spring a young girl's laugh rose clearly, and the big mountaineer said in a low tone, "Mr. Howitt, you've got education. It's easy to see that. I've always wanted to ask somebody like you, do you believe in hants? Do you reckon folks ever come back once they're dead and gone?"

17

The man from the city saw that his big host was terribly in earnest, and answered quietly, "No, I do not believe in such things, Mr. Matthews; but if it should be true, I do not see why we should fear the dead."

The other shook his head. "I don't know—I don't know, sir. I always said I didn't believe, but some things is mighty queer." He seemed to be shaping his thought for further speech, when again the girl's laugh rang clear along the mountainside. The young people were returning from the spring.

The mountaineer relighted his pipe, while Young Matt and Sammy seated themselves on the step, and Mrs. Matthews coming from the house joined the group.

"We've just naturally got to find somebody to stay with them sheep, Dad," said the son. "There ain't nobody there tonight, and as near as I can make out there's three ewes and their lambs missing. There ain't a bit of use in us trying to depend on Pete."

"I'll ride over on Bear Creek tomorrow, and see if I can get that fellow Buck told us about," returned the father.

"You find it hard to get help on the ranch?" inquired the stranger.

"Yes, sir, we do," answered Old Matt. "We had a good 'nough man till about a month ago; since then we've been gettin' along the best we could. But with some a-stayin' out on the range, an' not comin' in, an' the wolves a'gettin' into the corral at night, we'll lose mighty nigh all the profits this year. The worst of it is, there ain't much show to get a man; unless that one over on Bear Creek will come. I reckon, though, he'll be like the rest." He sat staring gloomily into the night.

"Is the work so difficult?" Mr. Howitt asked.

"Difficult, no; there ain't nothing to do but tendin' to the sheep. The man has to stay at the ranch of nights, though."

Mr. Howitt was wondering what staying at the ranch nights could have to do with the difficulty, when, up from

18

"Poor boy, poor boy."

the valley below, from out of the darkness and the mists, came a strange sound; a sound as if someone were singing a song without words. So wild and weird was the melody; so passionately sweet the voice, it seemed impossible that the music should come from human lips. It was more as though some genie of the forest-clad hills wandered through the mists, singing as he went with the joy of his possessions.

Mrs. Matthews came close to her husband's side, and placed her hand upon his shoulder as he half rose from his chair, his pipe fallen to the floor. Young Matt rose to his feet and moved closer to the girl, who was also standing. The stranger alone kept his seat and he noted the agitation of the others in wonder.

For some moments the sound continued, now soft and low, with the sweet sadness of the wind in the pines; then clear and ringing, it echoed and re-echoed along the mountain; now pleadingly, as though a soul in darkness prayed a gleam of light; again rising, swelling exultingly, as in glad triumph, only to die away once more to that moaning wail, seeming at last to hopelessly lose itself in this mists.

Slowly Old Matt sank back into his seat and the stranger heard him mutter, "Poor boy, poor boy." Aunt Mollie was weeping. Suddenly Sammy sprang from the steps and running down the walk to the gate sent a clear, piercing call over the valley: "O—h—h, Pete." The group on the porch listened intently. Again the girl called, and yet again: "O—h—h, Pete." But there was no answer.

"It's no use, honey," said Mrs. Matthews, breaking the silence. "It just ain't no use;" and the young girl came slowly back to the porch.

4

A Chat with Aunt Mollie

When the stranger looked from his window the next morning, the valley was still wrapped in its gray blanket. But when he and his host came from the house after breakfast, the sun had climbed well above the ridge, and, save a long, loosely twisted rope of fog that hung above the distant river, the mists were gone. The city man exclaimed with delight at the beauty of the scene.

As they stood watching the sheep—white specks in the distance—climbing out of the valley where the long shadows still lay, to the higher, sunlit pastures, Mr. Matthews said, "We've all been a-talkin' about you this morning', Mr. Howitt, and we'd like mighty well to have you stop with us for a spell. If I understood right, you're just out for your health anyway, and you'll go a long ways, sir, before you find a healthier place than this right here. We ain't got much such as you're used to, I know, but what we have is yourn, and we'd be proud to have you make yourself to home for as long as you'd like to stay. You see it's been a good while since we met up with anybody like you, and we count it a real favor to have you."

Mr. Howitt accepted the invitation with evident pleasure, and, soon after, the mountaineer rode away to Bear Creek, on his quest for a man to herd sheep. Young Matt had already gone with his team to the field on the hillside west of the house, and the brown pony stood at the gate ready for Sammy Lane to return to her home on Dewey Bald.

"I'd like the best in the world to stay, Aunt Mollie," she said, in answer to Mrs. Matthews' protest, "but you know there is no one to feed the stock, and besides Mandy Ford will be back sometime today."

The older woman's arm was around the girl as they went down the walk. "You must come over real often, now, honey; you know it won't be long 'til you'll be a-leavin' us for good. How do you reckon you'll like bein' a fine lady, and livin' in the city with them big folks?"

The girl's face flushed, and her eyes had that wide questioning look, as she answered slowly, "I don't know, Aunt Mollie; I ain't never seen a sure 'nough fine lady. I reckon them city folks are a heap different from us, but I reckon they're just as human. It would be nice to have lots of money and pretties, but somehow I feel like there's a heap more than that to think about. Anyhow," she added brightly, "I ain't goin' for quite a spell yet, and you know 'Preachin' Bill' says, 'There ain't no use to worry 'bout the choppin' 'til the dogs has treed the coon.' I'll sure come over every day."

Mrs. Matthews kissed the girl, and then, standing at the gate, watched until pony and rider had disappeared in the forest.

Later Aunt Mollie, with a woman's fondness for a quiet chat, brought the potatoes she was preparing for dinner, to sit with Mr. Howitt on the porch. "I declare I don't know what we'll do without Sammy," she said. "I just can't bear to think of her goin' away."

The guest, feeling that some sort of a reply was expected, asked, "Is the family moving from the neighborhood?"

"No, sir, there ain't no family to move. Just Sammy and her Pa, and Jim Lane won't never leave this country again. You see Ollie Stewart's uncle, his father's brother it is, ain't got no children of his own, and he wrote for Ollie to come and live with him in the city. He's to go to school and learn the business, foundry and machine shops, or something like that it is; and if the boy does what's right, he's to get it all some day. Ollie and Sammy has been promised ever since the talk first began about his goin'; but they'll wait now until he gets through his schoolin'. It'll be mighty nice for Sammy, marryin' Ollie, but we'll miss her awful; the whole country will miss her, too. She's just the life of the neighborhood, and everybody 'lows there never was another girl like her. Poor child, she ain't had no mother since she was a little trick, and she has always come to me for everything like, us bein' such close neighbors, and all. But law! sir, I ain't a blamin' her a mite for goin', with her daddy a-runnin' with that ornery Wash Gibbs the way he does."

Again the man felt called upon to express his interest. "Is Mr. Lane in business with this man Gibbs?"

"Law, no! That is, don't nobody know about any business. I reckon it's all on account of those old Bald Knobbers; they used to hold their meetin's on top of Dewey yonder, and folks do say a man was burned there once, because he told some of their secrets. Well, Jim and Wash's daddy, and Wash, all belonged, 'though Wash himself wasn't much more than a boy then; and when the government broke up the gang, old man Gibbs was killed, and Jim went to Texas. It was there that Sammy's ma died. When Jim come back it wasn't long before he was mighty thick again with Wash and his crowd down on the river, and he's been that way ever since. There's them that say it's the same old gang, what's left of them, and some thinks too that Jim and Wash knows about the old Dewey mine."

Mr. Howitt, remembering his conversation with Jed Holland, asked encouragingly, "Is this mine a very rich one?"

"Don't nobody rightly know about that, sir," answered Aunt Mollie. "This is how it was: away back when the Injuns was makin' trouble 'cause the government was movin' them west to the territory, this old man Dewey lived up there somewhere on that mountain. He was a mighty queer old fellow; didn't mix up with the settlers at all, except Uncle Josh Hensley's boy who wasn't right smart, and didn't nobody know where he come from nor nothing; but all the same, 'twas him that warned the settlers of the trouble, and helped them all through it, scoutin' and such. And one time when they was about out of bullets and didn't have nothin' to make more out of, Colonel Dewey took a couple of men and some mules up on that mountain yonder in the night, and when they got back they was just loaded down with lead, but he wouldn't tell nobody where he got it, and as long as he was with them, the men didn't dare tell. Well, sir, them two men was killed soon after by the Injuns, and when the trouble was finally over, old Dewey disappeared, and ain't never been heard tell of since. They say the mine is somewhere's in a big cave, but nobody ain't never found it, though there's them that says the Bald Knobbers used the cave to hide their stuff in, and that's how Jim Lane and Wash Gibbs knows where it is. It's all mighty queer. You can see for yourself that Lost Creek down yonder just sinks clean out of sight all at once. There must be a big hole in there somewhere."

Aunt Mollie pointed with her knife to the little stream that winds like a thread of light down into the Hollow. "I tell you, sir, these hills is pretty to look at, but there ain't much here for a girl like Sammy, and I don't blame her a mite for wantin' to leave. It's a mighty hard place to live, Mr. Howitt, and dangerous, too, sometimes."

"The city has its hardships and its dangers too, Mrs. Matthews. Life there demands almost too much at times; I often wonder if it is worth the struggle."

"I guess that's so," replied Aunt Mollie, "but it don't seem like it could be so hard as it is here. I tell Mr. Matthews we've clean forgot the ways of civilized folks; altogether, though, I suppose we've done as well as most, and we hadn't ought to complain."

The old scholar looked at the sturdy figure in its plain calico dress; at the worn hands, busy with their homely task; and the patient, kindly face, across which time had plowed many a furrow, in which to plant the seeds of character and worth. He thought of other women who had sat with him on hotel verandas, at fashionable watering places; women gowned in silks and laces; women whose soft hands knew no heavier task than the filmy fancy work they toyed with, and whose greatest care, seemingly, was that time should leave upon their faces no record of the passing years. "And this is the stuff," he said to himself, "that makes possible the civilization that produces them." Aloud, he said, "Do you ever talk of going back to your old home?"

"No, sir, not now." She rested her wet hands idly on the edge of the pan of potatoes and turned her face toward the clump of pines. "We used to think we'd go back sometime; seemed like at first I couldn't stand it; then the children come, and every time we laid one of them over there I thought less about leavin', until now we never talk about it no more. Then there was our girl, too, Mr. Howitt. No, sir, we won't never leave these hills now."

"Oh, you had a daughter, too? I understood from Mr. Matthews that your children were all boys."

Aunt Mollie worked a few moments longer in silence, then arose and turned toward the house. "Yes, sir, there was a girl; she's buried under that biggest pine you see off there a little to one side. We—we—don't never talk about her. Mr. Matthews can't stand it. Seems like he ain't never been the same since—since—it happened. 'Tain't natural for him to be so rough and short; he's just as good and kind inside as any man ever was or could be. He's real taken with you, Mr. Howitt, and I'm mighty glad you're goin' to stop a spell, for it will do him good. If it hadn't been for Sammy Lane runnin' in every day or two, I don't guess he could have stood it at all. I sure don't know what we'll do now that she's goin' away. Then there's—there's—that at the ranch in Mutton Hollow; but I guess I'd better not try to tell you about that. I wish Mr. Matthews would, though; maybe he will. You know so much more than us; I know you could help us or tell us about things."

5

"Jest Nobody"

After the midday meal, while walking about the place, Mr. Howitt found a well-worn path; it led him to the group of pines not far from the house, where five rough headstones marked the five mounds placed side by side. A little apart from these was another mound, alone.

Beneath the pines the needles made a carpet, firm and smooth, figured by the wild woodbine that clambered over the graves. Moss had gathered on the headstones, and the wind, in the dark branches above, moaned ceaselessly. About the little plot of ground a rustic fence of poles was built, and the path led to a stile by which one might enter the enclosure.

The stranger seated himself upon the rude steps. Below and far away he saw the low hills, rolling ridge on ridge like the waves of a great sea, until in the blue distance they were so lost in the sky that he could not say which was mountain and which was cloud. His poet heart was stirred at sight of the vast reaches of the forest all shifting light and shadows; the cool depths of the nearby woods with the sunlight filtering through the leafy arches in streaks and patches of gold on green; and the wide, wide sky with fleets of cloud ships sailing to unseen ports below the hills.

The man sat very still, and as he looked the worn face changed; once, as if at some pleasing memory, he smiled. A gray squirrel with bright eyes full of curious regard peeped over the limb of an oak; a red bird hopping from bush to bush whistled to his mate; and a bob-white's quick call came from a nearby thicket.

The dreamer was aroused at last by the musical tinkle of a bell. He turned his face toward the sound, but could see nothing. The bell was coming nearer; it came nearer still. Then he saw here and there through the trees small, moving patches of white; an old ewe followed by two lambs came from behind a clump of bushes, and the moving patches of white shaped themselves into other sheep feeding in the timber.

Mr. Howitt sat quite still, and, while the old ewe paused to look at him, the lambs took advantage of the opportunity, until their mother was satisfied with her inspection, and by moving on, upset them. Soon the whole flock surrounded him, and, after the first lingering look of inquiry, paid no heed to his presence.

Then from somewhere among the trees came the quick, low bark of a dog. The man looked carefully in every direction; he could see nothing but the sheep, yet he felt himself observed. Again came the short bark; and this time a voice—a girl's voice, Mr. Howitt thought—said, "It's all right, Brave; go on, brother." And from behind a big rock not far away a shepherd dog appeared, followed by a youth of some fifteen years.

He was a lightly built boy; a bit tall for his age, perhaps, but perfectly erect; and his every movement was one of indescribable grace, while he managed, somehow, to wear his rough backwoods garments with an air of distinction as remarkable as it was charming. The face was finely molded, almost girlish, with the large gray eyes, and its frame of yellow, golden hair. It was a sad face when in repose, yet wonderfully responsive to every passing thought and mood. But the eyes, with their strange expression, and shifting light, proclaimed the lad's mental condition.

As the boy came forward in a shy, hesitating way, an expression of amazement and wonder crept into the

27

stranger's face; he left his seat and started forward. "Howard," he said. "Howard!"

"That ain't his name, mister. His name's Pete," returned the youth, in low, soft tones.

In the voice and manner of the lad, no less than in his face and eyes, Mr. Howitt read his story. Unconsciously he echoed the words of Mr. Matthews, "Poor Pete."

The dog lifted his head and looked into the man's face, while his tail wagged a joyful greeting, and, as the man stooped to pat the animal and speak a few kind words, a beautiful smile broke over the delicate features of the youth. Throwing himself upon the ground, he cried, "Come here, Brave"; and taking the dog's face between his hands, said in confidential tones, ignoring Mr. Howitt's presence, "He's a good man, ain't he brother?" The dog answered with wagging tail. "We sure like him, don't we?" The dog gave a low bark. "Listen, Brave, listen." He lifted his face to the treetops, then turned his ear to the ground, while the dog too, seemed to hearken. Again that strange smile illuminated his face. "Yes, yes, Brave, we sure like him. And the tree things like him, too, brother; and the flowers, the little flower things that know everything; they're all a-singin' to Pete 'cause he's come. Did you see the flower things in his eyes, and hear the tree things a-talkin' in his voice, Brave? And see, brother, the sheep like him too!" Pointing toward the stranger, he laughed aloud. The old ewe had come quite close to the man, and one of the lambs was nibbling at his trouser leg.

Mr. Howitt seated himself on the stile again, and the dog, released by the youth, came to lie down at his feet; while the boy seemed to forget his companions, and appeared to be listening to voices unheard by them, now and then nodding his head and moving his lips in answer.

The old man looked long and thoughtfully at the youth, his own face revealing a troubled mind. This then was Pete, Poor Pete. "Howard," whispered the man, "the perfect image." Then again he said, half aloud, "Howard."

The boy turned his face and smiled. "That ain't his name, mister; his name's Pete. Pete seen you yesterday over on Dewey, and Pete he heard the big hills and the woods a-singin' when you talked. But Jed he didn't hear. Jed he don't hear nothin' but himself; he can't. But Pete he heard and all Pete's people, too. And the gray mist things come out and danced along the mountain, 'cause they was so glad you come. And Pete went with you along the Old Trail. Course, though, you didn't know. Do you like Pete's people, mister?" He waved his hands to include the forest, the mountains and the sky; and there was a note of anxiety in the sweet voice as he asked again: "Do you like Pete's friends?"

"Yes, indeed, I like your friends," replied Mr. Howitt heartily, "and I would like to be your friend too, if you will let me. What is your other name?"

The boy shook his head. "Not me; not me," he said. "Do you like Pete?"

The man was puzzled. "Are you not Pete?" he asked.

The delicate face grew sad. "No, no, no," he said in a low, moaning tone, "I'm not Pete; Pete, he lives in here." He touched himself on the breast. "I am—I am—" A look of hopeless bewilderment crept into his eyes. "I don't know who I am; I'm jest nobody. Nobody can't have no name, can he?" He stood with downcast head. Then suddenly he raised his face and the shadows lifted, as he said, "But Pete he knows, mister, ask Pete."

A sudden thought came to Mr. Howitt. "Who is your father, my boy?"

Instantly the brightness vanished; again the words were a puzzled moan. "I ain't got no father, mister; I ain't me; nobody can't have no father, can he?"

The other spoke quickly. "But Pete had a father; who was Pete's father?" Instantly the gloom was gone and the face was bright again. "Sure, mister, Pete's got a father; don't you know? Everybody knows that. Look!" he pointed upward to a break in the trees, to a large cumulus cloud

"Are you not Pete?"

that had assumed a fantastic shape. "He lives in them white hills, up there. See him, mister? Sometimes he takes Pete with him up through the sky, and course I go along. We sail, and sail, and sail, with the big bird things up there, while the sky things sing; and sometimes we play with the cloud things, all day in them white hills. Pete says he'll take me away up there where the star things live, some day, and we won't never come back again; and I won't be nobody no more; and Aunt Mollie says she reckons Pete knows. Course, I'd hate mighty much to go away from Uncle Matt and Aunt Mollie and Matt and Sammy, 'cause they're mighty good to me; but I jest got to go where Pete goes, you see, 'cause I ain't nobody, and nobody can't be nothin', can he?"

The stranger was fascinated by the wonderful charm of the boy's manner and words. As the lad's sensitive face glowed or was clouded by each wayward thought, and the music of his sweet voice rose and fell, Mr. Howitt told himself that one might easily fancy the child some wandering spirit of the woods and hills. Aloud, he asked, "Has Pete a mother, too?"

The youth nodded toward the big pine that grew to one side of the group, and, lowering his voice, replied, "That's Pete's mother."

Mr. Howitt pointed to the grave. "You mean she sleeps there?"

"No, no, not there; there!" He pointed up to the big tree itself. "She never sleeps; don't you hear her?" He paused. The wind moaned through the branches of the pine. Drawing closer to the stranger's side, the boy whispered, "She always talks that a-way, always, and it makes Pete feel bad. She wants somebody. Hear her callin', callin', callin'? He'll sure come someday, mister; he sure will. Say, do you know where he is?"

The stranger, startled, drew back. "No, no, my boy, certainly not; what do you mean; who are you?"

Like the moaning of the pines came the reply, "Nothin',

31

mister, nobody can't mean nothin', can they? I'm jest nobody. But Pete lives in here; ask Pete."

"Is Pete watching the sheep?" asked Mr. Howitt, anxious to divert the boy's mind to other channels.

"Yes, we're a-tendin' them now; but they can't trust us, you know; when they call Pete, he just goes, and course I've got to go 'long."

"Who is it calls Pete?"

"Why, they, don't you know? I 'lowed you knowed about things. They called Pete last night. The moonlight things was out, and all the shadow things; didn't you see them, mister? The moonlight things, the wind, the stars, the shadow things, and all the rest played with Pete in the shiny mists, and, course, I was along. Didn't you hear singin'? Pete he always sings that a-way, when the moonlight things is out. Seems like he just can't help it."

"But what becomes of the sheep when Pete goes away?"

The boy shook his head sadly. "Sometimes they get so lost that Young Matt can't never find 'em; sometimes wolves get 'em; it's too bad, mister, it sure is." Then laughing aloud, he clapped his hands. "There was a feller at the ranch to keep 'em, but he didn't stay. Ho! Ho! he didn't stay, you bet he didn't. Pete didn't like him, Brave didn't like him, nothing didn't like him, the trees wouldn't talk when he was around, the flowers died when he looked at 'em, and all the birds stopped singin' and went away over the mountains. He didn't stay, though." Again he laughed. "You bet he didn't stay! Pete knows."

"Why did the man go?" asked Mr. Howitt, thinking to solve a part of the mystery, at least. But the only answer he could draw from the boy was, "Pete knows; Pete knows."

Later when the stranger returned to the house, Pete went with him; at the big gate they met Mr. Matthews, returning unsuccessful from his trip.

"Hello, boy!" said the big man. "How's Pete today?"

The lad went with glad face to the giant mountaineer. It was clear that the two were the warmest friends. "Pete's mighty glad today, 'cause he's come." He pointed to Mr. Howitt.

"Does Pete like him?"

The boy nodded. "All Pete's people like him. Ask him to keep the sheep, Uncle Matt. He won't be scared at the shadow things in the night."

Mr. Matthews smiled, as he turned to his guest. "Pete never makes a mistake in his judgment of men, Mr. Howitt. He's different from us ordinary folks, as you can see; but in some things he knows a heap more. I'm mighty glad he's took up with you, sir. All day I've been thinking I'd tell you about some things I don't like to talk about; I feel after last night like you'd understand, maybe, and might help me, you having education. But still I've been a little afraid, us being such strangers. I know I'm right now, 'cause Pete says so. If you weren't the kind of a man I think you are, he'd never took to you like he has."

That night the mountaineer told the stranger from the city the story that I have put down in the next chapter.

6

The Story

Slowly the big mountaineer filled his cob pipe with strong, homegrown tobacco, watching his guest keenly the while, from under heavy brows.

Behind the dark pines the sky was blood red, and below, Mutton Hollow was fast being lost in the gathering gloom.

When his pipe was lighted, Old Matt said, "Well, sir, I reckon you think some things you seen and heard since you come last night are mighty queer. I ain't sayin' neither, but what you got reasons for thinkin' so."

Mr. Howitt made no reply. And, after puffing a few moments in silence, the other continued, "If it weren't for what you said last night makin' me feel like I wanted to talk to you, and Pete a-takin' up with you the way he has, I wouldn't be a-tellin' you what I am goin' to now. There's some trails, Mr. Howitt, that ain't pleasant to go back over. I didn't 'low to ever go over this one again. Did you and Pete talk much this afternoon?"

In a few words Mr. Howitt told of his meeting with the strange boy, and their conversation. When he had finished, the big man smoked in silence. It was as if he found it hard to begin. From a tree on the mountainside below, a screech owl sent up his long, quavering call; a bat darted past in the dusk; and away over on Compton Ridge a hound bayed. The mountaineer spoke. "That's Sam Wilson's dog, Ranger; must 'a' started a fox." The sound died away in the distance. Old Matt began his story.

"Our folks all live back in Illinois. And if I do say so, they are as good stock as you'll find anywhere. But there was a lot of us, and I always had a notion to settle in a new country where there was more room like and land wasn't so dear; so when wife and I was married we come out here. I recollect we camped at the spring below Jim Lane's cabin on yon side of Old Dewey, there. That was before Jim was married, and a wild young buck he was too, as ever you see. The next day wife and I rode along the Old Trail 'til we struck this gap, and here we've been ever since.

"We've had our ups and downs like most folks, sir, and sometimes it looked like they was mostly downs; but we got along, and last fall I bought in the ranch down there in the Hollow. The boy was just eighteen and we thought then that he'd be makin' his home there some day. I don't know how that'll be now, but there was another reason too why we wanted the place, as you'll see when I get to it.

"There was five other boys, as I told you last night. The oldest two would have been men now. The girl"—his voice broke—"the girl she come third; she was twenty when we buried her over there. That was fifteen year ago come the middle of next month.

"Everybody 'lowed she was a mighty pretty baby, and, bein' the only girl, I reckon we made more of her than we did of the boys. She growed up into a mighty fine young woman too; strong, and full of fire and go, like Sammy Lane. Seems to wife and me when Sammy's 'round that it's our own girl come back and we've always hoped that she and Grant would take the ranch down yonder; but I reckon that's all over, now that Ollie Stewart has come into such a fine thing in the city. Anyway, it ain't got nothing to do with this that I'm a-tellin' you.

"She didn't seem to care nothin' at all for none of the neighbor boys like most girls do; she'd go with them and have a good time all right, but that was all. 'Peared like she'd rather be with her brothers or her mother or me.

"Well, one day, when we was out on the range a ridin' for stock—she'd often go with me that way—we met a stranger over there at the deer lick in the big low gap, coming along the Old Trail. He was as fine a lookin' man as you ever see, sir; big and grand like, with lightish hair, kind of wavy, and a big mustache like his hair, and fine white teeth showing when he smiled. He was sure good lookin', damn him! And with his fine store clothes and a smooth easy way of talkin' and actin' he had, 'tain't no wonder she took up with him. We all did. I used to think God never made a finer body for a man. I know now that Hell don't hold a meaner heart than the one in the same fine body. And that's somethin' that bothers me a heap, Mr. Howitt.

"As I say, our girl was built like Sammy Lane, and so far as looks goes she was his dead match. I used to wonder when I'd look at them together if there ever was such another fine-lookin' pair. I ain't a-goin' to tell you his name; there ain't no call to, as I can see. There might be some decent man named the same. But he was one of these here artist fellows and had come into the hills to paint, he said."

A smothered exclamation burst from the listener.

Mr. Matthews, not noticing, continued: "He sure did make a lot of pictures and they seemed mighty nice to us, though of course we didn't know nothin' about such things. There was one big one he made of Maggie that was as natural as life. He was always drawin' of her in one way or another, and had a lot of little pictures that didn't amount to much, and that he didn't never finish. But this big one he worked at off and on all summer. It was sure fine, with her a-standin' by the ranch spring, holdin' out a cup of water, and smilin' like she was offerin' you a drink."

It was well that the night had fallen. At Old Matt's words the stranger shrank back in his chair, his hands raised as if to ward off a deadly blow. He made a sound in his throat as if he would cry out, but could not from horror or fear. But the darkness hid his face, and the mountaineer, with mind intent upon his story, did not heed.

"He took an old cabin at the foot of the hill near where the sheep corral is now, and fixed it up to work in. The shack had been built first by old man Dewey, him that the mountain's named after. It was down there he painted the big picture of her a-standin' by the big spring. We never thought nothin' about her bein' with him so much. Country folks is that way, Mr. Howitt, though we ought to knowed better; we sure ought to knowed better." The old giant paused and for some time sat with his head bowed, his forgotten pipe on the floor.

"Well," he begain again, "he stopped with us all that summer, and then one day he went out as usual and didn't come back. We hunted the hills out for signs, thinkin' maybe he met up with some trouble. He'd sent all his pictures away the week before, Jim Lane haulin' them to the settlement for him.

"The girl was nigh about wild and rode with me all during the hunt, and once when we saw some buzzards circlin', she gave a little cry and turned so white that I suspicioned maybe she got to thinkin' more of him than we knew. Then one afternoon when we were down yonder in the Hollow, she says, all of a sudden like, 'Daddy, it ain't no use a-ridin' no more. He ain't met up with no trouble. He's left all the trouble with us.' She looked so piqued and her eyes were so big and starin' that it come over me in a flash what she meant. She saw in a minute that I sensed it, and just hung her head, and we come home.

"She just kept a-gettin' worse and worse, Mr. Howitt; 'peared to fade away like, like I watched them big glade lilies do when the hot weather comes. About the only time she would show any life at all was when someone would go for the mail, when she'd always be at the gate a-waitin' for us.

"Then one day, a letter come. I brung it myself. She give a little cry when I handed it to her, and run into the house, 'most like her old self. I went on out to the barn to put up my horse, thinkin' maybe it was goin' to be all right after

37

all; but pretty soon, I heard a scream and then a laugh. 'Fore God, sir, that laugh's a-ringin' in my ears yet. She was ravin' mad when I got to her, a-laughin', and a-screechin', and tryin' to hurt herself, all the while callin' for him to come.

"I read the letter afterwards. It told over and over how he loved her and how no woman could ever be to him what she was; said they was made for each other, and all that; and then it went on to say how he couldn't never see her again; and told about what a grand old family his was, and how his father was so proud and expected such great things from him, that he didn't dare tell, them bein' the last of this here old family, and her bein' a backwoods girl, without any schoolin' or nothin'."

"My God! O my God!" faltered the stranger's voice in the darkness.

Old Matt talked on in a hard, easy tone. "Course it was all wrote out nice and smooth like he talked, but that's the sense of it. He finished it by sayin' that he would be on his way to the old country when the letter reached her, and that it would be no use to try to find him.

"The girl quieted down after a spell, but her mind never come back. She wasn't just to say plumb crazy' but she seemed kind o' dazed and lost like, and wouldn't take no notice of nobody. Acted all the time like she was expectin' him to come. And she'd stand out there by the gate for hours at a time, watchin' the Old Trail and talkin' low to herself.

"Pete is her boy, Mr. Howitt, and as you've seen he ain't just right. Seems like he was marked some way in his mind like you've seen other folks marked in their bodies. We've done our best by the boy, sir, but I don't guess he'll ever be any better. Once for a spell we tried keepin' him to home, but he got right sick and would o' died sure, if we hadn't let him go; it was pitiful to see him. Everybody 'lows there won't nothin' in the woods hurt him nohow; so we let him come and go, as he likes; and he just stops with the neighbors wherever he happens in. Folks are all as good to him as they can be, 'cause everybody knows how it is. You see, sir, people here don't think nothin' of a wood's colt, nohow, but we was raised different. As wife says, we've most forgot civilized ways, but I guess there's some things a man that's been raised right can't never forget.

"She died when Pete was born, and the last thing she said was, 'He'll come, Daddy, he'll sure come.' Pete says the wind singin' in that big pine over her grave is her a-callin' for him yet. It's mighty queer how the boy got that notion, but you see that's the way it is with him.

"And that ain't all, sir." The big man moved his chair nearer the other, and lowered his voice to a hoarse whisper. "Folks say she's come back. There's them that swears they've seen her 'round the old cabin where they used to meet when he painted her picture, the big one, you know. Just before I bought the ranch, it was first; and that's why we can't get no one to stay with the sheep.

"I don't know, Mr. Howitt; I don't know. I've thought a heap about it, I ain't never seen it myself, and it 'pears to me that if she *could* come back at all, she'd sure come to her old daddy. Then again I figure it that bein' took the way she was, part of her dead, so to speak, from the time she got that letter, and her mind so set on his comin' back, that maybe somehow—you see—that maybe she *is* sort a waitin' for him there. Many's the time I have prayed all night that God would let me meet him again just once, or that proud father of his'n, just once, sir. I'd glad go to Hell if I could only meet them first. If she is waitin' for him down there, *he'll come; he'll sure come. Hell couldn't hold him against such as that, and when he comes—*"

Unconsciously, as he spoke the last sentences, the giant's voice took a tone of terrible meaning, and he slowly rose from his seat. When he uttered the last word he was standing erect, his muscles tense, his powerful frame shaken with passion.

There was an inarticulate cry of horror, as the mountain-

39

"I'd glad go to hell if I could only meet them first."

eer's guest started to his feet. A moment he stood, then sank back into his chair, a cowering, shivering heap.

Long into the night, the stranger walked the floor of his little room under the roof, his face drawn and white, whispering half aloud things that would have startled his unsuspecting host. "My boy—my boy-*mine!* To do such a thing as that! Howard—Howard! O Christ! That I should live to be glad that you are dead! And that picture! His masterpiece, the picture that made his fame, the picture he would never part with, and that we could never find! I see it all now! Just God, what a thing to carry on one's soul!"

Once he paused to stand at the window, looking down upon the valley. The moon had climbed high above the mountain, but beneath the flood of silver light the shadows lay dark and deep in Mutton Hollow. Then as he stood there, from out the shadowy gloom, came the wild weird song they had heard the evening before. The man at the window groaned. The song sank to a low, moaning wail, and he seemed to hear again the wind in the pine above the grave of the murdered girl. She was calling, calling—would he come back? Back from the grave, could he come? The words of the giant mountaineer seemed burned into the father's brain: *Hell couldn't hold him against such as that.*"

Then the man with the proud face, the face of a scholar and poet, drew back from the window, shaking with a fear he could not control. He crept into a corner and crouched upon the floor. With wide eyes, he stared into the dark. He prayed.

And this is how it came about that the stranger, who followed the Old Trail along the higher sunlit ground, followed, also, the other trail down into the valley where the gloomy shadows are; there to live at the ranch near the haunted cabin—the shepherd of Mutton Hollow.

41

7

What Is Love?

Sammy Lane rode very slowly on her way home from the
Matthews place that morning after the stranger had arrived.
She started out at her usual reckless gait, but that was
because she knew that Young Matt was watching her.

Once in the timber, the brown pony was pulled to a
walk, and by the time they came out into the open again,
the little horse, unrebuked by his mistress, was snatching
mouthfuls of grass as he strolled along the trail. Sammy was
thinking; thinking very seriously. Aunt Mollie's parting question had stirred the girl deeply.

Sammy had seen few people who did not belong to the
backwoods. The strangers she had met were hunters or cat-
tlemen, and these had all been, in dress and manner, not
unlike the natives themselves. This man, who had come so
unexpectedly out of the mists the night before, was unlike
anyone the young woman had ever known. Like Jed Holland, she felt somehow as if he were a superior being. The
Matthews family were different in many ways from those
born and raised in the hills. And Sammy's father, too, was
different. But this stranger—it was quite as though he
belonged to another world.

Coming to the big, low gap, the girl looked far away to
the blue line of hills, miles and miles away. The stranger
had come from over there, she thought; and then she fell
to wondering what that world beyond the farthest cloud-

like ridge was like.

Of all the people Sammy had ever known, young Stewart was the only one who had seen even the edge of that world to tell her about it. Her father and her friends, the Matthews, never talked of the old days. She had known Ollie from a child. With Young Matt they had gone to and from the log schoolhouse along the same road. Once, before Mr. Stewart's death, the boy had gone with his father for a day's visit to the city, and ever after had been a hero to his backwoods schoolmates. It was this distinction, really, that first won Sammy's admiration, and made them sweethearts before the girl's skirts had touched the tops of her shoes. Before the woman in her was fairly awake she had promised to be his wife; and they were going away now to live in that enchanted land.

Spying an extra choice bunch of grass a few steps to one side of the path, Brownie turned suddenly toward the valley, and the girl's eyes left the distant ridge for the little cabin and the sheep corral in Mutton Hollow. Sammy always spoke of that cabin as "Young Matt's house." And, all unbidden now, the thought came, who would live with the big fellow down there in the valley when she had gone far away to make her home with Ollie and his people in the city?

An impatient tug at the reins informed Brownie that his mistress was aware of his existence, and, for a time, the pony was obliged to pass many a luscious bunch of grass. But soon the reins fell slack again. The little horse moved slowly, and still more slowly, until, by the relaxed figure of his rider, he knew it was safe to again browse on the grass along the path.

So, wondering, dreaming, Sammy Lane rode down the trail that morning—the trail that is nobody knows how old. And on the hill back of the Matthews house a team was standing idle in the middle of the field.

At the big rock on the mountainside, where the trail seems to pause a moment before starting down to the valley, the girl slipped from her saddle, and, leaving Brownie to wander at will, climbed to her favorite seat. Half reclining in the warm sunshine, she watched the sheep feeding near, and laughed aloud as she saw the lambs with wagging tails, greedily sucking at their mothers' sides; nearby in a black-haw bush a mother bird sat on her nest; a gray mare, with a week-old colt following on unsteady legs, came over the ridge; and not far away a mother sow with ten squealing pigs came out of the timber. Keeping very still the young woman watched until they disappeared around the mountain. Then, lifting her arms above her head, she stretched her lithe form out upon the warm rocky couch with the freedom and grace of a wild thing of the woods.

Sammy Lane knew nothing of the laws and customs of the so-called best society. Her splendid young womanhood was not the product of those social traditions and rules that kill the instinct of her kind before it is fairly born. She was as free and as physically perfect as any of the free creatures that lived in the hills. And, keenly alive to the life that throbbed and surged about her, her woman's heart and soul responded to the spirit of the season. The droning of the bees in the blossoms that grew in a cranny of the rock; the tinkle, tinkle of the sheep bells, as the flock moved slowly in their feeding; and the soft breathing of Mother Earth was in her ears; while the gentle breeze that stirred her hair came heavy with the smell of growing things. Lying so, she looked far up into the blue sky where a buzzard floated on lazy wings. If she were up there she perhaps could see that world beyond the hills. Then suddenly a voice came to her, Aunt Mollie's voice, "How do you reckon you'll like bein' a fine lady, Sammy, and a-livin' in the city with the big folks?"

The girl turned on her side and rising on one elbow looked again at Mutton Hollow with its little cabin half hidden in the timber. And, as she looked, slowly her rich red life colored cheek, and neck, and brow. With a gesture of impatience, Sammy turned away to her own home on

44

the southern slope of the mountain, just in time to see a young woman ride into the clearing and dismount before the cabin door. It was her friend, Mandy Ford. The girl on the rock whistled to her pony, and, mounting, made her way down the hill.

All that day the strange guest at the Matthews place was the one topic of conversation between the two girls.

"Shucks," said Mandy, when Sammy had finished a very minute description of Mr. Howitt, "he's jest some revenue, like's not."

Sammy tossed her head. "Revenue! You ought to see him! Revenues don't come in no such clothes as them, and they don't talk like him, neither."

"Can't tell 'bout revenues," retorted the other. "Don't you mind how that'n fooled everybody over on th' bend last year? He was jest as common as common, and folks all 'lowed he was just one of 'em."

"But this one ain't like anybody that we ever met up with, and that's jest it," returned Sammy.

Mandy shook her head. "You say he ain't huntin'; he sure ain't buyin' cattle this time o' year; and he ain't a-wantin' t' locate a-comin' in on foot; what else can he be but revenue?"

To which Sammy replied with an unanswerable argument: "Look-a here, Mandy Ford; you jest tell me, would a low down revenue ask a blessin' like Parson Bigelow does?"

At this Mandy gave up the case, saying in despair, "Well, what is he a-doin' here then? 'Tain't likely he's done come into th' woods for nothin'."

"He told Old Matt that he was sick and tired of it all," answered the other.

"Did he look like he was ailin'?"

Sammy replied slowly, "I don't reckon it's that kind of sickness he meant; and when you look right close into his eyes, he does 'pear kind o' used up like."

In connection with this discussion, it was easy to speak of Miss Lane's fairy prospects, for was not the stranger

"Mandy, what is love, anyhow?"

from the city? And was not Sammy going to live in that land of wonders? The two girls were preparing for the night, when Sammy, who was seated on the edge of the bed, paused, with one shoe off, to ask thoughtfully, "Mandy, what is love, anyhow?"

Mandy looked surprised. "I reckon you ought to know," she said with a laugh. "Ollie's been a-hangin' round you ever since I can remember."

Sammy was struggling with a knot in the other shoelace. "Yes," she admitted slowly, "I reckon I had ought to know; but what do you say it is, Mandy?"

"Why, hit's—hit's—jest a-caring fer somebody more'n fer ary one else in th' whole world."

"Is that all?" The knot was still stubborn.

"No, hit ain't all. Hit's a-goin' t' live with somebody an' a-lettin' him take care o' you, 'stead o' your folks." Sammy was still struggling with the knot. "An' hit's a-cookin' an' a-scrubbin' an' a-mendin' fer him, an'—an'—sometimes hit's a-splittin' wood, an' a-doin' chores, too; an' I reckon that's all."

Just here the knot came undone, and the shoe dropped to the floor with a thud. Sammy sat upright. "No, it ain't, Mandy. It's a heap more'n that; it's a-nursin' babies, and a-takin' care of 'em 'til they're growed up, and then when they're big enough to take care o' themselves, and you're old and in the way, like Grandma Bowles, it's a-lookin' back over it all, an bein' glad you done married the man you did. It's a heap more'n livin' with a man, Mandy; it's a-doin' all that, without ever once wishin' he was somebody else."

This was too much for Mandy; she blushed and giggled, then remarked, as she gazed admiringly at her friend, "You'll look mighty fine, Sammy, when you get fixed up with all them pretties you'll have when you an' Ollie git married. I wish my hair was bright an' shiny like yourn. How do you reckon you'll like bein' a fine lady anyhow?"

Here it was again. Sammy turned upon her helpless friend

47

with, "How do I know if I would like it or not? What is bein' a fine lady, anyhow?"

"Why, bein' a fine lady is—is livin' in a big house with carpets on th' floor, an' lookin' glasses, an' not havin' no work t' do, an' wearin' pretty clothes, with lots of rings an' things, an'—an'," she paused, then finished in triumph, 'an' a-ridin' in a carriage."

That wide questioning look was in Sammy's eyes as she returned, "It's a heap more'n that, Mandy. I don't jest sense what it is, but I know 'tain't all them things that makes a sure 'nough lady. 'Tain't the clothes he wears that makes Mr. Howitt different from the folks we know. He don't wear no rings, and he walks. He's jest different 'cause he's different; and would be, no matter what he had on or where he was."

This, too, was beyond Mandy. Sammy continued, as she finished her preparations for retiring, "This here house is plenty big enough for me, leastwise it would be if it had one more room like the cabin in Mutton Hollow; carpets would be mighty dirty and unhandy to clean when the men folks come trampin' in with their muddy boots; I wouldn't want to wear no dresses so fine I couldn't knock round in the brush with them; and it would be awful to have nothin' to do. As for a carriage, I wouldn't swap Brownie for a whole city full of carriages." She slipped into bed and stretched out luxuriously. "Do you reckon I could be a fine lady, and be as I am now, a-livin' here in the hills?"

The next day Mandy went back to her home on Jake Creek. And in the evening Sammy's father, with Wash Gibbs, returned, both men and horses showing the effects of a long, hard ride.

8

"Why Ain't We Got No Folks?"

Preachin' Bill says, "There's a heap o' difference in most men, but Jim Lane now he's more different than ary man you ever seed. Ain't no better neighbor'n Jim anywhere. Ride out o' his way any time t' do you a favor. But you bet there ain't ary man lives can ask Jim any fool questions while Jim's a-lookin' at him. Tried it onct myself. Jim was a'waitin' at th' ferry fer Wash Gibbs, an' we was a-talkin' 'long right peart 'bout crops an' th' weather an' such, when I says, says I, like a dumb ol' fool, 'How'd you like it down in Texas, Jim, when you was there that time?' I gonies! His jaw shet with a click like he'd cocked a pistol, an' that look o' hisn, like he was a-seein' plumb through you, come int' his eyes, an' he says, says he, quiet like, 'D' you reckon that rain over on James yesterday raised th' river much?' An' 'fore I knowed it, I was a-tellin' him how that ol' red bull o' mine treed th' Perkins boys when they was a-possum huntin'."

Many stories of the Bald Knobber days, when the law of the land was the law of rifle and rope, were drifting about the countryside, and always, when these tales were recited, the name of Jim Lane was whispered; while the bolder ones wondered beneath their breath where Jim went so much with that Wash Gibbs, whose daddy was killed by the Government.

Mr. Lane was a tall man, well set up, with something in

his face and bearing that told of good breeding; southern blood, one would say, by the dark skin, and the eyes, hair, and drooping mustache of black.

His companion, Wash Gibbs, was a gigantic man. Taller and heavier, even, than the elder Matthews, but more loosely put together than Old Matt; with coarse, heavy features, and, as Grandma Bowles said, "the look of a sheep-killin' dog." Grandma, being very near her journey's end, could tell the truth even about Wash Gibbs, but others spoke of the giant only in whispers, save when they spoke in admiration of his physical powers.

As the two men swung stiffly from their saddles, Sammy came running to greet her father with a kiss of welcome. This little exhibition of affection between parent and child was one of the many things that marked the Lanes as different from the natives of that region. Your true back-woodsman carefully hides every sign of his love for either family or friends. Wash Gibbs stood looking on with an expression upon his brutal face that had very little of the human in it.

Releasing his daughter, Mr. Lane said, "Got anything to eat, honey? We're powerful hungry. Wash 'lowed we'd better tie up at the river, but I knew you'd be watching for me. The horses are plumb beat." And Gibbs broke in with a coarse laugh, "I wouldn't mind killin' a hoss neither, if I was t' git what you do at th' end o' the ride."

To this, Jim made no reply but began loosening the saddle girths, while Sammy only said, as she turned toward the house, "I'll have supper ready for you directly, Daddy."

While his host was busy caring for his tired horse, the big man, who did not remove the saddle from his mount, followed the girl into the cabin. "Can't you even tell a feller howdy?" he exclaimed, as he entered the kitchen.

"I did tell you howdy," replied the girl sharply, stirring up the fire.

" 'Pears like you might 'a' been a grain warmer about hit," growled the other, seating himself where he could

50

"I'll have supper ready for you directly, Daddy."

51

watch her. "If I'd been Young Matt er that skinny Ollie Stewart, you'd 'a' been keen enough."

Sammy turned and faced him with angry eyes. "Look-a here, Wash Gibbs, I done tol' you last Thursday when you come for Daddy that you'd better let me alone. I don't like you, and I don't aim to ever have anything to do with you. You done fixed yourself with me that time at the Cove picnic. I'll tell Daddy about that if you don't mind. I don't want to make no trouble, but you just got to quit pestering me."

The big fellow sneered. "I 'lowed you might change your mind 'bout that someday. Jim ain't goin' t' say nothin' t' me, an' if he did, words don't break no bones. I'm a heap th' best man in this neck o' th' woods, an' your paw knows hit. You know hit, too."

Under his look, the blood rushed to the girl's face in a burning blush. In spite of her anger she dropped her eyes, and without attempting a reply, turned to her work.

A moment later, Mr. Lane entered the room. A single glance at his daughter's face, a quick look at Wash Gibbs, as the bully sat following with wolfish eyes every movement of the girl, and Jim stepped quietly in front of his guest. At the same moment, Sammy left the house for a bucket of water, and Wash turned toward his host with a start to find the dark-faced man gazing at him with a look that few men could face with composure. Without a word, Jim's right hand crept stealthily inside his hickory shirt, where a button was missing.

For a moment Gibbs tried to return the look. He failed. Something he read in the dark face before him—some meaning light in those black eyes—made him tremble and he felt, rather than saw, Jim's hand resting quietly now inside the hickory shirt near his left armpit. The big man's face went white beneath the tan, his eyes wavered and shifted, he hung his head and shuffled his feet uneasily, like an overgrown schoolboy brought sharply to task by the master.

Then Jim, his hand still inside his shirt, drawled softly, but with a queer metallic ring in his voice, "Do you reckon it's going t' storm again?"

At the commonplace question, the bully drew a long breath and looked around. "We might have a spell o' weather," he muttered, "but I don't guess it'll be t'night."

Then Sammy returned and they had supper.

Next to his daughter, Jim Lane loved his violin, and with good reason, for the instrument had once belonged to his great-grandfather, who, tradition says, was a musician of no mean ability.

Preachin' Bill " 'lowed there was a heap o' difference between a-playin' a violin an' jest fiddlin'. You wouldn't know some fellers was a-makin' music, if you didn't see 'em a-pattin' their foot; but hit ain't that-a way with Jim Lane. He sure do make music, real music." As no one ever questioned Bill's judgment, it is safe to conclude that Mr. Lane inherited something of his great-grandfather's ability along with his treasured instrument.

When supper was over, and Wash Gibbs had gone on his way, Jim took the violin from its peg above the fireplace, and, tucking it lovingly under his chin, gave himself up to his favorite pastime, while Sammy moved busily about the cabin, putting things right for the night.

When her evening tasks were finished, the girl came and stood before her father. At once the music ceased and the violin was laid carefully aside. Sammy seated herself on her father's knee.

"Law, child, but you're sure growin' up," said Jim, with a mock groan at her weight.

"Yes, Daddy, I reckon I'm about growed; I'll be nineteen come Christmas."

"Oh, shucks!" ejaculated the man. "It wasn't more'n last week that you was washin' doll clothes, down by the spring."

The young woman laughed. "I didn't wash no doll clothes last week," she said. Then her voice changed, and that

53

wide, questioning look, the look that made one think so of her father, came into her eyes. "There's something I want to ask you, Daddy Jim. You—you know—Ollie's goin' away, an'—an'—an' I was thinkin' about it all day yesterday, an', Daddy, why ain't we got no folks?"

Mr. Lane stirred uneasily. Sammy continued, "There's the Matthews, they've got kin back in Illinois; Mandy Ford's got uncles and aunts over on Long Creek; Jed Holland's got a grandad and mam, and even Preachin' Bill talks about a pack o' kinfolks over in Arkansaw. Why ain't we got no folks, Daddy?"

The man gazed long and thoughtfully at the fresh young face of his child; and the black eyes looked into the brown eyes keenly, as he answered her questions with another question, "Do you reckon you love him right smart, honey? Are you sure, dead sure you ain't thinkin' of what he's got 'stead of what he is? I know it'll be mighty nice for you to be one of the fine folks and they're big reasons why you ought, but it's goin' to take a mighty good man to match you—a mighty good man. And it's the man you've got to live with, not his money."

"Ollie's good, Daddy," she returned in a low voice, her eyes fixed upon the floor.

"I know, I know," replied Jim. "He wouldn't do nobody no harm; he's good enough that way, and I ain't a-faultin' him. But you ought to have a *man*, a sure enough good man."

"But tell me, Daddy, why ain't we got no folks?"

The faintest glimmer of a smile came into the dark face. "You're sure growed up, girl; you're sure growed up, girl; you sure are. An' I reckon you might as well know." Then he told her.

9

Sammy Lane's Folks

It began on a big southern plantation, where there were several brothers and sisters, with a gentleman father of no little pride, and a lady mother of equal pride and great beauty.

With much care for detail, Jim drew a picture of the big mansion with its wide lawns, flower gardens and tree-bordered walks; with its wealth of culture, its servants, and distinguished guests; for, said he, "When you get to be a fine lady, you ought to know that you got as good blood as the best of the thoroughbreds." And Sammy, interrupting his speech with a kiss, bade him go on with his story.

Then he told how the one black sheep of that proud southern flock had been cast forth from the beautiful home while still hardly grown; and how, with his horse, gun and violin, the wanderer had come into the heart of the Ozark wilderness, when the print of moccasin feet was still warm on the Old Trail. Jim sketched broadly here, and for some reason did not fully explain the cause of his banishment; neither did he comment in any way upon its justice or injustice.

Time passed, and a strong, clear-eyed, clean-limbed, deep-bosomed mountain lass, with all the mastering passion of her kind, mated the free, half wild, young hunter; and they settled in the cabin by the spring on the southern slope of Dewey. Then the little one came, and in her veins there was mingled the blue blood of the proud southerners and the warm red life of her wilderness mother.

Again Jim's story grew rich in detail. Holding his daughter at arm's length, and looking at her through half-closed eyes, he said, "You're like her honey; you're mighty like her; same eyes, same hair, same mouth, same build, same way of movin', strong, but smooth and free like. She could run clean to the top of Dewey, or sit a horse all day. Do you ever get tired, girl?"

Sammy laughed, and shook her head. "I've run from here to the signal tree, lots of times, Daddy."

"You're like the old folks, too," mused Jim; "like them in what you think and say."

"Tell me more," said the girl. "Seems like I remember bein' in a big wagon, and there was a woman there too; was she my mother?"

Jim nodded, and unconsciously lowered his voice, as he said, "It was in the old Bald Knobber time. Things happened in them days, honey. Many's the night I've seen the top of old Dewey yonder black with men. It was when things was broke up, that—that your mother and me thought we could do better in Texas; so we went." Jim was again sketching broadly.

"Your mother left us there, girl. Seemed like she couldn't stand it, bein' away from the hills or somethin', and she just give up. I never did rightly know how it was. We buried her out there, way out on the big plains."

"I remember her a little," whispered Sammy.

Jim continued: "Then after a time you and me come back to the old place. Your mother named you Samantha, girl, but bein' as there wasn't no boy, I always called you Sammy. It seems right enough that way now, for you've sure been more'n a son to me since we've been alone; and that's one reason why I learned you to ride and shoot with the best of them.

"There's them that says I ain't done right by you, bringing you up without any woman about the place; and I don't know as I have, but somehow I couldn't never think of no woman as I ought, after living with your mother. And then there was Aunt Mollie to learn you how to cook and do things about the house. I counted a good bit, too, on the old stock, and it sure showed up right. You're like the old folks, girl, in the way you think, but you're like your mother in the way you look."

Sammy's arms went around her father's neck. "You're a good man, Daddy Jim; the best Daddy a girl ever had; and if I ain't all bad, it's on account of you." There was a queer look on the man's dark face. He had sketched some parts of his tale with a broad hand, indeed.

The girl raised her head again. "But, Daddy, I wish you'd do something for me. I—I don't like Wash Gibbs to be a-comin' here. I wish you'd quit ridin' with him, Daddy. I'm—I'm afeared of him; he looks at me so. He's a sure bad one—I know he is, Daddy."

Jim laughed and again there was that odd metallic note in his voice. "I've knowed him a long time, honey. Me and his daddy was—was together when he died; and you used to sit on Wash's knee when you was a little tad. Not that he's so mighty much older than you, but he was a man's size at fifteen. You don't understand, girl, but I've got to go with him sometimes. But don't you fret; Wash Gibbs ain't goin' to hurt me, and he won't come here more'n I can help, either." Then he changed the subject abruptly. "Tell me what you've been doin' while I was away."

Sammy told of her visit to their friends at the Matthews place, and of the stranger who had come into the neighborhood. As the girl talked, her father questioned her carefully, and several times the metallic note crept into his soft, drawling speech, while into his eyes came that peculiar, searching look, as if he would draw from his daughter even more than she knew of the incident. Once he rose, and, going to the door, stood looking out into the night.

Sammy finished with her answer to Mandy Ford's opinion of the stranger. "You don't reckon a revenue would ask a blessin', do you, Daddy? Seems like he just naturally wouldn't dast; God would make the victuals stick in his throat and choke him sure."

Jim laughed, as he replied, "I don't know, girl; I never heard of a revenue's doin' such. But a feller can't tell."

When Sammy left him to retire for the night, her father picked up the violin again, and placed it beneath his chin as if to play; but he did not touch the strings, and soon hung the instrument in its place above the mantel. Then, going to the doorway, he lighted his pipe, and, for a full hour, sat looking up the Old Trail toward the Matthews place, his right hand thrust into the bosom of his hickory shirt, where the button was missing.

10

A Feat of Strength and a Challenge

What the club is to the city man, and the general store or post office to the citizens of the country village, the mill is to the native of the backwoods.

Made to saw the little rough lumber he needs in his primitive building, or to grind his corn into the rough meal that is his staff of life, the mill does more for the settler than this; it brings together the scattered population, it is the news center, the heart of the social life, and the hub of the industrial wheel.

On grinding day, the Ozark mountaineer goes to mill on horseback, his grist in a sack behind the saddle, or, indeed, taking place of the saddle itself. The rule is, first come, first served. So, while waiting his turn, or waiting for a neighbor who will ride in the same direction, the woodsman has time to contribute his share to the gossip of the countryside, or to take part in the discussions that are of more or less vital interest. When the talk runs slow, there are games; pitching horseshoes, borrowed from the blacksmith shop—there is always a blacksmith shop nearby; running or jumping contests, or wrestling or shooting matches.

Fall Creek Mill, owned and operated by Mr. Matthews and his son, was located on Fall Creek in a deep, narrow valley, about a mile from their home.

A little old threshing engine, one of the very first to take the place of the horse power, and itself in turn already pushed to the wall by improved competitors, rolled the saw or the burr. This engine, which had been rescued by Mr. Matthews from the scrap pile of a Springfield machine shop, was accepted as evidence beyond question of the superior intelligence and genius of the Matthews family. In fact, Fall Creek Mill gave the whole Mutton Hollow neighborhood such a tone of up-to-date enterprise, that folks from the Bend, or the mouth of the James, looked upon the Mutton Hollow people with no little envy and awe, not to say even jealousy.

The settlers came to the Matthews mill from far up the creek, crossing and recrossing the little stream; from Iron Spring and from Gardner, beyond Sand Ridge, following faint, twisting bridle paths through the forest; from the other side of Dewey Bald, along the Old Trail; from the Cove and from the Post Office at the Forks, down the wagon road, through the pinery; and from Wolf Ridge and the head of Indian Creek beyond, climbing the rough mountains. Even from the river bottoms they came, yellow and shaking with ague, to swap tobacco and yarns, and to watch with never failing interest the crazy old engine, as Young Matt patted, and coaxed, and flattered her into doing his will.

They began coming early that grinding day, two weeks after Mr. Howitt had been installed at the ranch. But the young engineer was ready, with a good head of steam in the old patched boiler, and the smoke was rising from the rusty stack, in a long, twisting line, above the motionless treetops.

It was a great day for Young Matt; great because he knew that Sammy Lane would be coming to mill; he would see her and talk with her; perhaps if he were quick enough, he might even lift her from the brown pony.

It was a great day, too, because Ollie Stewart would be saying good-by, and before tomorrow would be on his way out of the hills. Not that it mattered whether Ollie went or not. It was settled that Sammy was going to marry young Stewart; that was what mattered. And Young Matt had given her up. And, as he had told his father in the barn that day, it was all right. But still—still it was a great day, because Ollie would be saying good-by.

It was a great day in Young Matt's life, too, because on that day he would issue his challenge to the acknowledged champion of the countryside, Wash Gibbs. But Young Matt did not know this until afterwards, for it all came about in a very unexpected way.

The company had been discussing the new arrival in the neighborhood, and speculating as to the probable length of Mr. Howitt's stay at the ranch, and while Young Matt was in the burr-house with his father, they had gone over yet again the familiar incidents of the ghost story; how "Budd Wilson seen her as close as from here t' th' shop yonder." How "Joe Gardner's mule had gone plumb hog-wild when he tried to ride past the ol' ruins near th' ranch." And "how Lem Wheeler, while out hunting that roan steer o' hisn, had heard a moanin' an' a wailin' under the bluff."

Upon Young Matthews returning to his engine, the conversation had been skillfully changed to Ollie Stewart and his remarkable good fortune. From Ollie and his golden prospects, it was an easy way to Sammy Lane and her coming marriage.

Buck Thompson was just concluding a glowing tribute to the girl's beauty of face and form when Young Matt reached for an axe lying near the speaker. Said Buck, "Preachin' Bill 'lowed t'other day hit didn't make no difference how much money th' ol' man left Ollie he'd be a poor sort of a man anyhow; an' that there's a heap better men than him right here in th' hills that Sammy could 'a' had fer th' askin'."

"How 'bout that, Matt?" called a young fellow from the river.

The big man's face flushed at the general laugh which followed, and he answered hotly, as he swung his axe, "You'd better ask Wash Gibbs; I hear he says he's the best man in these woods."

"I reckin as how Wash can back his jedgment there," said Joe.

"Wash is a sure good man," remarked Buck, "But there's

another not so mighty far away that'll pretty nigh hold his level." He looked significantly to where Young Matt was making the big chips fly.

"Huh," grunted Joe. "I tell you, gentlemen, that there man, Gibbs, is powerful; yes, sir, he sure is. Tell you what I seed him do." Joe pulled a twist of tobacco from his hip pocket, and settled down upon his heels, his back against a post.

"Wash an' me was a-goin' to th' settlement last fall, an' jest this side th' camp house, on Wilderness Road, we struck a threshin' crew stuck in th' mud with their engine. Had a breakdown o' some kind. Somethin' th' matter with th' hind wheel. An' jest as Wash an' me drove up, th' boss of th' outfit was a-tellin' 'em t' cut a big pole for a pry t' lift th' hind ex, so's they could block it up, an' fix th' wheel.

"Wash he looked at 'em a minute an' then says, says he, 'Hold on, boys; you don't need ary pole.'

" 'What do you know 'bout an engine, you darned hillbilly,' says th' old man, kind o' short.

" 'Don't know nothin' 'bout an engine, you prairie hopper,' says Wash, 'but I know you don't need no pole t' lift that thing.'

" 'How'd you lift it then?' says t'other.

" 'Why I'd jest catch holt an' lift,' says Wash.

"The gang like t' bust theirselves laughin'. 'Why you blame fool,' says the boss, 'do you know what that engine'll weight?'

" 'Don't care a cuss *what* she'll weigh,' says Wash. 'She ain't *planted* there, is she?' An' with that he climbs down from th' wagon, an' dad burn me if he didn't take holt o' that hind ex an' lift one whole side o' that there engine clean off th' ground. Them fellers jest stood 'round an' looked at him t' beat th' stir. 'Well,' says Wash, still a-keepin' his holt, 'slide a block under her an' I'll mosey along!'

"That boss didn't say a word 'til he'd got a bottle from a box on th' wagon an' handed hit t' Wash; then he says kind o' scared like, 'Where in hell are you from, mister?'

" 'Oh, I'm jest a kid from over on Roark,' says Wash, handin' th' bottle t' me. 'You ought t' see some o' th' *men* in

62

my neighborhood!' Then we went on."

When the speaker had finished, there was quiet for a little. Then the young man from the river drawled, "How much did you say that there engine'd weigh, Joe?"

There was a general laugh at this, which the admirer of Gibbs took good-naturedly. "Don't know what she'd weight but she was 'bout the size o' that one there," he answered.

With one accord everyone turned to inspect the mill engine. "Pretty good lift, Joe. Let's you an' me take a pull at her, Budd," remarked Lem Wheeler.

The two men lifted and strained at the wheel. Then another joined them, and, amid the laughter and good-natured raillery of the crowd, the three tried in vain to lift one of the wheels; while Mr. Matthews, seeing some unusual movement, came into the shed and stood with his son, an amused witness of their efforts.

"Sure this engine ain't bigger'n t'other, Joe?" asked one of the group.

"Don't believe she weighs a pound more," replied the mountaineer with conviction. "I tell you, gentlemen, that man Gibbs is a wonder, he sure is."

Old Matt and his son glanced quickly at each other, and the boy shook his head with a smile. This little byplay was lost on the men who were interested in the efforts of different ones, in groups of three, to move the wheel. When they had at last given it up, the young man from the river drawled, "You're right sure hit weren't after th' boss give you that bottle that Wash lifted her, are you, Joe? Or wasn't hit on th' way home from th' settlement?"

When the laugh at this insinuation had died out, Buck said thoughtfully, "Tell you what, boys; I'd like t' see Young Matt try that lift."

Mr. Matthews, who was just starting back to the burr-house, paused in the doorway. All eyes were fixed upon his son. "Try her, Matt. Show us what you can do," called the men in chorus. But the young man shook his head, and found something that needed his immediate attention.

All that morning at intervals the mountaineers urged the big fellow to attempt the feat, but he always put them off with some evasive reply, or was too busy to gratify them.

But after dinner, while the men were pitching horseshoes in front of the blacksmith shop, Buck Thompson approached the young engineer alone. "Look-a here, Matt," he said, "why don't you try that lift? Durned me if I don't believe you'd fetch her."

The young giant looked around. "I know I can, Buck; I lifted her yesterday while Dad fixed the blockin'; I always do it that way."

Buck looked at him in amazement. "Well, why in thunder don't you show th' boys, then?" he burst forth at last.

" 'Cause if I do Wash Gibbs'll hear of it sure, and I'll have to fight him to settle which is the best man."

"Good Lord!" ejaculated Buck, with a groan. "If you're afraid o' Wash Gibbs, it's th' first thing I ever knowed you t' be scared o'."

Young Matt looked his friend steadily in the eyes, as he replied, "I ain't afraid of Wash Gibbs; I'm afraid of myself. Mr. Howitt says, 'No man needn't be afraid of nobody but himself.' I've been a-thinkin' lately, Buck, an' I see some things that I never see before. I figure it that if I fight Wash Gibbs or anybody else just to see which is th' best man, I ain't no better'n he is. I reckon I'll have to whip him some day, all right, an' I ain't a-carin' much how soon it comes; but I ain't a-goin' to hurt nobody for nothin' just because I can."

Buck made no reply to this. Such sentiment was a little too much for his primitive notions. He went back to the men by the blacksmith shop.

It was not long, however, until the players left their game, to gather once more about the engine. Lem Wheeler approached Young Matt with a serious air. "Look-a here," he said, "we all want t' see you try that lift."

"I ain't got no time for foolin'," replied the young man. "Dad's just pushin' to get done before dark."

"Shucks!" reported the other. "Hit won't take a minute t'

64

"Them colts 'll make a fine team, Buck."

try. Jest catch hold an' show us what you can do."

"What are you all so keen about my liftin' for, anyhow?" demanded the big fellow suspiciously. "I ain't never set up as the strong man of this country."

"Well, you see it's this way; Buck done bet me his mule colt agin mine that you could lift her; an' we want you to settle th' bet!" exclaimed Lem.

Young Matthew shot a glance at the mountaineer, who grinned joyously. "Yep," said Buck, "that's how it is; I'm a-backin' you. Don't want you t' hurt yourself for me, but I sure do need that colt o' Lem's; hit's a dead match for mine."

The giant looked at his friend a moment in silence, then burst into a laugh of appreciation at Buck's hint. "Seein' as how you're backin' me, Buck, I'll have t' get you that mule if I can."

He shut off steam, and, as the engine came to a stop, stooped, and, with apparent ease, lifted the rear wheel a full four inches from the ground.

Loud exclamations of admiration came from the little group of men in the shed. Lem turned with a long face. "Them colts'll make a fine team, Buck," he said.

"You bet; come over an' hep me break 'em," replied Buck, with another grin of delight.

"Wait 'til Wash Gibbs hears 'bout this, an' he'll sure be for breakin' Young Matt," put in another.

"Better get your fightin' clothes on, Matt; Wash'll never rest easy until you've done showed him." These and similar remarks revealed the general view of the situation.

While the men were discussing the matter, a thin, high-pitched voice from the edge of the crowd broke in, "That there's a good lift all right, but hit ain't nothin' t' what I seed when I was t' th' circus in th' city."

Young Matt, who had started the engine again, turned quickly. Ollie Stewart was sitting on a horse nearby, and at his side, on the brown pony, was Miss Sammy Lane. They had evidently ridden up just in time to witness the exhibition of the giant's strength.

11

Ollie Stewart's Good-by

Beside the splendidly developed young woman, Ollie Stewart appeared but a weakling. His shoulders were too narrow and he stooped; his limbs were thin; his hair black and straight; and his eyes dull.

As Young Matt stepped forward, Ollie dismounted quickly, but the big fellow was first at the brown pony's side. Sammy's eyes shone with admiration, and, as the strong man felt their light, he was not at all sorry that he had won the mule colt for Buck.

"No," she said, declining his offered assistance, she did not wish to get down; they were going to the Post Office and would call for the meal on their way home.

Young Matt lifted the sack of corn from Brownie's back and carried it into the shed. When he returned to the group, Ollie was saying in his thin voice, "In th' circus I seen in the city there was a feller that lifted a man, big as Jed here, clean above his head with one hand."

Buck turned to his big friend. His look was met by a grim smile that just touched the corners of the lad's mouth, and there was a gleam in the blue eyes that betrayed the spirit within. The lean mountaineer again turned to the company, while the boy glanced at Sammy. The girl was watching him and had caught the silent exchange between the two friends.

"Shucks!" said Buck, "Matt could do that easy." "Try it,

THE SHEPHERD OF THE HILLS

Matt." "Try Jed here." "Try hit once," called the chorus.

This time the big fellow needed no urging. With Sammy looking on, he could not resist the opportunity which Ollie himself had presented. Without a word, but with a quick tightening of the lips, he stepped forward and caught Jed by the belt with his right hand; and then, before anyone could guess his purpose, he reached out with his other hand, and grasped Ollie himself in the same manner. There was a short step forward, a quick upward swing, and the giant held a man in each hand at full arm's length above his head. Amid the shouts of the crowd, still holding the men, he walked deliberately to the blacksmith shop and back; then lowering them easily to their feet, turned to his engine.

Ollie and Sammy rode away together, up the green arched road, and the little company in the mill shed stood watching them. As the finely formed young woman and her inferior escort passed from sight, a tall mountaineer, from the other side of Compton Ridge, remarked, "I done heard Preachin' Bill say t'other day, that 'mighty nigh all this here gee-hawin', balkin', and kickin' 'mongst th' married folks comes 'cause th' teams ain't matched up right.' Bill he 'lowed God 'lmighty'd fixed hit somehow so th' birds an' varmints don't make no mistake, but left hit plumb easy for men an' women t' make durned fools o' theirselves."

Everybody grinned in appreciation, and another spoke up. "According t' that, I'll bet four bits if them two yonder ever do get into double harness, there'll be pieces o' th' outfit strung from th' parson's clean t' th' buryin' ground."

When the laughter had subsided, Buck turned to see Young Matt standing just outside the shed, ostensibly doing something with the belt that led to the burr, but in reality looking up the creek.

"Law!" ejaculated Buck, under his breath, "what a team *they'd* make!"

"Who?" said Lem, who was standing nearby.

"Them mule colts," returned Buck with a grin.

"They sure will, Buck. There ain't two better in the

country; they're a dead match. I'll come over an' hep you break 'em when they're big 'nough." And then he wondered why Buck swore with such evident delight.

One by one the natives received their meal, and, singly, or in groups of two or three, were swallowed up by the great forest. Already the little valley was in the shadow of the mountain, though the sun still shone brightly on the treetops higher up, when Ollie and Sammy returned from the Forks. Mr. Matthews had climbed the hill when the last grist was ground, leaving his son to cool down the engine and put things right about the mill.

"Come on, Matt," said Ollie, as the big fellow brought out the meal. "It's time you was a-goin' home."

The young giant hung back, saying, "You folks better go on ahead. I'll get home all right."

"Didn't think nothin' would get you," laughed Ollie. "Come on, you might as well go 'long with us."

The other muttered something about being in the way, and started back into the shed.

"Hurry up," called Sammy, "we're waitin'."

After this there was nothing else for the young man to do but join them. And the three were soon making their way up the steep mountain road together.

For a time they talked of commonplace things, then Young Matt opened the subject that was on all their hearts. "I reckon, Ollie, this is the last time that you'll ever be a climbin' this old road." As he spoke he was really thinking of the time to come when Sammy would climb the road for the last time.

"Yes," returned Stewart. "I go tomorrow 'fore sun up."

The other continued, "It'll sure be fine for you to live in the city and get your schoolin' and all that. Us folks here in the woods don't know nothin'. We ain't got no chance to learn. You'll be forgettin' us all mighty quick, I reckon, once you get to livin' with your rich kin."

" 'Deed, I won't!" returned Ollie warmly. "Sammy an' me was a-talkin' 'bout that this evenin'. We aim t' always

69

"I don't guess you need to count on me bein' more than I am."

come back t' Mutton Holler onct a year, an' be just like
other folks; don't we, Sammy?"

The brown pony, stepping on a loose stone, stumbled
toward the man walking by his side. And the big fellow put
out his hand quickly to the little horse's neck. For an
instant, the girl's hand rested on the giant's shoulder, and
her face was close to his. Then Brownie recovered his footing, and Young Matt drew farther away.

Ollie continued, "We aim t' have you come t' th' city
after a while. I'm goin' t' get Uncle Dan t' give you a job
in th' shops, an' you can get out o' these hills an' be
somebody like we'uns."

The tone was unmistakably patronizing. The big mountaineer lifted his head proudly, and turned toward the
speaker, but before he could reply, Sammy broke in eagerly, "Law! but that would sure be fine, wouldn't it, Matt?
I know you'd do somethin' big if you only had the chance.
I just know you would. You're so—so kind o' big every
way," she laughed. "It's a plumb shame for you to be buried alive in these hills."

There was nothing said after this, until, coming to the
top of the ridge, they stopped. From here Ollie and Sammy
would take the Old Trail to the girl's home. Then, with his
eyes on the vast sweep of forest-clad hills and valleys, over
which the blue haze was fast changing to purple in the level
rays of the sun, Young Matt spoke.

"I don't guess you'd better figure on that. Some folks are
made to live in the city, and some ain't. I reckon I was
built to live in these hills. I don't somehow feel like I could
get along without them; and besides, I'd always be knockin'
against somethin' there." He laughed grimly, and stretched
out his huge arms. "I've got to have room. Then there's the
folks yonder." He turned his face toward the log house,
just showing through the trees. "You know how it is, me
bein' the only one left, and Dad gettin' old. No, I don't
guess you need to count on me bein' more than I am."

Then suddenly he wheeled about and looked from one

face to the other; and there was a faint hint of definance in his voice, as he finished, "I got an idea, too, that the backwoods needs men same as the cities. I don't see how there ever could *be* a city even, if it wasn't for the men what cleared the brush. Somebody's got to lick Wash Gibbs some day, or there just naturally won't be no decent livin' in the neighborhood ever."

He held up his big hand to the man on the horse. "Good-by, and good luck to you, Ollie." The horses turned down the Old Trail and with their riders, passed from sight.

That night Sammy Lane said farewell to her lover, and, with many promises for the future, Ollie rode away to his cabin home, to leave the next morning for that world that lies so far—so far away from the world of Young Matt and his friends, the world that is so easy to get into after all, and so impossible to get out of ever.

12

The Shepherd and His Flock

All that spring and summer things went smoothly in the
Mutton Hollow neighborhood. The corn was ready to
gather, and nothing had happened at the ranch since Mr.
Howitt took charge, while the man who had appeared so
strangely in their midst had made a large place for himself
in the hearts of the simple mountaineers.

At first they were disposed to regard him with some dis-
trust, as one apart; he was so unlike themselves. But when
he had changed his dress for the rough garb of the hillsman, and, meeting them kindly upon their own ground,
had entered so readily into their life, the people by common consent dropped the distinguishing title "Mister" for
the more familiar one of the backwoods, "Dad." Not that
they lacked in respect or courtesy; it was only their way.
And the quiet shepherd accepted the title with a pleased
smile, seeming to find in the change an honor to be received not lightly. But while showing such interest in all
that made up their world, the man never opened the door
for anyone to enter his past. They knew no more of his
history than the hints he had given Mr. Matthews the night
he came out of the mists.

At the occasional religious meetings in the schoolhouse at
the Forks, Mr. Howitt was always present, an attentive listener to the sermons of the backwoods preacher. And then,
seeing his interest, they asked him to talk to them one day

when Parson Bigelow failed to make his appointment. "He don't holler so much as a regular parson," said Uncle Josh Hensley, "but he sure talks so we'uns can understand." From that time they always called upon him at their public gatherings.

So the scholar from the world beyond the ridges slipped quietly into the life of the mountain folk, and took firm root in their affections. And in his face, so "Preachin' Bill" said, was the look of one who had "done fought his fight to a finish, an' war too dead beat t' even be glad it war all over."

Between the giant Mr. Matthews and his shepherd, the friendship, begun that night, grew always stronger. In spite of the difference in education and training, they found much in common. Some bond of fellowship, unknown to the mountaineer, at least, drew them close, and the two men spent many evenings upon the front porch of the log house in quiet talk, while the shadows crept over the valley below, and the light went from the sky back of the clump of pines.

From the first Young Matt was strongly drawn to the stranger, who was to have such influence over his life, and Pete—Pete said that "God lived with Dad Howitt in Mutton Hollow."

Pete somehow knew a great deal about God these days. A strange comradeship had come to be between the thoughtful gentleman who cared for the sheep, and the ignorant, sorely afflicted, and nameless backwoods boy. The two were always together, out on the hillside and in the little glens and valleys, during the day with the sheep, or at the ranch in the Hollow, when the flock was safely folded and the nights slipped quietly over the timbered ridges. Mr. Howitt had fixed a bunk in his cabin for the boy, so that he could come and go at will. Often the shepherd awoke in the morning to find that some time during the night his strange friend had come in from his roving. Again, after seeing the boy soundly sleeping, the shepherd would arise in the morning to find the bunk empty.

Sammy Lane, too, had fallen under the charm of the man with the white hair and poet's face.

Sammy was not so often at the Matthews place after Ollie had gone to the city. The girl could not have told why. She had a vague feeling that it was better to stay away. But this feeling did not prevent her climbing the Old Trail to the Lookout on the shoulder of Dewey, and she spent hours at the big rock, looking over the valley to where the smoke from Aunt Mollie's kitchen curled above the trees. And sometimes, against the sky, she could see a man and a team moving slowly to and fro in the field back of the house. When this happened, Sammy always turned quickly away to where the far-off line of hills lay like a long, low cloud against the sky.

Every week the girl rode her brown pony to the Post Office at the Forks; and when she had a letter, things were different. She always stopped then at the Matthews home.

One day when this happened, Dad and Pete were on the ridge above the Old Trail, just where the north slope of Dewey shades into the rim of the Hollow. The elder man was seated on the ground in the shade of an oak, with his back against the trunk of the tree, while the boy lay full length on the soft grass, looking up into the green depths of foliage where a tiny brown bird flitted from bough to bough. In his quaint way, Pete was carrying on a conversation with his little friend in the treetop, translating freely the while for his less gifted, but deeply interested, companion on the ground below, when Brave, the shepherd dog, lying near, interrupted the talk by a short bark. Looking up, they saw Young Matt riding along the summit of the ridge.

The young man paused when he heard the dog, and caught sight of the two under the tree; then he came to them, and seated himself on the grass at Pete's side. He spoke no word of greeting, and the look on his face was not good to see.

Pete's eyes went wide with fear at the manner of his big friend, and he drew back as if to run, but when Young Matt, throwing himself over on the grass, had hidden his face, a half sad, half knowing look came into the lad's delicate features; reaching forth a hand, as slim as a girl's, he stroked the shaggy, red-brown head, as he murmured softly, "Poor Matt. Poor Matt. Does it hurt? Is Matt hurt? It'll be better by and by."

The great form on the grass stirred impatiently. The shepherd spoke no word. Pete continued, stroking the big head, and talking in low, soothing tones, as one would hush a child, "Pete don't know what's a-hurtin' Young Matt, but it'll be all right, some day. It'll sure grow over after awhile. Ain't nothing won't grow over after awhile; 'cause God he says so."

Still the older man was silent. Then the giant burst forth in curses, and the shepherd spoke. "Don't do that, Grant. It's not like you, lad. You cannot help your trouble that way."

Young Matt turned over to face his friend. "I know it, Dad," he growled defiantly, "but I just got to say somethin'. I ain't meanin' no disrespect to God 'lmighty, and I reckon He ought to know it, but—" He broke forth again.

Pete drew back in alarm. "Look your trouble in the face, lad," said the shepherd. "Don't let it get you down like this."

"Look it in the face!" roared the other. "Good God! that's just it! Ain't I a lookin' it in the face every day? You don't know about it, Dad. If you did, you—you'd cuss too." He started in again.

"I know more than you think, Grant," said the other, when the big fellow had stopped swearing to get his breath. While he spoke, the shepherd was looking away along the Old Trail. "There comes your trouble now," he added, pointing to a girl on a brown pony, coming slowly out of the timber near the deer lick. The young man made no reply. Pete, at sight of the girl, started to his feet, but the

big fellow pulled him down again, and made the boy understand that he must not betray their position.

When Sammy reached the sheep, she checked her pony,
and searched the hillside with her eyes, while her clear call
went over the mountain, "Oh—h—h—Dad!"

Young Matt shook his head savagely at his companion,
and even Brave was held silent by a low "Be still" from his
master.

Again Sammy looked carefully on every side, but lying
on the higher ground, and partly hidden by the trees, the
little group could not be seen. When there was no answer
to her second call, the girl drew a letter from her pocket,
and, permitting the pony to roam at will, proceeded to
read.

The big man, looking on, cursed again beneath his breath.
"It's from Ollie," he whispered to his companions. "She
stopped at the house. He says his uncle will give me a job
in the shops, and that it'll be fine for me, 'cause Ollie will
be my boss himself. He my boss! Why, dad burn his sneak-
in' little soul, I could crunch him with one hand. I'd see
him in hell before I'd take orders from him. I told her so,
too," he finished savagely.

"And what did she say?" asked the shepherd quietly, his
eyes on the girl below.

"Just said, kind o' short like, that she reckoned I could.
Then I come away."

The girl finished her letter, and, after another long call
for Dad, moved on over the shoulder of the mountain.
Pete, who had withdrawn a little way from his companions,
was busily talking in his strange manner to his unseen
friends.

Then Young Matt opened his heart to the shepherd and
told him all. It was the old, old story; and, as Mr. Howitt
listened, dreams that he had thought dead with the death of
his only son, stirred again in his heart, and his deep voice
was vibrant with emotion as he sought to comfort the lad
who had come to him.

While they talked, the sun dropped until its lower edge touched the top of the tallest pine on Wolf Ridge, and the long shadows lay over the valley below. "I'm mighty sorry I let go and cuss, Dad," finished the boy. "But I keep a-holdin' in, and a-holdin' in, 'til I'm plumb wild; then something happens like that letter, and I go out on the range and bust. I've often wished you knowed. Seems like your just knowin' about it will help me to hold on. I get scared at myself sometimes, Dad, I do, honest."

"I'm glad, too, that you have told me, Grant. It means more to me than you can guess. I—I had a boy once, you know. He was like you. He would have come to me this way, if he had lived."

The sheep had begun working toward the lower ground. The shepherd rose to his feet. "Take them home, Brave. Come on, boys, you must eat with me at the ranch tonight." Then the three friends, the giant mountaineer, the strangely afflicted youth, and the old scholar went down the mountainside together. As they disappeared in the timber on the lower level, the bushes, near which they had been sitting, parted silently, and a man's head and shoulders appeared from behind a big rock. The man watched the strange companions out of sight. Then the bushes swayed together, and the mountain seemed to have swallowed him up.

The three friends had just finished their supper when Pete saw Sammy entering the ranch clearing. Young Matt caught up his hat. At the rear door he paused. "I've got to go now, Dad," he said awkwardly. "I can't see her any more today. But if you'll let me, I'll come again when things get too hot."

The shepherd held out his hand, "I understand. Come always, my boy."

The big fellow, with Pete, slipped away into the timber at the rear of the cabin, a moment before Sammy appeared at the open door in front.

13

Sammy Lane's Ambition

"Law sakes!" cried Sammy, looking at the table. "You don't use all them dishes, do you, Dad? You sure must eat a lot."

"Oh, I eat enough," laughed Mr. Howitt, "but it happens that I had company this evening. Young Matt and Pete were here for supper." He brought two chairs outside the cabin.

"Shucks!" exclaimed Sammy, as she seated herself, and removed her sunbonnet. "They must've eat and run. Wish'd I'd got here sooner. Young Matt run away from me this afternoon. And I wanted to see him 'bout Mandy Ford's party next week. I done promised Mandy that I'd bring him. I reckon he'd go with me if I asked him."

"There is not the least doubt about that," observed the man. "I'm sure anyone would be glad for such charming company."

The girl looked up suspiciously. "Are you a-jokin'?" she said.

"Indeed, I am not; I am very much in earnest." Then, taking a cob pipe from his pocket, he added, politely, "May I smoke?"

Heh? O law! yes. What you ask *me* for?" She watched him curiously, as he filled and lighted the pipe. "I reckon that's because you was raised in the city," she added slowly. "Is that the way folks do there?"

"Folks smoke here, sometimes, do they not?" he returned

79

between puffs.

"I don't mean that. Course they smoke and chew, too. And the women dip snuff, some of 'em. Aunt Mollie Matthews don't, though, and I ain't never goin' to, 'cause she don't. But nobody don't ask nobody else if they can. They just go ahead. That ain't the only way you're different from us, though," she continued, looking at Mr. Howitt, with that wide, questioning gaze. "You're different in a heap o' ways. 'Tain't that you wear different clothes, for you don't, no more. Nor, 'taint that you act like you were any better'n us. I don't know what it is, but it's somethin'. Take your stayin' here in Mutton Hollow, now; honest, Dad, ain't you afear'd to stay here all alone at nights?"

"Afraid? Afraid of what?" He looked at her curiously.

"Hants," said the girl, lowering her voice, "down there." She pointed toward the old ruined cabin under the bluff. "*She's* sure been seen there. What if *he* was to come, too? Don't you believe in hants?"

The shepherd's face was troubled, as he answered, "I don't know, Sammy. I scarcely know what I believe. Some marvelous experiences are related by apparently reliable authorities; but I have always said that I could not accept the belief. I—I am not so sure now. After all, the unseen world is not so very far away. Strange forces, of which we know nothin, are about us everywhere. I dare not say that I do not believe."

"But you ain't scared?"

"Why should I fear?"

Sammy shook her head. "Ain't nother man or woman in the whole country would dast spend the night here, Dad; except Pete, of course. Not even Young Matt, nor my daddy would do it; and I don't guess they're afraid of anything— anything that's alive, I mean. You're sure different, Dad; plumb different. I reckon it must be the city that does it. And that's what I've come to see you about this evenin'. You see Ollie's been a-tellin' me a lot about folks and things way over there." She waved her hand toward the ridges that shut in the Hollow. "And Ollie he's changed a heap himself since he went there to live. I got a letter today, and, when I went home, I hunted up the first one he wrote, and I can tell there's a right smart difference already. You know all about Ollie and me goin' to get married, I reckon?"

Mr. Howitt admitted that he had heard something of that nature; and Sammy nodded. "I 'lowed you'd know. But you don't know how mighty proud and particular Ollie always is. I figure that bein' in the city with all them fine folks ain't goin' to make him any less that way than he was. And if he stays there and keeps on a-changin', and I stay here, and don't change none, why it might be that I— I—" She faltered and came to a dead stop, twisting her bonnet strings nervously in her confusion. "Ollie he ain't like Young Matt, nohow," she said again. "Such as that wouldn't make no difference with him. But Ollie—well, you see—"

There was a twinkle, now, in the shepherd's eye, as he answered, "Yes, I see; I am quite sure that I see."

The girl continued, "You know all about these things, Dad. And there ain't nobody else here that does. Will you learn me to be a sure 'nough lady, so as Ollie won't—so he won't—" Again she paused in confusion. It was evident, from the look on Mr. Howitt's face, that, whatever he saw, it was not this.

"I feel somehow like I could do it, if I had a chance," she murmured.

There was no answer. After a time, Sammy stole a look at her quiet companion. What could the man in the chair be thinking about? His pipe was neglected; his gray head bowed.

"Course," said the young woman, with just a little lifting of her chin, "Course, if I couldn't never learn, there ain't no use to try."

The old scholar raised his head and looked long at the girl. Her splendid form, glowing with the rich life and

81

strength of the wilderness, showed in every line the proud old southern blood. Could she learn to be a fine lady? Mr. Howitt thought of the women of the cities, pale, sickly, colorless, hothouse posies, beside this mountain flower. What would this beautiful creature be, had she their training? What would she gain? What might she not lose? Aloud he said, "My dear child, do you know what it is that you ask?"

Sammy hung her head, abashed at his serious tone. "I 'lowed it would be right smart trouble for you," she said. "But I could let you have Brownie in pay; he ain't only five years old, and is as sound as a button. He's all I've got, Mr. Howitt. But I'd be mighty proud to swap him to you."

"My girl, my girl," said the shepherd, "You misunderstand me. I did not mean that. It would be a pleasure to teach you. I was thinking how little you realized what the real life of the city is like, and how much you have that the 'fine ladies,' as you call them, would give fortunes for, and how little they have after all that could add one ray of brightness to your life."

Sammy laughed aloud, as she cried, "Me got anything that anybody would want? Why, Dad, I ain't got nothin' but Brownie, and my saddle, and—and that's all. I sure ain't got nothing to lose."

The man smiled in sympathy. Then slowly a purpose formed in his mind. "And if you should lose, you will never blame me?" he said at last.

"Never, never," she promised eagerly.

"All right, it is a bargain. I will help you."

The girl sprang to her feet. "I knew you would. I knew you would. I was plumb sure you would," she cried, fairly quivering with life and excitement. "It's got to be a sure 'nough lady, Dad. I want to be a really truly fine lady, like them Ollie tells about in his letters, you know."

"Yes, Sammy. I understand, a 'sure enough' lady, and we will do it, I am sure. But it will take a great deal of hard work on your part, though."

"My dear child, do you know what it is that you ask?"

"I reckon it will," she returned soberly, coming back to her seat. Then drawing her chair a little closer, she leaned toward her teacher, "Begin now," she commanded. "Tell me what I must do first."

Mr. Howitt carefully searched his pockets for a match, and lighted his pipe again, before he said, "First you must know what a 'sure enough' lady is. You see, Sammy, there are several kinds of women who call themselves ladies, but are not real ladies after all; and they all look very much like the 'sure enough' kind; that is, they look like them to most people."

Sammy nodded, "Just like them Thompsons down by Flat Rock. They're all mighty proud, 'cause they come from Illinois the same as the Matthews. You'd think to hear 'em that Old Matt couldn't near run the ranch without 'em, and some folks, strangers like, might believe it. But we all know they ain't nothing but just low down trash, all the time, and no better than some of them folks over on the Bend."

The shepherd smiled, "Something like that. I see you understand. Now a real lady, Sammy, is a lady in three ways: First, in her heart; I mean just to herself, in the things that no one but she could ever know. A 'sure enough' lady does not *pretend* to be; she *is*."

Again the girl broke in eagerly, "That's just like Aunt Mollie, ain't it? Couldn't no one ever have a finer lady heart than her."

"Indeed, you are right," agreed the teacher heartily. "And that is the thing that lies at the bottom of it all, Sammy. The lady heart comes first."

"I won't never forget that," she returned. "I couldn't forget Aunt Mollie, nohow. Tell me more, Dad."

"Next, the 'sure enough' lady must have a lady mind. She must know how to think and talk about the things that really matter. All the fine dresses and jewels in the world can't make a real lady, if she does not think, or if she thinks only of things that are of no value. Do you see?"

Again the girl nodded, and, with a knowing smile, answered quickly, "I know a man like that. And I see now that that is what makes him so different from other folks. It's the things he thinks about all to himself that does it. But I've got a heap to learn, I sure have. I could read all right, if I had something to read, and I reckon I could learn to talk like you if I tried hard enough. What else is there?"

Then, continued the shepherd, "A lady will keep her body as strong and as beautiful as she can, for this is one way that she expresses her heart and mind. Do you see what I mean?"

Sammy answered slowly, "I reckon I do. You mean I mustn't get stooped over and thin chested, and go slouching around, like so many of the girls and women around here do, and I mustn't let my clothes go without buttons, 'cause I am in a hurry, and I must always comb my hair, and keep my hands as white as I can. Is that it?"

"That's the idea," said the shepherd.

Sammy gazed ruefully at a large rent in her skirt, and at a shoe half laced. Then she put up a hand to her tumbled hair. "I—I didn't think it made any difference, when only home folks was around," she said.

"That's just it, my child," said the old man gently. "I think a 'sure enough' lady would look after these things whether there was anyone to see her or not; just for herself, you know. And this is where you can begin. I will send for some books right away, and when they come we will begin to train your mind."

"But the heart, how'll I get a lady heart, Dad?"

"How does the violet get its perfume, Sammy? Where does the rose get its color? How does the bird learn to sing its song?"

For a moment she was puzzled. Then her face lighted. "I see!" she exclaimed. "I'm just to catch it from folks like Aunt Mollie, and—and someone else I know. I'm just to *be*, not to make believe or let on like I was, but to *be* a real lady inside. And then I'm to learn how to talk and look like I know myself to be." She drew a long breath as she rose to go. "It'll be mighty hard, Dad, in some ways; but it'll sure be worth it all when I get out 'mong the folks. I'm mighty thankful to you, I sure am. And I hope you won't never be sorry you promised to help me."

As the girl walked swiftly away through the thickening dusk of the evening, the shepherd watched her out of sight; then turned toward the corral for a last look at the sheep, to see that all was right for the night. "Brave, old fellow," he said to the dog who trotted by his side, "are we going to make another mistake, do you think? We have made so many, so many, you know." Brave looked up into the master's face, and answered with his low bark, as though to declare his confidence. "Well, well, old dog, I hope you are right. The child has a quick mind, and a good heart; and, if I am not mistaken, good blood. We shall see. We shall see."

Suddenly the dog whirled about, the hair on his back bristling as he gave a threatening growl. A man on a dun-colored mule was coming up the road.

14

The Common Yeller Kind

Mr. Howitt stood quietly by the corral gate when the horse-man rode up. It was Wash Gibbs, on his way home from an all day visit with friends on the river.

When the big mountaineer took the short cut through Mutton Hollow, he thought to get well past the ranch before the light failed. No matter how well fortified with the courage distilled by his friend, Jennings, the big man would never have taken the trail by the old ruined cabin alone after dark. He had evidently been riding at a good pace, for his mule's neck and flanks were wet with sweat. Gibbs himself seemed greatly excited, and one hand rested on the pistol at his hip, as he pulled up in front of the shepherd.

Without returning Mr. Howitt's greeting, he pointed toward the two empty chairs in front of the house, demand-ing roughly, "Who was that with you before you heard me comin'?"

"Sammy Lane was here a few minutes ago," replied the shepherd.

Gibbs uttered an oath, "She was, was she? Well, who was th' man?"

"There was no man," returned the other. "Young Matt and Pete were here for supper, but they went as soon as the meal was finished, before Sammy came."

"Don't you try to lie to me!" exclaimed the big man, with another burst of language, and a threatening movement with the hand that rested on the pistol.

Mr. Howitt was startled. Never in his life before had such words been addressed to him. He managed to reply with quiet dignity, "I have no reason for deceiving you, or anyone else, Mr. Gibbs. There has been no man here but myself, since Matt and Pete left after supper." The shepherd's manner carried conviction, and Gibbs hesitated, evidently greatly perplexed. During the pause, Brave growled again, and faced toward the cliff below the corral, his hair bristling.

"What's th' matter with that dog?" said Gibbs, turning uneasily in his saddle, to face in the direction the animal was looking.

"What is it, Brave?" said Mr. Howitt. The only answer was an uneasy whine, followed by another growl, all of which said plainly, in dog talk, "I don't know what it is, but there is something over there on that cliff that I don't like."

"It must be some animal," said the shepherd.

"Ain't no animal that makes a dog act like that. Did anybody pass while you was a-sittin' there, jest before I come in sight?"

"Not a soul," answered the other. "Did you meet someone down the road?"

The big man looked at the shepherd hard before he answered, in a half-frightened, half-bullying tone, "I seed something in th' road yonder, an' hit disappeared right by th' old shack under th' bluffs." He twisted around in his saddle again, facing the cliff with its dense shadows and dim twilight forms, as he muttered, "If I was only right sure, I—" Then swinging back he leaned toward the man on the ground. "Look a-here, mister. There's them that 'lows there's things in this here Holler t' be afeared of, an' I reckon hit's so. There's sure been hell t' pay at that there cabin down yonder. I ain't a-sayin' what hit was I seed, but if hit war anywhere else, I'd a-said hit was a man; but if hit was a man, I don't know why you didn't see him when he come past; er else you're a-lyin'. I jest want t' tell you, you're right smart of a stranger in these here parts, even if you have been a-workin' fer Ol' Matt all summer. You're too blame careful 'bout talkin' 'bout yourself, o' tellin' whar you come from, t' suit some folks. Some strangers are all right, an' again some ain't. But we don't aim t' have nobody in this here neighborhood what jumps into th' brush when they see an honest man a-comin'."

As he finished speaking, Gibbs straightened himself in the saddle, and before Mr. Howitt could reply, the dun mule, at a touch of the spur, had dashed away up the road in the direction taken by Sammy Lane.

It was quite dark in the heavy timber of the Hollow by the time Sammy had reached the edge of the open ground on the hill side, but once on the higher level, clear of the trees, the strong glow of the western sky still lighted the way. From here it was not far to the girl's home, and, as she climbed a spur of Dewey, Sammy saw the cabin, and heard distinctly the sweet strains of her father's violin. On top of the rise, the young woman paused a moment to enjoy the beauties of the evening, which seemed to come to her with a new meaning that night. As she stood there, her strong young figure was clearly outlined against the sky to the man who was riding swiftly along the road over which she had just passed.

Sammy turned when she heard the quick beating of the mule's feet; then, recognizing the huge form of the horseman, as he came out of the woods into the light, she started quickly away towards her home; but the mule and its rider were soon beside her.

"Howdy, Sammy." Gibbs leaped from the saddle, and, with the bridle rein over his arm, came close to the girl. "Fine evening for a walk."

"Howdy," returned the young woman coolly, quickening her pace.

"You needn't t' be in such a powerful hurry," growled Wash. "If you've got time t' talk t' that old cuss at th'

"You needn't be in such a powerful hurry."

ranch, you sure got time t' talk t' me."

Sammy turned angrily. "You'd better get back on your mule, and go about your business, Wash Gibbs. When I want you to walk with me, I'll let you know."

"That's all right, honey," exclaimed the other insolently. "I'm goin' your way just th' same; an' we'll mosey 'long t'gether. I was a-goin' home, but I've got business with your paw now."

"Worse thing for Daddy, too," flashed the girl. "I wish you'd stay away from him."

Wash laughed. "Your daddy couldn't keep house 'thout me, nohow. Who was that feller talkin' with you an' th' old man down yonder?"

"There wasn't nobody talkin' to us," replied Sammy shortly.

"That's what he said, too," growled Gibbs, "but I sure seed somebody a-sneakin' into th' brush when I rode up. I thought when I was down there hit might o' been a hant; but I know hit was a man, now. There's somethin' mighty funny a-goin' on around here, since that feller come int' th' neighborhood; an' he'll sure find somethin' in Mutton Holler more alive than Ol' Matt's gal if he ain't careful."

The girl caught her breath quickly. She knew the big ruffian's methods, and with good reason feared for her old friend, should he even unconsciously incur the giant's displeasure.

As they drew near the house, Wash continued, "Young Matt he was there too. Let me tell you I ain't forgot 'bout his big show at th' mill last spring; he'll have t' do a heap better'n he done then, when I get 'round t' him."

Sammy laughed scornfully, " 'Pears like you ain't been in no hurry t' try it on. I ain't heard tell of Young Matt's leaving th' country yet. You'd better stay away from Jennings' still though, when you do try it." Then, while the man was tying his mule to the fence, she ran into the cabin to greet her father with a hysterical sob that greatly astonished Jim. Before explanations could be made, a step was

91

heard approaching the door, and Sammy had just time to say, "Wash Gibbs," in answer to her father's inquiring look, when the big man entered. Mr. Lane arose to hang his violin on its peg.

"Don't stop fer me, Jim," said the newcomer. "Jest let her go. Me an' Sammy's been havin' a nice little walk, an' some right peart music would sound mighty fine." Gibbs was angered beyond reason at Sammy's last words, or he would have exercised greater care.

Sammy's father made no reply until the girl had left the room, but whatever it was that his keen eye read in his daughter's face, it made him turn to his guest with anything but a cordial manner, and there was that in his voice that should have warned the other.

"So you and Sammy went for a walk, did you?"

"She was comin' home from th' sheep ranch, an' I caught up with her," explained Gibbs. "I 'lowed as how she needed company, so I come 'long. I seemed t' be 'bout as welcome as usual," he added with an ugly grin.

"Meanin' that my girl don't want your company, and told you so?" asked the other softly.

Wash answered with a scowl, "Sammy's gettin' too dad burned good fer me since Ollie's uncle took him in. An' now, this here old man from nowhere has come, it's worse than ever. She'll put a rope 'round our necks th' first thing you know."

Jim's right hand slipped quietly inside his hickory shirt, where the button was missing, as he drawled, "My girl always was too good for some folks. And it's about time you was a-findin' it out. She can't help it. She was born that way. She's got mighty good blood in her veins, that girl has; and I don't aim to ever let it be mixed up with none of the low down common yeller kind."

The deliberate purpose of the speaker was too evident to be mistaken. The other man's hand flew to his hip almost before Mr. Lane had finished his sentence. But Wash was not quick enough. Like a flash Jim's hand was withdrawn from inside the hickory shirt, and the giant looked squarely into the muzzle of Jim Lane's ever ready, murderous weapon.

In the same even voice, without the slightest allusion to the unfinished movement of the other, Mr. Lane continued, "I done told you before that my girl would pick her own company, and I ain't never feared for a minute that she'd take up with such as you. Ollie Stewart ain't so mighty much of a man, maybe, but he's clean, he is, and the stock's pretty good. Now you can just listen to me, or you can mosey out of that door, and the next time we meet, we will settle it for good, without any further arrangement."

As Sammy's father talked, the big figure of his visitor relaxed, and when Jim had finished his slow speech, Wash was leaning forward with his elbows on his knees, his hands clasped in front. "We ain't got no call t' fight, now, Jim," he said in a tone of respect. "We got something else t' think about; an' that's what I come here fer t'night. I didn't aim t', 'til I seed what I did at th' ranch down yonder. I tell you hit's time we was a-doin' somethin'."

At this, Mr. Lane's face and manner changed quickly. He put up his weapon, and the two men drew their chairs close together, as though Death had not a moment before stretched forth his hand to them.

For an hour they sat talking in low tones. Sammy in the next room had heard the conversation up to this point, but now only an occasional word reached her ears. Gibbs seemed to be urging some action, and her father was as vigorously protesting. "I tell you, Jim, hit's th' only safe way. You didn't use t' be so squeamish." Several times the old shepherd was mentioned, and also the stranger whom Wash had seen that evening. And once, the trembling girl heard Young Matt's name. At length the guest rose to go, and Mr. Lane walked with him to the gate. Even after the big man was mounted, the conversation still continued; Wash still urging and Jim still protesting.

When his visitor was gone, Mr. Lane came slowly back

93

to the house. Extinguishing the light, he seated himself in the open doorway, and filled his pipe. Sammy caught the odor of tobacco, and a moment later Jim heard a light, quick step on the floor behind him. Then two arms were around his neck. "What is it, Daddy? What is it? Why don't you drive that man away?"

"Did you hear us talkin'?" asked the man, an anxious note in his voice.

"I heard you talkin' to him about pesterin' me, but after that, you didn't talk so loud. What is the matter Daddy, that he could stay and be so thick with you after the things you said? I was sure he'd make you kill him."

Jim laughed softly. "You're just like your mother, girl. Just like her, with the old blood a-backin' you up." Then he asked a number of questions about Mr. Howitt, and her visit to the ranch that evening.

As Sammy told him of her ambition to fit herself for the place that would be hers, when she married, and repeating the things that Mr. Howitt had told her, explained how the shepherd had promised to help, Jim expressed his satisfaction and delight. "I knowed you was a-studyin' about something, girl," he said, "but I didn't say nothin', 'cause I 'lowed you'd tell me when you got ready."

"I didn't want to say nothing 'til I was sure, you see," replied the daughter. "I aimed to tell you as soon as I got home tonight, but Wash Gibbs didn't give me no chance."

The man held her close. "Dad Howitt sure puts the thing just right, Sammy. It'll be old times come back, when you're a lady in your own house with all your fine friends around; and you'll do it, girl; you sure will. Don't never be afraid to bank on the old blood. It'll see you through." Then his voice broke. "You won't never be learned away from your old daddy, will you, honey? Will you always stand by daddy, like you do now? Will you let me and Young Matt slip round once in a while, just to look at you, all so fine?"

"Daddy Jim, if you don't—hush—I'll—I'll—" She hid her face on his shoulder.

THE COMMON YELLER KIND

"There, there, honey; I was only funnin'. You'll always be my Sammy. You just naturally couldn't be nothin' else."

Long after his daughter had gone to her room and to her bed, the mountaineer sat in the doorway, looking into the dark. He heard the short bark of a fox in the brush back of the stable; and the wild cry of a catamount from a cliff farther down the mountain was answered by another from the timber below the spring. He saw the great hills heaving their dark forms into the sky, and in his soul he felt the spirit of the wilderness and the mystery of the hour. At last he went into the house to close and bar the door.

Away down in Mutton Hollow a dog barked, and high up on Old Dewey near Sammy's Lookout, a spot of light showed for a moment, then vanished.

15

The Party at Ford's

Young Matt would have found some excuse for staying at home the night of the party at Ford's, but the shepherd said he must go.

The boy felt that the long evening with Sammy would only hurt. He reasoned with himself that it would be better for him to see as little as possible of the girl who was to marry Ollie Stewart. Nevertheless, he was singing as he saddled the big white-faced sorrel to ride once more over the trail that is nobody knows how old.

Mr. Lane was leading the brown pony from the stable as Young Matt rode up to the gate; and from the doorway of the cabin Sammy called to say that she would be ready in a minute.

"Ain't seen you for a coon's age, boy," said Jim, while they were waiting for the girl. "Why don't you never come down the Old Trail no more?"

The big fellow's face reddened, as he answered, "I ain't been nowhere, Jim. 'Pears like I just can't get away from the place no more; we're that busy."

Sammy's father looked his young neighbor squarely in the eye with that peculiar searching gaze. "Look-a here, Grant. I've knowed you ever since you was born, and you ought to know me a little. 'Tain't your way to dodge, and 'tain't mine. I reckon you know you're welcome, same as always, don't you?"

Young Matt returned the other's look fairly. "I ain't never doubted it, Jim. But things is a heap different now, since it's all done and settled, with Ollie gone."

The two understood each other perfectly. Said Jim, drawing a long breath, "Well, I wish you'd come over just the same, anyway. It can't do nobody no harm as I can see."

"It wouldn't do me no good," replied the young man.

"Maybe not," assented Jim. "But I'd like mighty well to have you come just the same." Then he drew closer to his young friend. "I've been aimin' to ride over and see you, Matt; but Sammy said you was a-comin' this evenin', and I 'lowed this would be soon enough. I reckon you know what Wash Gibbs is tellin' he aims to do first chance he gets."

The giant drew himself up with a grim smile, "I've heard a good bit, Jim. But you don't need to mind about me; I know I ain't quite growed, but I am a-growin'."

The older man surveyed the great form of the other with a critical eye, as he returned, "Durned if I don't believe you'd push him mighty close, if he'd only play fair. But—but I 'lowed you ought to know it was a-comin'."

"I have knowed it for a long time," said the other cheerfully, "but I heard 'Preachin' Bill' say once, that if a feller don't fuss about what he knows for sure, the things he don't know ain't apt to bother him none. It's this here guessin' that sure gets a man down."

"Preachin' Bill, hits it every pop, don't he?" exclaimed Jim admiringly. "But there's somethin' else you ought to know, too, Matt. Wash has done made his threats agin the old man down there."

"You mean Dad Howitt?" said Young Matt sharply. "What's Wash got agin Dad, Jim?"

Mr. Lane shifted uneasily. Some fool notion of hisn. You mind old man Lewis, I reckon?"

The big man's muscles tightened. "Dad told us about his stoppin' at the ranch the other night. Wash Gibbs better keep his hands off Mr. Howitt."

97

"I ain't told nobody about this, Grant, and you can do as you like about tellin' your father, and the old man. But if anything happens, get word to me, quick."

Before more could be said, Sammy appeared in the doorway, and soon the two young people were riding on their way. Long after they had passed from sight in the depth of the forest, the dark mountaineer stood at the big gate, looking in the direction they had gone.

Young Matt was like a captive, tugging at his bonds. Mr. Lane's words had stirred the fire, and the girl's presence by his side added fuel to the flame. He could not speak. He dared not even look at her, but rode with his eyes fixed upon the ground, where the sunlight fell in long bars of gold. Sammy, too, was silent. She felt something that was strangely like fear, when she found herself alone with her big neighbor. Now and then she glanced timidly up at him and tried to find some word with which to break the silence. She half wished that she had not come. So they rode together through the lights and shadows down into the valley, the only creatures in all the free life of the forest who were not free.

At last the girl spoke. "It's mighty good of you to take me over to Mandy's tonight. There ain't no one else I could 'o' gone with." There was no reply, and Sammy, seeming not to notice, continued talking in a matter-of-fact tone that soon—for such is the way of a woman—won him from his mood, and the two chatted away like the good comrades they had always been.

Just after they had crossed Fall Creek at Slick Rock Ford, some two miles below the mill, Young Matt leaned from his saddle, and for a little way studied the ground carefully. When he sat erect again, he remarked, with the air of one who had reached a conclusion, "wouldn't wonder but there'll be doin's at Ford's tonight, sure enough."

"There's sure to be," returned the girl. "Everybody'll be there. Mandy's folks from over on Long Creek are comin', and some from the mouth of the James. Mandy wanted

Daddy to play for 'em, but he says he can't play for parties no more, and they got that old fiddlin' Jake from the Flag neighborhood, I guess."

"There'll be somethin' a heap more excitin' than fiddlin' and dancin', accordin' to my guess," returned Young Matt.

"What do you mean?" asked Sammy.

Her escort pointed to the print of a mule's shoe in the soft soil of the low bottom land. "That there's Wash Gibb's dun mule, and he's headed down the creek for Jennings still. Wash'll meet a lot of his gang from over on the river, and like's not they'll go from there to the party. I wish your dad was goin' to do the playin' tonight."

It was full dark before they reached the Ford clearing. The faint, faraway sound of a violin, seeming strange and out of place in the gloomy solitude of the great woods, first told them that other guests had already arrived. Then as they drew nearer and the tones of the instrument grew louder, they could hear the rhythmic swing and beat of heavily shod feet upon the rough board floors, with the shrill cries of the caller, and the half savage, half pathetic singsong of the backwoods dancers, singing "Missouri Gal."

Reaching the edge of the clearing, they involuntarily checked their horses, stopping just within the shadow of the timber. Here the sound of the squeaking fiddle, the shouting caller, the stamping feet, and the swinging dancers came with full force; and, through the open door and windows of the log house, they could see the wheeling, swaying figures of coatless men and calico gowned women, while the light, streaming out, opened long lanes in the dusk. About them in the forest's edge, standing in groups under the trees, were the shadowy forms of saddle horses and mules, tied by the bridle reins to the lower branches; and nearer to the cabin, two or three teams, tied to the rail-fence, stood hitched to big wagons in which were splint-bottom chairs for extra seats.

During the evening, the men tried in their rough, good-natured way, to joke Young Matt about taking advantage of

Ollie Stewart's absence, but they very soon learned that, while the big fellow was ready to enter heartily into all the fun of the occasion, he would not receive as a jest any allusion to his relation to the girl whom he had escorted to the party. Sammy, too, when her big companion was not near, suffered from the crude wit of her friends.

"Ollie Stewart don't own me yet," she declared with a toss of the head, when someone threatened to write her absent lover.

"No," replied one of her tormentors, "but you ain't aimin' to miss your chance o' goin' to' th' city t' live with them big-bugs."

In the laugh that followed, Sammy was claimed by a tall woodsman for the next dance, and escaped to take her place on the floor.

"Well, Ollie'll sure make a good man for her," remarked another joker. "If he don't walk th' chalk, she can take him 'cross her knee an' wallop him."

"She'll surely marry him, all right," said the first " 'cause he's got th' money, but she's goin' t' have a heap o' fun makin' Young Matt play th' fool before she leaves th' woods. He ain't took his eyes off her t'night. Everybody's laughin' at him."

"I notice they take mighty good care t' laugh behind his back," flashed little black-eyed Annie Brooks from the Cove neighborhood.

Young Matt, who had been dancing with Mandy Ford, came up behind the group just in time to hear their remarks. Two or three who saw him within hearing tried to warn the speakers, but while everybody around them saw the situation, the two men caught the frantic signals of their friends too late. The music suddenly stopped. The dancers were still. By instinct every eye in the room was fixed upon the little group, as the jokers turned to face the object of their jests.

The big mountaineer took one long step toward the two who had spoken, his brow dark with rage, his huge fists clenched. But, even as his powerful muscles contracted for the expected blow, the giant came to a dead stop. Slowly, his arm relaxed. His hand dropped to his side. Then, turning deliberately, he walked to the door, the silent crowd parting to give him way.

As the big man stepped from the room, a gasp of astonishment escaped from the company, and the two jokers, with frightened faces, broke into a shrill, nervous laughter. Then a buzz of talk went round; the fiddlers struck up again; the callers shouted; the dancers stamped, and bowed, and swung their partners as they sang.

And out in the night under the trees, at the edge of the gloomy forest, the strongest man in the hills was saying over and over to the big, white-faced sorrel, "I don't dare do it. I don't dare. Dad Howitt wouldn't. He sure wouldn't."

Very soon two figures left the house, and hurried toward a bunch of saddle horses near by. They had untied their animals, and were about to mount, when suddenly a huge form stepped from the shadows to their horses' heads. "Put up your guns, boys," said Young Matt calmly. "I reckon you know that if I'd wanted trouble, it would o' been all over before this."

The weapons were not drawn, and the big man continued, "Dad Howitt says a feller always whips himself every time he fights when there ain't no—no principle evolved. I don't guess Dad would see ary principle in this, 'cause there might be some truth in what you boys said. I reckon I am somethin' at playin' a fool, but it would o' been a heap safer for you to let folks find it out for themselves."

"We all were jest a-foolin', Matt," muttered one.

"That's all right," returned the big fellow. "But you'd better tie up again and go back into the house and dance a while longer. Folks might think you was scared if you was to leave so soon."

16

On the Way Home

Not until the party was breaking up, and he saw Sammy in the doorway, did Young Matt go back to the house.

When they had ridden again out of the circle of light, and the laughter and shouting of the guests was no longer heard, Sammy tried in vain to arouse her silent escort, chatting gaily about the pleasures of the evening. But all the young man's reserve had returned. When she did force him to speak, his responses were so short and cold that at last the girl, too, was silent. Then, man-like, he wished she would continue talking.

By the time they reached Compton Ridge the moon was well up. For the last two miles Sammy had been watching the wavering shafts of light that slipped through tremulous leaves and swaying branches. As they rode, a thousand fantastic shapes appeared and vanished along the way, and now and then as the sound of their horses' feet echoed through the silent forest, some wild thing in the underbrush leaped away into the gloomy depth.

Coming out on top of the narrow ridge, the brown pony crowded closer to the big, white-faced sorrel, and the girl, stirred by the weird loveliness of the scene, broke the silence with an exclamation. "Oh, Matt! Ain't it fine? Look there!" She pointed to the view ahead. "Makes me feel like I could keep on a-goin', and goin', and never stop."

The man, too, felt the witchery of the night. The horses

*"Makes me feel like I could
keep on a-goin', and goin', and never stop."*

were crowding more closely together now, and, leaning forward, the girl looked up into his face. "What's the matter, Matt? Why don't you talk to me? You know it ain't true what them folks said back there."

The sorrel was jerked farther away. "It's true enough, so far as it touches me," returned the man shortly. "When are you goin' to the city?"

"I don't know," she replied. "Let's don't talk about that, tonight. I don't want even to think about it, not tonight. You—you don't believe what they was a-sayin', Matt; you know you don't. You mustn't ever believe such as that. I—I never could get along without you and Aunt Mollie and Uncle Matt, nohow." The brown pony was again crowding closer to his mate. The girl laid a hand on her companion's arm. "Say you don't blame me for what they said, Matt. You know I wouldn't do no such a thing even if I could. There musn't anything ever come between you and me; never—never. I—I want us always to be like we are now. You've been so good to me ever since I was a little trick, and you whipped big Lem Wheeler for teasin' me. I—I don't guess I could get along without knowin' you was around somewhere." She finished with a half sob.

It was almost too much. The man swung around in his saddle, and the horses, apparently of their own accord, stopped. Without a word, the big fellow stretched forth his arms, and the girl, as if swept by a force beyond her control, felt herself swaying toward him.

The spell was broken by the trampling of horses and the sound of loud voices. For a moment they held their places, motionless, as if rudely awakened from a dream. The sound was coming nearer. Then Young Matt spoke. "It's Wash Gibbs and his crowd from the still. Ride into the brush quick."

There was no time for flight. In the bright moonlight, they would have been easily recognized, and a wild chase would have followed. Leaving the road, they forced their horses into a thick clump of bushes, where they dismounted, to hold the animals by their heads. Scarcely had they gained this position when the first of the crowd reached the spot where they had been a moment before. Wash Gibbs was easily distinguished by his gigantic form, and with him were ten others, riding two and two, several of whom were known to Young Matt as the most lawless characters in the country. All were fired by drink and were laughing and talking, with now and then a burst of song, or a vulgar jest.

"I say, Wash," called one, "what'll you do if Young Matt's there?" The unseen listeners could not hear the leader's reply; but those about the speaker laughed and shouted with great glee. Then the two in the bushes distinctly heard the last man in the line ask his companion, "Do you reckon he'll put up a fight?" and as they passed from sight, the other answered, "Wash don't aim t' give him no show."

When the sounds had died away, Young Matt turned to the girl. "Come on; we've got to keep 'em in sight."

But Sammy held back. "Oh, Matt, don't go yet. We must not. Didn't you hear what that man said? It's you they're after. Let's wait here until they're clean gone."

"No, 'tain't; they ain't a-wantin' me," the big fellow replied. And before the young woman could protest further, he lifted her to the saddle as easily as if she were a child. Then, springing to the back of his own horse, he led the way at a pace that would keep them within hearing of the company of men.

"Who is it, Matt? Who is it, if it ain't you?" asked the girl.

"Don't know for sure yet, but I'll tell you pretty soon."

They had not gone far when Young Matt stopped the horses to listen intently; and soon by the sound he could tell that the party ahead had turned off from the ridge road and were following the trail that leads down the eastern side of the mountain. A moment longer the mountaineer listened, as if to make sure; then he spoke. "Them devils are goin' to the ranch after Dad Howitt. Sammy, you've got to ride hard tonight. They won't hear you now, and they're getting farther off every minute. There ain't no other way, and I know you'll do it for the old man. Get home as quick as you can and tell Jim what's up. Tell him I'll hold 'em until he gets there." Even as he spoke, he sprang from his horse and began loosening the saddle girths.

"But, Matt," protested the girl, "how can you? You can't get by them. How're you going to get there in time?"

"Down the mountain; short cut," he answered as he jerked the heavy saddle from his horse and threw it under some nearby bushes.

"But they'll kill you. You can't never face that whole crowd alone."

"I can do it better'n Dad, and him not a-lookin' for them."

Slipping the bridle from the sorrel, he turned the animal loose, and, removing his coat and hat, laid them with the saddle. Then to the girl on the pony he said sharply, "Go on, Sammy. Why don't you go on? Don't you see how you're losin' time? Them devils will do for Dad Howitt like they done for old man Lewis. Your father's the only man can stop 'em now. Ride hard, girl, and tell Jim to hurry. And—and good-by, Sammy." As he finished, he spoke to her horse and struck him such a blow that the animal sprang away.

For a moment Sammy attempted to pull up her startled pony. Then Young Matt saw her lean forward in the saddle, and urge the little horse to even greater speed. As they disappeared down the road, the giant turned and ran crashing through the brush down the steep side of the mountain. There was no path to follow. And with deep ravines to cross, rocky bluffs to descend or scale, and, in places, wild tangles of vines and brush and fallen trees, the trip before him would have been a hard one even in the full light of day. At night, it was almost impossible, and he must go like a buck with the dogs in full cry.

When Sammy came in sight of her home, she began calling to her father, and, as the almost exhausted horse dashed up to the big gate, the door of the cabin opened, and Jim came running out. Lifting his daughter from the trembling pony, he helped her into the house, where she sobbed out her message.

At the first word, "Wash Gibbs," Jim reached for a cartridge belt, and, by the time Sammy had finished, he had taken his Winchester from its brackets over the fireplace. Slipping a bridle on his horse that was feeding in the yard, he sprange upon the animal's back without waiting for a saddle. "Stay in the cabin, girl, put out the light, and don't open the door until I come," he said and he was gone.

As Sammy turned back into the house, from away down in Mutton Hollow, on the night wind, came the sound of guns.

17

What Happened at the Ranch

It was after midnight when Mr. Howitt was rudely awakened. The bright moon shining through the windows lit up the interior of the cabin and he easily recognized Young Matt standing by the bed, with Pete, who was sleeping at the ranch that night, nearby.

"Why, Matt, what is the matter?" exclaimed the shepherd, sitting up. He could not see that the big fellow's clothing was torn, that his hat was gone, and that he was dripping with perspiration; but he could hear his labored breathing. Strong as he was, the young giant was nearly exhausted by the strain of his race over the mountains.

"Get up quick, Dad. I'll tell you while you're puttin' on your clothes," the woodsman answered; and while the shepherd dressed, he told him in a few words, finishing with, "Call Brave inside, and get your gun, with all the shells you can find. Don't show a light for a minute. They'll be here any time now, and it'll be a good bit yet before Sammy can get home." He began fastening the front door.

The peaceful-minded scholar could not grasp the meaning of the message; it was to him an impossible thought. "You must be mistaken, Grant," he said. "Surely you are excited and unduly alarmed. Wash Gibbs has no reason to attack me."

Young Matt replied gruffly, "I ain't makin' no mistake in the woods, Dad. You ain't in the city now, and there ain't no one can hear you holler. Don't think I am scared neither, if that's what you mean. But there's ten of them in that bunch, and they're bad ones. You'd better call Brave, sir. He'll be some help when it comes to the rush."

But the other persisted, "You must be mistaken, lad. Why should anyone wish to harm me? Those men are only out fox hunting, or something like that. If they should be coming here, it is all a mistake; I can easily explain."

"Explain, hell!" ejaculated the mountaineer. "I ask your pardon, Dad; but you don't know, not being raised in these woods like me. Old man Lewis hadn't done nothing neither, and he explained, too; only he never got through explainin'. They ain't got no reason. They're drunk. You've never seen Wash Gibbs drunk, and tonight he's got his whole gang with him. I don't know why he's comin' after you, but, from what you told me 'bout his stoppin' here that evenin', and what I've heard lately, I can guess. I know what he'll do when he gets here, if we don't stop him. It'll be all the same to you whether he's right or wrong."

Brave came trotting into the cabin through the rear door, and lay down in his corner by the fireplace. "That's mighty funny," said Young Matt. Then, as he glanced quickly around, "Where's Pete?"

The boy had slipped away while the two men were talking. Stepping outside, they called several times; but, save the "Wh-w-h-o—w-h-o-o" of an owl in a big tree near the corral, there was no answer.

"The boy's all right, anyway," said the young man. "Nothin' in the woods ever hurts Pete. He's safer there than he would be here, and I'm glad he's gone."

The shepherd did not reply. He seemed not to hear, but stood as though fascinated by the scene. He still could not grasp the truth of the situation, but the beauty of the hour moved him deeply. "What a marvelous, what a wonderful sight!" he said at last in a low tone. "I do not wonder the boy loves to roam the hills a night like this. Look, Grant! See how soft the moonlight falls on that patch of grass this side of the old tree yonder, and how black the shadow is under that bush, like the mouth of a cave, a witch's cave. I am sure there are ghosts and goblins in there, with fairies and gnomes, and perhaps a dragon or two. And see, lad, how the great hills rise into the sky. How grand, how beautiful the world is! It is good to live, Matt, though life be sometimes hard, still—still it is good to live."

At the old scholar's words and manner, the mountaineer, too, forgot for a moment the thing that had brought him there, and a look of awe and wonder came over his rugged features, as the shepherd, with his face turned upward and his deep voice full of emotion, repeated, "The heavens declare the glory of God; and the firmament showeth his handiwork. Day unto day uttereth speech, and night unto night showeth knowledge."

The owl left his place in the old tree and flew across the moonlit clearing into the deeper gloom of the woods. Inside the cabin the dog barked, and through the still night, from down the valley, where the ranch trail crosses the creek, came the rattle of horses' feet on the rocky floor of the little stream, and the faint sound of voices. Young Matt started, and again the man of the wilderness was master of the situation. "They're comin', Dad. We ain't got no time to lose."

Re-entering the cabin, Mr. Howitt quieted the dog, while his companion fastened the rear door, and, in the silence, while they waited, a cricket under the corner of the house sang his plaintive song. The sound of voices grew louder as the horses drew nearer. Brave growled and would have barked again, but was quieted by the shepherd, who crouched at his side, with one hand on the dog's neck.

The older man smiled to himself. It all seemed to him so like a child's game. He had watched the mountaineer's preparation with amused interest, and had followed the young woodsman's directions, even to the loaded shotgun in his hand, as one would humor a boy in his play. The scholar's mind, trained to consider the problems of civilization, and to recognize the dangers of the city, refused to entertain seriously the thought that there, in the peaceful woods, in

110

the dead of night, a company of ruffians was seeking to do him harm.

The voices had ceased, and the listeners heard only the sound of the horses' feet, as the party passed the ruined cabin under the bluff. A moment or two later the riders stopped in front of the ranch house. Brave growled again, but was silenced by the hand on his neck.

Young Matt was at the window. "I see them," he whispered. "They're gettin' off their horses, and tyin' them to the corral fence." The smile on the shepherd's face vanished, and he experienced a queer sensation; it was as though something gripped his heart.

The other continued his whispered report; "They're bunchin' up now under the old tree, talkin' things over. Don't know what to make of the dog not bein' around, I reckon. Now they're takin' a drink. It takes a lot of whiskey to help ten men jump onto one old man, and him a stranger in the woods. Now Wash is sendin' two of them around to the back, so you can't slip out into the brush. Sh—h—h, here comes a couple more to try the front door." He slipped quietly across the room to the shepherd's side. The visitors came softly up to the front door, and tried it gently. A moment later the rear door was tried in the same way.

"Let Brave speak to them," whispered Young Matt; and the dog, feeling the restraining hand removed, barked fiercely.

Mr. Howitt, following his companion's whispered instructions, spoke aloud, "What's the matter, Brave?"

A bold knock at the front door caused the dog to redouble his efforts, until his master commanded him to be still. "Who is there?" called the shepherd.

"Young Matt's took powerful bad," answered a voice, "an they want you t' come up t' th' house, an' doctor him."

A drunken laugh came from the old tree, followed by a smothered oath.

The giant at Mr. Howitt's side growled under his breath, "Oh, I'm sick, am I? There's them that'll be a heap sicker before mornin'. Keep on a-talkin', Dad. We've got to make

111

"We've got to stand them off as long as we can."

all the time we can, so's Jim can get here."

The shepherd called again, "I do not recognize your voice. You must tell me who you are."

Outside there was a short consultation, followed by a still louder knock. "Open up. Why don't you open up an' see who we are?" while from under the tree came a call, "Quit your foolin' an' bring him out o' there, you fellers." This command was followed by a still more vigorous hammering at the door, and the threats, "Open up, ol' man. Open up, or we'll sure bust her in."

Mr. Howitt whispered to his companion, "Let me open the door and talk to them, Grant. Surely they will listen to reason."

But the woodsman returned, "Talk to a nest of rattlers! Jim Lane's the only man that can talk to them now. We've got to stand them off as long as we can." As he spoke he raised his revolver, and was about to fire a shot through the door, when a slight noise at one side of the room attracted his attention. He turned just in time to catch a glimpse of a face as it was withdrawn from one of the little windows. The noise at the door ceased suddenly, and they heard the two men running to join the group under the tree.

"They've found you ain't alone," whispered the big fellow, springing to the window again. And, as a wild drunken yell came from the visitors, he added, "Seems like they're some excited about it, too. They're holding' a regular powwow. What do you reckon they're thinkin'? Hope they'll keep it up 'til Jim—Sh—h—h. Here comes another. It's that ornery Jim Bowles from the mouth of Indian Creek."

The man approached the cabin, but stopped some distance away and called, "Hello, ol' man!"

"Well, what do you want?" answered Mr. Howitt.

"Who's that there feller you got with you?"

"A friend."

"Yes! We all 'lowed hit war a friend, an' we all want t' see him powerful bad. Can't he come out an' play with us, mister?" Another laugh came from the group under the tree.

Young Matt whispered, "Keep him a-talkin', Dad," and Mr. Howitt called, "He doesn't feel like playing tonight. Come back tomorrow."

At this the spokesman dropped his bantering tone, "Look-a here, ol' man. We'uns ain't got no time t' be a-foolin' here. We know who that feller is, an' we're a-goin' t' have him. He's been a-sneakin' 'round this here neighborhood long enough. As fer you, mister, we 'low your health'll be some better back where you come from; an' we aim t' hep you leave this neck o' th' woods right sudden. Open up, now, an' turn that there feller over t' us; an' we'll let you off easy like. If you don't, we'll bust in th' door, an' make you both dance t' th' same tune. There won't be ary thing under you t' dance on, nuther."

The old shepherd was replying kindly, when his speech was interrupted by a pistol shot, and a command from the leader, at which the entire gang charged toward the cabin, firing as they came, and making the little valley hideous with their drunken oaths and yells.

From his window, Young Matt coolly emptied his revolver, but even as the crowd faltered, there came from their leader another volley of oaths. "Go on, go on," yelled Wash. "Their guns are empty, now. Fetch 'em out 'fore they can load again." With an answering yell, the others responded. Carrying a small log they made for the cabin at full speed. One crashing blow—the door flew from its hinges, and the opening was filled with the drunken, sweating, swearing crew. The same instant, Young Matt dropped his useless revolver, and springing forward, met them on the threshold. The old shepherd—who had not fired a shot — could scarcely believe his eyes, as he saw the giant catch the nearest man by the shoulder and waist, and, lifting him high above his head, fling him with terrifc force full into the faces of his bewildered companions.

Those who were not knocked down by the strange weapon scattered in every direction, crouching low. For a moment the big fellow was master of the situation, and,

114

standing alone in the doorway, in the full light of the moon, was easily recognized.

"Hell, boys! Hit's Young Matt hisself!" yelled the one who had raised a laugh, by saying that Young Matt was sick and the shepherd was wanted to doctor him.

"Yes! It's me, Bill Simpson. I'm sure ailin' tonight. I need somebody to go for a doctor powerful bad," returned the young giant.

"We never knowed it war you," whined the other, carefully lengthening the distance between the big man on the doorstep and himself.

"No, I reckon not. You all planned to find an old man alone, and do for him like you've done for others. A fine lot you are, ten to one, and him not knowin' the woods."

While he was speaking, the men slowly retreated, to gather about their big leader under the tree, two of them being assisted by their companions, and one other limping painfully. Young Matt raised his voice, "I know you, Wash Gibbs, and I know this here is your dirty work. You've been a-braggin' what you'd do when you met up with me. I'm here now. Why don't you come up like a man? Come out here into the light and let's you and me settle this thing right now. You all—" *Crack!* A jet of flame leaped out of the shadow, and the speaker dropped like a log.

With a cry the shepherd ran to the side of his friend; but in a moment the crowd had again reached the cabin, and the old man was dragged from his fallen companion. With all his strength, Mr. Howitt struggled with his captors, begging them to let him go to the boy. But his hands were bound tightly behind his back, and when he still pleaded with those who held him, Wash Gibbs struck him full in the mouth, a blow that brought the blood.

They were leading the stunned and helpless old man away, when someone, who was bending over Young Matt, exclaimed, "You missed him, Wash! Jest raked him. He'll be up in a minute. An' hell 'll be to pay in th' wilderness if he ain't tied. Better fix him quick."

The big fellow already showed signs of returning consciousness, and, by the time they had tied his arms, he was able to struggle to his feet. For a moment he looked dizzily around, his eyes turning from one evil, triumphant face to another, until they rested upon the bleeding countenance of his old friend. The shepherd's eyes smiled back a message of cheer, and the kind old man tried to speak, when Wash Gibbs made another threatening motion, with his clenched fist.

At this, a cry like the roar of a mad bull came from the young giant. In his rage, he seemed suddenly endowed with almost superhuman strength. Before a man of the startled company could do more than gasp with astonishment, he had shaken himself free from those who held him, and, breaking the rope with which he was bound, as though it were twine, had leaped to the shepherd's side.

But it was uselss. For a moment, no one moved. Then a crashing blow, from the butt of a rifle in the hands of a man in the rear of the two prisoners, sent Young Matt once more to the ground. When he again regained consciousness, he was so securely bound that, even with his great strength, he was helpless.

Leading their captives to the old tree, the men withdrew for a short consultation, and to refresh themselves with another drink. When they had finished, Gibbs addressed the two friends. "We'uns didn't aim to hurt you, Young Matt, but seein' how you're so thick with this here feller, an' 'pear to know so much 'bout him, I reckon we can't hep ourselves nohow." He turned to the shepherd. "There's been too dad burned much funny work, at this ranch, since you come, mister, an' we'uns 'low we'll just give warnin' that we don't want no more strangers snoopin' round this neighborhood, an' we don't aim t' have 'em neither. We'uns 'low we can take care o' ourselves, without ary hep from th' dad burned government."

The shepherd tried to speak, but Gibbs, with an oath, roared, "Shut up, I tell you. Shut up. I've been a-watchin', an' I know what I know. Fix that there rope, boys, an' we'll get through, an' mosey 'long out o' here. Ain't no use to palaver, nohow."

A rope was thrown over a limb above their heads and a man approached the shepherd with the noose. Young Matt struggled desperately. With an evil grin, Gibbs said, "Don't you worry, sonny; you're a goin', too." And at his signal another rope was fixed, and the noose placed over the young man's head. The men took their places, awaiting the word from their leader.

The shepherd spoke softly to his companion, "Thank you, my boy." The giant began another desperate struggle.

Wash Gibbs, raising his hand, opened his lips to give the signal. But no word came. The brutal jaw dropped. The ruffian's eyes fairly started from his head, while the men who held the ropes stood as if turned to stone, as a long wailing cry came from the dark shadows under the bluff. There was a moment of death-like silence. Then another awful, sobbing groan, rising into a blood-curdling scream, came from down the road, and, from the direction of the ruined cabin, advanced a ghostly figure. Through the deep shadows and the misty light, it seemed to float toward them, moaning and sobbing as it came.

A shuddering gasp of horror burst from the frightened crew under the tree. Then, at a louder wail from the approaching apparition, they broke and ran. Like wild men they leaped for their horses, and flinging themselves into their saddles, fled in every direction.

Young Matt and the shepherd sank upon the ground in helpless amazement.

As the outlaws fled, the specter paused. Then it started onward toward the two men. Again it hesitated. For a moment it remained motionless, then turned and vanished, just as Jim Lane came flying out of the timber, into the bright light of the little clearing.

18

Learning to Be a Lady

The books sent for by Mr. Howitt came a few days after the adventure at the ranch, and Sammy, with all the intensity of her nature, plunged at once into the work mapped out for her by the shepherd.

All through the long summer and autumn, the girl spent hours with her teacher out on the hillside. Seated on some rocky bench, or reclining on the grassy slope, she would recite the lessons he gave her, or listen to him, as he read aloud from character-forming books, pausing now and then to slip in some comment to make the teaching clear, or to answer her eager questions.

At other times, while they followed the sheep, leisurely, from one feeding ground to another, he provoked her to talk of the things they were reading, and, while he thus led her to think, he as carefully guarded her speech and language.

At first they took the old familiar path of early intellectual training, but, little by little, he taught her to find the way for herself. Always as she advanced, he encouraged her to look for the life that is more than meat, and always, while they read and talked together, there was opened before them the great book wherein God has written, in the language of mountain, and tree, and sky, and flower, and brook, the things that make truly wise those who pause to read.

From her mother, and from her own free life in the hills, Sammy had a body beautiful with the grace and strength of perfect physical womanhood. With this, she had inherited from many generations of gentlefolk a mind and spirit susceptible of the highest culture. Unspoiled by the hothouse, forcing process, that so often leaves the intellectual powers jaded and weak, before they have fully developed, and free from the atmosphere of falsehood and surface culture, in which so many souls struggle for their very existence, the girl took what her teacher had to offer and made it her own. With a mental appetite uninjured by tidbits and dainties, she digested the strong food, and asked eagerly for more.

Her progress was marvelous, and the old scholar often had cause to wonder at the quickness with which his pupil's clear mind grasped the truths he showed her. Often before he could finish speaking, a bright nod, or word, showed that she had caught the purpose of his speech, while that wide eager look, and the question that followed, revealed her readiness to go on. It was as though many of the things he sought to teach her slept already in her brain, and needed only a touch to arouse them to vigorous life.

In time, the girl's very clothing, and even her manner of dressing her hair, came to reveal the development and transformation of her inner self; not that she dressed more expensively; she could not do that; but in the selection of materials, and in the many subtle touches that give distinction even to the plainest apparel, she showed her awakening. To help her in this, there was Aunt Mollie and a good ladies' magazine, which came to her regularly, through the kindness of her teacher.

Sammy's father, too, came unconsciously under the shepherd's influence. As his daughter grew, the man responded to the change in her, as he always responded to her every thought and mood. He talked often now of the old home in the southland, and sometimes fell into the speech of other days, dropping, for a moment, the rougher expres-

119

sions of his associates. But all this was to Sammy alone. To the world, there was no change in Jim, and he still went on his long rides with Wash Gibbs. By fall, the place was fixed up a bit; the fence was rebuilt, the yard trimmed, and another room added to the cabin.

So the days slipped away over the wood-fringed ridges. The soft green of tree, and of bush and grassy slope changed to brilliant gold, and crimson, and russet brown, while the gray blue haze that hangs always over the hollows took on a purple tone. Then in turn this purple changed to a deeper, colder blue, when the leaves had fallen, and the trees showed naked against the winter sky.

With the cold weather, the lessons were continued in the Lane cabin in the southern slope of Dewey. All day, while the shepherd was busy at the ranch, Sammy pored over her books; and every evening the old scholar climbed the hill to direct the work of his pupil, with Jim sitting, silent and grim, by the fireside, listening to the talk, and seeing who knows what visions of the long ago in the dancing flame.

And so the winter passed, and the spring came again; came, with its soft beauty of tender green; its wealth of blossoms, and sweet fragrance of growing things. Then came the summer; that terrible summer, when all the promises of spring were broken; when no rain fell for weary months, and the settlers, in the total failure of their crops, faced certain ruin.

19

The Drought

It began to be serious by the time corn was waist high. When the growing grain lost its rich color and the long blades rustled dryly in the hot air, the settlers looked anxiously for signs of coming rain. The one topic of conversation at the mill was the condition of the crops. The stories were all of past drought or tales of hardship and want.

The moon changed and still the same hot dry sky, with only now and then a shred of cloud floating lazily across the blue. The grass in the glades grew parched and harsh; the trees rattled their shriveled leaves; creek beds lay glaring white and dusty in the sun; and all the wild things in the wood sought the distant river bottom. In the Mutton Hollow neighborhood, only the spring below the Matthews place held water; and all day the stock on the range, crowding around the little pool, tramped out the narrow fringe of green grass about its edge, and churned its bright life into mud in their struggle.

Fall came and there was no relief. Crops were a total failure. Many people were without means to buy food for themselves and their stock for the coming winter and the months until another crop could be grown and harvested. Family after family loaded their few household goods into the big covered wagons, and, deserting their homes, set out to seek relief in more fortunate or more wealthy portions of the country.

The day came at last when Sammy found the shepherd in the little grove, near the deer lick, and told him that she and her father were going to move.

"Father says there is nothing else to do. Even if we could squeeze through the winter, we couldn't hold out until he could make another crop."

Throwing herself on the ground, she picked a big yellow daisy from a cluster, that, finding a little moisture oozing from a dirt-filled crevice of the rock, had managed to live, and began pulling it to piece.

In silence the old man watched her. He had not before realized how much the companionship of this girl was to him. To the refined and cultivated scholar, whose lot had been cast so strangely with the rude people of the mountain wilderness, the companionship of such a spirit and mind was a necessity. Unconsciously Sammy had supplied the one thing lacking, and by her demands upon his thought had kept the shepherd from mental stagnation and morbid brooding. Day after day she had grown into his life—his intellectual and spiritual child, and though she had dropped the rude speech of the native, she persisted still in calling him by his backwoods title, "Dad." But the little word had come to hold a new meaning for them both. He saw now, all at once, what he would lose when she went away.

One by one, the petals from the big daisy fell from the girl's hand, dull splashes of gold against her dress and on the grass.

"Where will you go?" he asked at last.

Sammy shook her head without looking up. "Don't know; anywhere that Daddy can earn a livin'—I mean living—for us."

"And when do you start?"

"Pretty soon now; there ain't nothin'—there is nothing to stay for now. Father told me when he went away day before yesterday that we would go as soon as he returned. He promised to be home sometime this evening. I—I couldn't tell you before, Dad, but I guess you knew."

The shepherd did know. For weeks they had both avoided the subject.

Sammy continued, "I—I've just been over to the Matthews place. Uncle Matt has been gone three days now. I guess you know about that, too. Aunt Mollie told me all about it. Oh, I wish, I wish I could help them." She reached for another daisy and two big tears rolled from under the long lashes to fall with the golden petals. "We'll come back in the spring when it's time to plant again, but what if you're not here?"

Her teacher could not answer for a time; then he said, in an odd, hesitating way, "Have you heard from Ollie lately?"

The girl raised her head, her quick, rare instinct divining his unspoken thought, and something she saw in her old friend's face brought just a hint of a smile to her own tearful eyes. She knew him so well. "You don't mean that, Dad," she said. "We just couldn't do that. I had a letter from him yesterday offering us money, but you know we could not accept it from him." And there the subject was dropped.

They spent the afternoon together, and in the evening, at Sammy's Lookout on the shoulder of Dewey, she bade him good-night, and left him alone with his flocks in the soft twilight.

That same evening Mr. Matthews returned from his trip to the settlement.

20

The Shepherd Writes a Letter

To purchase the sheep and the ranch in the Hollow, Mr. Matthews had placed a heavy mortgage not only upon the ranch land but upon the homestead as well. In the loss of his stock the woodsman would lose all he had won in years of toil from the mountain wilderness.

When the total failure of the crops became a certainty, and it was clear that the country could not produce enough feed to carry his flock through the winter until the spring grass, Mr. Matthews went to the settlement hoping to get help from the bank there, where he was known.

He found the little town in confusion and the doors of the bank closed. The night before a band of men had entered the building and, forcing the safe, had escaped to the mountains with their booty.

Old Matt's interview with the bank official was brief. "It is simply impossible, Mr. Matthews," said the man. "As it is, we shall do well to keep our own heads above water."

Then the mountaineer had come the long way home. As he rode slowly up the last hill, the giant form stooped with a weariness unusual, and the rugged face looked so worn and hopelessly sad, that Aunt Mollie, who was waiting at the gate, did not need words to tell her of his failure. The old man got stiffly down from his horse, and when he had removed saddle and bridle, and had turned the animal into the lot, the two walked toward the house. But they did not

124

enter the building. Without a word they turned aside from the steps and followed the little path to the graves in the rude enclosure beneath the pines, where the sunshine fell only in patches here and there.

That night after supper Mr. Matthews went down into the Hollow to see the shepherd. "It's goin' to be mighty hard on Mollie and me a-leavin' the old place up yonder," said the big man, when he had told of his unsuccessful trip. "It won't matter so much to the boy, 'cause he's young yet, but we've worked hard, Mr. Howitt, for that home—Mollie and me has. She's up there now a-sittin' on the porch and a-livin' it all over again, like she does when there ain't no one around, with her face turned toward them pines west of the house. It' mighty nigh a-breakin' her heart just to think of leavin', but she'll hide it all from me when I go up there, thinkin' not to worry me—as if I didn't know. An' it's goin' to be mighty hard to part with you, too, Mr. Howitt. I don't reckon you'll ever know, sir, how much you done for us; for me most of all."

The shepherd made as if to interrupt, but the big man continued, "Don't you suppose we can see, sir, how you've made over the whole neighborhood? There ain't a family for ten miles that don't come to you when they're in trouble.

An' there's Sammy Lane a-readin', an' talkin' just about the same as you do yourself, fit to hold up her end with anybody what's got education, and Jim himself's changed something wonderful. Same old Jim in lots of ways, but something more, somehow, through I can't tell it. Then there's my boy, Grant. I know right well what he'd been if it wasn't for you to show him what the best kind of a man's like. He'd-a sure never knowed it from me. I don't mean as he'd-a ever been a bad man like Wash Gibbs, or a no account triflin' one, like them Thompsons, but he couldn't never a been what he is now, through and through, if he hadn't a known you. There's a heap more, too, all over the country that you've talked to a Sunday, when the

"Are you sure there is no one who can help you over this hard time."

parson wasn't here. As for me, you—you sure been a God's blessin' to me and Mollie, Mr. Howitt."

Again the shepherd moved uneasily, as if to protest, but his big friend made a gesture of silence. "Let me say it while I got a chance, Dad." And the other bowed his head while Old Matt continued, "I can't tell how it is, an' I don't reckon you'd understand anyway, but stayin' as you have after our talk that first night you come, an' livin' down here on this spot alone, after what you know, it's— it's just like I was a little kid, an' you was a standin' big and strong like between me an' a great blackness that was somethin' awful. I reckon it looks foolish, me a-talkin' this way. Maybe it's because I'm gettin' old, but anyhow I wanted you to know."

The shepherd raised his head and his face was aglow with a glad triumphant light, while his deep voice was full of meaning, as he said gently, "It has been more to me, too, than you think, Mr. Matthews. I ought to tell you—I—I will tell you—" he checked himself and added, "someday." Then he changed the topic quickly.

"Are you sure there is no one who can help you over this hard time? Is there *no* way?"

The mountaineer shook his head. "I've gone over it all again an' again. Williams at the bank is the only man I know who had the money, an' he's done for now by this robbery. You see I can't go to strangers, Dad. I ain't got nothin' left for security."

"But, could you not sell the sheep for enough to save the homestead?"

"Who could buy? Or who would buy, if they could, in this country, without a bit of feed? And then look at 'em, they're so poor an' weak, now, they couldn't stand the drivin' to the shippin' place. They'd die all along the road. They're just skin an' bones, Dad; ain't no butcher would pay freight on 'em, even."

Mr. Howitt sat with knitted brow, staring into the shadows. Then he said slowly, "There is that old mine. If this

127

man Dewey were only here, do you suppose—?"

Again the mountaineer shook his head. "Colonel Dewey would be a mighty old man now, Dad, even if he were livin'. 'Tain't likely he'll ever come back, nor 'tain't likely the mine will ever be found without him. I studied all that out on the way home."

As he finished speaking, he rose to go, and the dog, springing up, dashed out of the cabin and across the clearing toward the bluff by the corral, barking furiously.

The two men looked at each other. "A rabbit," said Mr. Howitt. But they both knew that the well-trained shepherd dog never tracked a rabbit, and Old Matt's face was white when he mounted to ride away up the trail.

Long the shepherd stood in the doorway looking out into the night, listening to the voices of the wilderness. In his life in the hills he had found a little brightness, while in the old mountaineer's words that evening, he had glimpsed a future happiness, of which he had scarcely dared to dream. With the single exception of that one wild night, his life had been an unbroken calm. Now he was to leave it all. And for what?

He seemed to hear the rush and roar of the world beyond the ridges, as one in a quiet harbor hears outside the thunder of the stormy sea. He shuddered. The gloom and mystery of it all crept into his heart. He was so alone. But it was not the wilderness that made him shudder. It was the thought of the great, mad, cruel world that raged beyond the hills; that, and something else.

The dog growled again and faced threateningly toward the cliff. "What is it, Brave?" The only answer was an uneasy whine as the animal crouched close to the man's feet. The shepherd peered into the darkness in the direction of the ruined cabin. "God," he whispered, "how can I leave this place?"

He turned back into the house, closed and barred the door. With the manner of one making a resolution after a hard struggle, he took writing material from the top shelf of the cupboard, and, seating himself at the table, began to write. The hours slipped by, and page after page, closely written, came from the shepherd's pen, while, as he wrote, the man's face grew worn and haggard. It was as though he lifted again the burden he had learned to lay aside. At last it was finished. Placing the sheets in an envelope, he wrote the address with trembling hand.

While Mr. Howitt was writing his letter at the ranch, and Old Matt was tossing sleeplessly on his bed in the big log house, a horseman rode slowly down from the Compton Ridge road. Stopping at the creek to water, he pushed on up the mountain toward the Lane cabin. The horse walked with low-hung head and lagging feet; the man slouched half asleep in the saddle. It was Jim Lane.

21

God's Gold

The troubled night passed. The shepherd arose to see the sky above the eastern rim of the Hollow glowing with the first soft light of a new day. Away over Compton Ridge one last, pale star hung, caught in the upper branches of a dead pine. Not a leaf of the forest stirred. In awe the man watched the miracle of the morning, as the glowing colors touched cloud after cloud, until the whole sky was aflame, and the star was gone.

Again he seemed to hear, faint and far away, the roar and surge of the troubled sea. With face uplifted, he cried aloud, "O God, my Father, I ask thee not for the things that men deem great. I covet not wealth, nor honor, nor ease; only peace; only that I may live free from those who do not understand; only that I may in some measure make atonement; that I may win pardon. Oh, drive me not from this haven into the world again!"

"Again, again," came back from the cliff on the other side of the clearing, and, as the echo died away in the silent woods, a bush on top of the bluff stirred in the breathless air; stirred, and was still again. Somewhere up on Dewey a crow croaked hoarsely to his mate; a cow on the range bawled loudly and the sheep in the corral chorused in answer.

Re-entering the cabin, the old man quickly built a fire, then, taking the bucket, went to the spring for water. He

130

must prepare his breakfast. Coming back with the brimming pail, he placed it on the bench and was turning to the cupboard, when he noticed on the table a small oblong package. "Mr. Matthews must have left it last night," he thought. "Strange that I did not see it before."

Picking up the package he found that it was quite heavy, and, to his amazement, saw that it was addressed to himself, in a strange, cramped printing, such letters as a child would make. He ripped open the covering and read in the same crude writing: "This stuff is for you to give to the Matthews and Jim Lane, but don't tell anyone where you got it. And don't try to find out where it come from either, or you'll wish you hadn't. You needn't be afraid. It's good money all right." The package contained gold pieces of various denominations.

With a low exclamation, the shepherd let the parcel slip, and the money fell in a shining heap on the floor. He stood as in a dream looking from the gold to the letter in his hand. Then, going to the door, he gazed long and searchingly in every direction. Nothing unusual met his eye. Turning back into the cabin again, he caught up the letter he had written, and stepped to the fireplace, an expression of relief upon his face. But with his hand outstretched toward the flames, he paused, the letter still in his grasp, while the expression of relief gave way to a look of fear.

"The bank," he muttered, "the robbery." The shining pieces on the floor seemed to glisten mockingly. "No, no, no," said the man. "Better the other way, and yet—" He read the letter again. "It's good money, all right; you needn't be afraid."

In his quandary, he heard a step without and looking up saw Pete in the open door.

The boy's sensitive face was aglow, as he said, "Pete's glad this morning; Pete saw the sky. Did Dad see the sky?"

Mr. Howitt nodded; then, moved by a sudden impulse, pointed to the money, and said, "Does Pete see this? It's gold, all gold."

131

The boy drew near with curious eyes. "Dad doesn't know where it came from," continued the shepherd. "Does Pete know?"

The youth gave a low laugh of delight. "Course Pete knows. Pete went up on Dewey this morning; 'way up to the old signal tree, and course he took me with him. The sky was all soft and silvery, an' the clouds was full, plumb full of gold, like that there." He pointed to the yellow coins on the floor. "Didn't Dad see? Some of it must o' spilled out."

"Ah, yes, that was God's gold," said the older man softly.

The lad touched his friend on the arm, and with the other hand again pointed to the glittering heap on the floor. "Pete says that there's God's gold too, and Pete he knows."

The man started and looked at the boy in wonder. "But why, why should it come to me at such a time as this?" he muttered.

" 'Cause you're the Shepherd of Mutton Hollow, Pete says. Don't be scared, Dad. Pete knows. It's sure God's gold."

The shepherd turned to the fireplace and dropped the letter he had written upon the leaping flames.

22

A Letter from Ollie Stewart

The Post Office at the Forks occupied a commanding position in the northeast corner of Uncle Ike's cabin, covering an area not less than four feet square.

The fittings were in excellent taste, and the equipment fully adequate to the needs of the service: an old table, on legs somewhat rickety; upon the table, a rude box, set on end and divided roughly into eight pigeonholes, duly numbered; in the table, a drawer, filled a little with stamps and stationery, filled mostly with scraps of leaf tobacco, and an odd company of veteran cob pipes, now on the retired list, or home on furlough; before the table, a little old chair, wrought in some fearful and wonderful fashion from hickory sticks from which the bark had not been removed.

With every change of the weather, this chair, through some unknown but powerful influence, changed its shape, thus becoming in its own way a sort of government weather bureau. And if in all this "land of the free and home of the brave" there be a single throne, it must be this same curiously changeable chair. In spite of, or perhaps because of, its strange powers, that weird piece of furniture managed to make itself so felt that it was religiously avoided by every native who called at the Forks. Not the wildest "hillbilly" of them all dared to occupy for a moment this seat of Uncle Sam's representative. Here Uncle Ike reigned supreme over his four feet square of government property. And you may be very sure that the mighty mysterious thing known as the "gov'ment" lost none of its might, and nothing of its mystery, at the hands of its worthy official.

Uncle Ike left the group in front of the cabin and, hurriedly entering the office, seated himself upon his throne. A tall, thin, slow-moving mule was brought to before a certain tree with the grace and dignity of an ocean liner coming into her slip. Zeke Wheeler dismounted, and, with the saddle mail pouch over his arm, stalked solemnly across the yard and into the house, his spurs clinking on the gravel and rattling over the floor. Following the mail carrier, the group of mountaineers entered, and, with Uncle Ike's entire family, took their places at a respectful distance from the holy place of mystery and might, in the northeast corner of the room.

The postmaster, with a key attached by a small chain to one corner of the table, unlocked the flat pouch and drew forth the contents—five papers, three letters and one postal card.

The empty pouch was kicked contemptuously beneath the table. The papers were tossed to one side. All eyes were fixed on the little bundle of first class matter. In a breathless silence the official cut the string. The silence was broken.

"Ba thundas! Mary Liz Jolly'll sure be glad t' git that there letter. Her man's been gone nigh onto three months now, an' ain't wrote but once. That was when he was in Mayville. I see he's down in th' nation now at Auburn, sendin' Mary Liz some money, I reckon. Ba thundas, it's 'bout time! What!"

"James Creelman, E-S-Q., Wal, dad burn *me*. Jim done wrote t' that there house in Chicago more'n three weeks ago, 'bout a watch they're a-sellin' fer fo' dollars. Ba thundas! They'd sure answer *me* quicker'n that, er they'd hear turkey. What! I done tole Jim it was only a blamed ol' fo'-dollar house anyhow."

At this many nods and glances were exchanged by the

group in silent admiration of the "gov'ment," and one mountaineer, bold even to recklessness, remarked, "Jim must have a heap o' money t' be a-buyin' four-dollar watches. Must er sold that gray mule o' hisn; hit'd fetch 'bout that much, I reckon."

"Much you know 'bout it, Buck Boswell. Let me tell you, Jim he works, he does. He's the workingest man in this here county, ba thundas! What! Jim he don't sit round like you fellers down on th' creek an' wait fer pawpaws to git ripe, so he can git a square meal, ba thundas!" The bold mountaineer wilted.

Uncle Ike proceeded with the business of his office. "Here's Sallie Rhodes done writ her maw a card from th' Corners. Sallie's been a-visitin' her paw's folks. Says she'll be home on th' hack next mail, an' wants her maw t' meet her here. You can take th' hack next time, Zeke. An' ba thundas! Here's 'nother letter from that dummed Ollie Stewart. Sammy ain't been over yet after th' last one he wrote. Ba thundas! If it weren't for them blamed gov'ment inspectors, I'd sure put a spoke in his wheel. What! I'd everlastin'ly seva' th' connections between that gentleman an' these here Ozarks. Dad burn me, if I wouldn't. He'd better take one o' them new-fangled women in th' city, where he's gone to, an' not come back here for one o' our girls. I don't believe Sammy'd care much, nohow, ba thundas! What!" The official tossed the letter into a pigeon hole beside its neglected mate, with a gesture that fully expressed the opinion of the entire community, regarding Mr. Stewart and his intentions toward Miss Lane.

Sammy got the letters the next day, and read them over and over, as she rode slowly through the sweet-smelling woods. The last one told her that Ollie was coming home on a visit. "Thursday, that's the day after tomorrow," she said aloud. Then she read the letter again.

It was a very different letter from those Ollie had written when first he left the woods. Most of all it was different in that indefinable something by which a man reveals his place

135

in life in the letters he writes, no less than in the words he speaks, or the clothing he wears. As Sammy rode slowly through the pinery and down the narrow Fall Creek valley, she was thinking of these things, thinking of these things seriously.

The girl had been in a way conscious of the gradual change in Ollie's life, as it had been revealed in his letters, but she had failed to connect that change with her lover. The world into which young Stewart had gone, and by which he was being formed, was so foreign to the only world known to Sammy, that while she realized in a dim way that he was undergoing a transformation, she still saw him in her mind as the backwoods boy. With the announcement of his return, and the thought that she would soon meet him face to face, it burst upon her suddenly that her lover was a stranger. The man who wrote this letter was not the man whom she had promised to marry. Who was he?

Passing the mill and the blacksmith shop, the brown pony with his absorbed rider began to climb the steep road to the Matthews place. Halfway up the hill, the little horse, stepping on a loose stone, stumbled, catching himself quickly.

As a flash of lightning on a black night reveals well known landmarks and familiar objects, this incident brought back to Sammy the evening when, with Ollie and Young Matt, she had climbed the same way; when her horse had stumbled and her face had come close to the face of the big fellow whose hand was on the pony's neck. The whole scene came before her with a vividness that was startling; every word, every look, every gesture of the two young men, her own thoughts and words, the objects along the road, the very motion of her horse; she seemed to be actually living again those moments of the past. But more than this, she seemed not only to live again the incidents of that evening, but in some strange way to possess the faculty of analyzing and passing judgment upon her own thoughts and words.

Great changes had come to Sammy, too, since that night when her lover had said good-by. And now, in her deeper life, the young woman felt a curious sense of shame, as she saw how trivial were the things that had influenced her to become Ollie's promised wife. She blushed, as she recalled the motives that had sent her to the shepherd with the request that he teach her to be a fine lady.

Coming out on top of the ridge, Brownie stopped of his own accord, and the girl saw again the figure of a young giant, standing in the level rays of the setting sun, with his great arms outstretched, saying, "I reckon I was built to live in these hills. I don't guess you'd better count on me ever bein' more'n I am." Sammy realized suddenly that the question was no longer whether Ollie would be ashamed of her. It was quite a different question, indeed.

23

Ollie Comes Home

The day that Ollie was expected at the cabin on Dewey Bald, Mr. Lane was busy in the field.

"I don't reckon you'll need me at th' house nohow," he said with a queer laugh, as he rose from the dinner table; and Sammy, blushing, told him to go on to his work, or Young Matt would get his planting done first.

Jim went out to get his horse from the stable, but before he left, he returned once more to the house.

"What is it, Daddy? Forget something?" asked Sammy, as her father stood in the doorway.

"Not exactly," drawled Jim. "I ain't got a very good forgetter. Wish I had. It's somethin' I can't forget. Wish I could."

In a moment the girl's arms were about his neck, "You dear foolish old Daddy Jim. I have a bad forgetter, too. You thought when I began studying with Dad Howitt that my books would make me forget you. Well, have they?" A tightening of the long arm about her waist was the only answer. "And now you are making yourself miserable trying to think that Ollie Stewart and his friends will make me forget you; just as if all the folks in the world could ever be to me what you are; you, and Dad, and Uncle Matt, and Aunt Mollie, and Young Matt. Daddy, I am ashamed of you. Honest, I am. Do you think a real genuine lady could ever forget the father who had been so good to her? Daddy,

138

I am insulted. You must apologize immediately."

She pretended to draw away, but the long arm held her fast, while the mountaineer said in a voice that had in it pride and pain, with a world of love, "I know, I know, girl. But you'll be a-livin' in the city, when you and Ollie are married, and these old hills will be mighty lonesome with you gone. You see I couldn't never leave the old place. 'Tain't much, I know, so far as money value goes. But there's some things worth a heap more than their money value, I reckon. If you was only goin' t' live where I could ride over once or twice a week to see you, it would be different."

"Yes, Daddy; but maybe I won't go after all. I'm not married, yet, you know."

Something in her voice or manner caused Jim to hold his daughter at arm's length, and look full into the brown eyes. "What do you mean, girl?"

Sammy laughed in an uneasy and embarrassed way. She was not sure that she knew herself all that lay beneath the simple words. She tried to explain. "Why, I mean that— that Ollie and I have both grown up since we promised, and he has been living away out in the big world and going to school besides. He must have seen many girls since he left me. He is sure to changed greatly, and—and, maybe he won't want a backwoods wife."

The man growled something beneath his breath, and the girl placed a hand over his lips. "You mustn't say swear words, Daddy Jim. Indeed, you must not. Not in the presence of ladies, anyway."

"You're changed a heap in some ways, too," said Jim.

"Yes, I suppose I am; but my changes are mostly on the inside like and perhaps he won't see them."

"Would you care so mighty much, Sammy?" whispered the father.

"That's just it, Daddy. How can I tell? We must both begin all over again, don't you see?" Then she sent him away to his work.

Sammy had finished washing the dinner dishes, and was putting things in order about the house, when she stopped suddenly before the little shelf that held her books. Then, with a smile, she carried them every one into her own room, placing them carefully where they could not be seen from the open door. Going next to the mirror, she deliberately took down her hair, and arranged it in the old careless way that Ollie had always known. "You're just the same backwoods girl, Sammy Lane, so far as outside things go," she said to the face in the glass, "but you are not quite the same all the way through. We'll see if he—" She was interrupted by the loud barking of the dog outside, and her heart beat more quickly as a voice cried, "Hello, hello, I say; call off your dog!"

Sammy hurried to the door. A strange gentleman stood at the gate. The strangest gentleman that Sammy had ever seen. Surely this could not be Ollie Stewart; this slender, pale-faced man, with faultless linen, well-gloved hands and shining patent leathers. The girl drew back in embarrassment.

But there was no hesitation on the part of the young man. Before she could recover from her astonishment, he caught her in his arms and kissed her again and again, until she struggled from his embrace. "You—you must not," she gasped.

"Why not?" he demanded laughingly. "Has anyone a better right? I have waited a long while for this, and I mean to make up now for lost time."

He took a step toward her again, but Sammy held him off at arm's length, as she repeated, "No—no—you must not; not now." Young Stewart was helpless. And the discovery that she was stronger than this man brought to the girl a strange feeling, as of shame.

"How strong you are," he said petulantly, ceasing his efforts. Then carefully surveying the splendidly proportioned and developed young woman, he added, "And how beautiful!"

Under his look, Sammy's face flushed painfully, even to her neck and brow; and the man, seeing her confusion, laughed again. Then, seating himself in the only rocking chair in the room, the young gentleman leisurely removed his gloves, looking around the while with an amused expression on his face, while the girl stood watching him. At last, he said impatiently, "Sit down, sit down, Sammy. You look at me as if I were a ghost."

Unconsciously, she slipped into the speech of the old days, "You sure don't look much like you used to. I never see nobody wear such clothes as them. Not even Dad Howitt, when he first come. Do you wear 'em every day?"

Ollie frowned. "You're just like all the rest, Sammy. Why don't you talk as you write? You've improved a lot in your letters. If you talk like that in the city, people will know in a minute that you are from the country."

At this, Sammy rallied her scattered wits, and the wide, questioning look was her eyes, as she replied quietly, "Thank you. I'll try to remember. But tell me, please, what harm could it do, if people did know I came from the country?"

It was Ollie's turn to be amazed. "Why, you can talk!" he said. "Where did you learn?" And the girl answered simply that she had picked it up from the old shepherd.

This little incident put Sammy more at ease, and she skillfully led her companion to speak of the city and his life there. Of his studies the young fellow had little to say, and, to her secret delight, the girl found that she had actually made greater progress with her books than had her lover with all his supposed advantages.

But of other things, of the gaiety and excitement of the great city, of his new home, the wealth of his uncle, and his own bright prospects, Ollie spoke freely, never dreaming the girl had already seen the life he painted in such glowing colors through the eyes of one who had been careful to point out the froth and foam of it all. Neither did the young man discover in the quiet questions she asked that Sammy was seeking to know what in all this new world he

141

"Why, you can talk! Where did you learn?"

had found that he could make his own as the thing most worth while.

The backwoods girl had never seen that type of man to whom the life of the city, only, is life. Ollie was peculiarly fitted by nature to absorb quickly those things of the world, into which he had gone, that were most different from the world he had left; and there remained scarcely a trace of his earlier wilderness training.

But there is that in life that lies too deep for any mere change of environment to touch. Sammy remembered a lesson the shepherd had given her: "A gentle spirit may express itself in the rude words of illiteracy; it is not therefore rude. Ruffianism may speak the language of learning or religion; it is ruffianism still. Strength may wear the garb of weakness, and still be strong; and a weakling may carry the weapons of strength, but fight with a faint heart." So, beneath all the changes that had come to her backwoods lover, Sammy felt that Ollie himself was unchanged. It was as though he had learned a new language, but still said the same things.

Sammy, too, had entered a new world. Step by step, as the young man had advanced in his schooling, and, dropping the habits and customs of the backwoods, had conformed in his outward life to his new environment, the girl had advanced in her education under the careful hand of the old shepherd. Ignorant still of the false standards and the petty ambitions that are so large a part of the complex world, into which he had gone, she had been introduced to a world where the life itself is the only thing worth while. She had seen nothing of the glittering tinsel of that cheap culture that is death to all true refinement. But in the daily companionship of her gentle teacher, she had lived in touch with true aristocracy, the aristocracy of heart and spirit.

Young Matt and Jim had thought that, in Sammy's education, the bond between the girl and her lover would be strengthened. They had thought to see her growing farther and farther from the life of the hills; the life to which they felt that they must always belong. But that was because

Young Matt and Jim did not know the kind of education the girl was getting.

So Ollie had come back to his old home to measure things by his new standard; and he had come back, too, to be measured according to the old, old standard. If the man's eyes were dimmed by the flash and sparkle that play upon the surface of life, the woman's vision was strong and clear to look into the still depths.

Later in the day, as they walked together up the Old Trail to Sammy's Lookout, the girl tried to show him some of the things that had been revealed to her in the past months. But the young fellow could not follow where she led, and answered her always with some flippant remark, or with the superficial philosophy of his kind.

When he tried to turn the talk to their future, she skill-fully defeated his purpose, or was silent; and when he would claim a lover's privileges, she held him off. Upon his demanding a reason for her coldness, she answered, "Don't you see that everything is different now? We must learn to know each other over again."

"But you are my promised wife."

"I promised to be the wife of a backwoodsman," she answered. "I cannot keep that promise, for that man is dead. You are a man of the city, and I am scarcely acquainted with you."

Young Stewart found himself not a little puzzled by the situation. He had come home expecting to meet a girl beautiful in face and form, but with the mind of a child to wonder at the things he would tell her. He had found, instead, a thoughtful young woman trained to look for and recognize truth and beauty. Sammy was always his physical superior. She was now his intellectual superior as well. The change that had come to her was not a change by environment of the things that lay upon the surface, but it was a change in the deeper things of life—in the purpose and understanding of life itself. Like many of his kind, Ollie could not distinguish between these things.

24

What Makes a Man

Mr. Matthews and his son finished their planting early in the afternoon and the boy set out to find old Kate and the mule colt. Those rovers had not appeared at the home place for nearly two weeks, and someone must bring them in before they forgot their home completely.

"Don't mind if I ain't back for supper, Mother," said Young Matt. "I may eat at the ranch with Dad. I ain't been down there for quite a spell now, an' I'd kind o' like to know if that panther we've been a-hearin' is givin' Dad any trouble."

"Dad told me yesterday that he thought he heard old Kate's bell over on yon side of Cox's Bald," said Mr. Matthews. "I believe if I was you I'd take across Cox's along the far side of th' ridge, around Dewey an' down into the Hollow that way. Joe Gardner was over north yesterday, an' he said he didn't see no signs on that range. I reckon you'll find 'em on Dewey somewheres about Jim Lane's, maybe. You'd better saddle a horse."

"No, I'll take it afoot. I can ride old Kate in, if I find them," replied the big fellow; and, with his rifle in the hollow of his arm, he struck out over the hills. All along the eastern slope of the ridge, that forms one side of Mutton Hollow, he searched for the missing stock, but not a sound of the bell could he hear; not a trace of the vagabonds could he find. And that was because old Kate and the little

145

colt were standing quietly in the shade in a little glen below Sand Ridge not a quarter of a mile from the barn.

The afternoon was well on when Young Matt gave up the search, and shaped his course for the sheep ranch. He was on the farther side of Dewey, and the sun told him that there was just time enough to reach the cabin before supper.

Pushing straight up the side of the mountain, he found the narrow bench, that runs like a great cornice two-thirds of the way around the Bald Knob. The mountaineer knew that at that level, on the side opposite from where he stood, was Sammy's Lookout, and from there it was an easy road down to the sheep ranch in the valley. Also, he knew that from that rocky shelf, all along the southern side of the mountain, he would look down upon Sammy's home; and, who could tell, he might even catch a glimpse of Sammy herself. Very soon he rounded the turn of the hill, and saw far below the Lane homestead; the cabin and the barn in the little clearing looking like tiny doll houses.

Young Matt walked slowly now. The supper was forgotten. Coming to the clump of cedars just above the Old Trail where it turns the shoulder of the hill from the west, he stopped for a last look. Beyond this point, he would turn his back upon the scene that interested him so deeply.

The young man could not remember when he had not loved Sammy Lane. She seemed to have been always a part of his life. It was the season of the year when all the wild things of the forest choose their mates, and as the big fellow stood there looking down upon the home of the girl he loved, all the splendid passion of his manhood called for her. It seemed to him that the whole world was slipping away to leave him alone in a measureless universe. He almost cried aloud. It is the same instinct that prompts the panther to send his mating call ringing over the hills and through the forest, and leads the moose to issue his loud challenge.

At last Young Matt turned to go, when he heard the

sound of voices. Someone was coming along the Old Trail that lay in full view on the mountainside not two hundred yards away. Instinctively the woodsman drew back into the thick foliage of the cedars.

The voices grew louder. A moment more and Sammy with Ollie Stewart appeared from around the turn of the hill. They were walking side by side and talking earnestly. The young woman had just denied the claims of her former lover, and was explaining the change in her attitude toward him; but the big fellow on the ledge above could not know that. He could not hear what they were saying. He only saw his mate, and the man who had come to take her from him.

Half crouching on the rocky shelf in the dark shadow of the cedar, the giant seemed a wild thing ready for his spring; ready and eager, yet held in check by something more powerful still than his passion. Slowly the two, following the Old Trail, passed from sight, and Young Matt stood erect. He was trembling like a frightened child. A moment longer he waited, then turned and fairly ran from the place. Leaving the ledge at the Lookout, he rushed down the mountain and through the woods as if mad, to burst in upon the shepherd, with words that were half a cry, half a groan. "He's come, Dad; he's come. I've just seen him with her."

Mr. Howitt sprang up with a startled exclamation. His face went white. He grasped the table for support. He tried to speak, but words would not come. He could only stare with frightened eyes, as though Young Matt himself were some fearful apparition.

The big fellow threw himself into a chair, and presently the shepherd managed to say in a hoarse whisper, "Tell me about it, Grant, if you can."

"I seen them up on Dewey just now, goin' down the Old Trail from Sammy's Lookout to her home. I was huntin' stock."

The old scholar leaned toward his friend, as he almost

shouted, "Saw them going to Sammy's home! Saw whom, lad? Whom did you see?"

"Why—why—Sammy Lane and that—that Ollie Stewart, of course. I tell you he's come back. Come to take her away."

The reaction was almost as bad as the shock. Mr. Howitt gasped as he dropped back into his seat. He felt a hysterical impulse to laugh, to cry out. Young Matt continued, "He's come home, Dad, with all his fine clothes and city airs, and now she'll go away with him, and we won't never see her again."

As he began to put his thoughts into words, the giant got upon his feet, and walked the floor like one insane. "He shan't have her," he cried; clenching his great fists; "he shan't have her. If he was a man I could stand it, Dad. But look at him! Look at him, will you? The little white-faced, washed-out runt, what is he? He ain't no man, Dad. He ain't even as much of a man as he was. And Sammy is— God! What a woman she is! You've been a-tellin' me that I could be a gentleman, even if I always lived in the back-woods. But you're wrong, Dad, plumb wrong. I ain't no gentleman. I can't never be one. I'm just a man. I'm a—a savage, a damned beast, and I'm glad of it." He threw back his shaggy head, and his white teeth gleamed through his parted lips, as he spoke in tones of mad defiance.

"Dad, you say there's some things bigger'n learnin', and such, and I reckon this here's one of them. I don't care if that little whelp goes to all the schools there is, and gets to be a president or a king; I don't care if he's got all the money there is between here and hell; put him out here in the woods, face to face with life where them things don't count, and what is he? What is he, Dad? He's nothin'! Plumb nothin'!"

The old shepherd waited quietly for the storm to pass. The big fellow would come to himself after a time; until then, words were useless. At last Young Matt spoke in calmer tones, "I run away, Dad. I had to. I was afraid I'd hurt him. Something inside o' me just fought to get at him, and I couldn't-a held out much longer. I don't want to hurt nobody, Dad. I reckon it was a-seein' 'em together that did it. It's a God's blessin' I come away when I did; it sure is." He dropped wearily into his chair again.

Then the teacher spoke, "It is always a God's blessing, lad, when a man masters the worst of himself. You are a strong man, my boy. You hardly know your strength. But you need always to remember that the stronger the man, the easier it is for him to become a beast. Your manhood depends upon this, and upon nothing else, that you conquer and control the animal side of yourself. It will be a sad moment for you, and for all of us who love you, if you ever forget. Don't you see, lad, it is this victory only that gives you the right to think of yourself as a man. Mind, I say to think of yourself, as a man. It doesn't much matter what others think of you. It is what one can honestly think of one's self that matters."

So they spent the evening together, and the big mountaineer learned to see still more deeply into the things that had come to the older man in his years of study and painful experience.

When at last Young Matt arose to say good-night, the shepherd tried to persuade him to sleep at the ranch. But he said, no, the folks at home would be looking for him, and he must go. "I'm mightly glad I come, Dad," he added. "I don't know what I'd do if it wasn't for you; go plumb hog wild, and make a fool of myself, I reckon. I don't know what a lot of us would do, either. Seems like you're a sort of shepherd to the whole neighborhood. I reckon, though, I'm 'bout the worst in the flock," he finished with a grim smile.

Mr. Howitt took his hat from the nail. "If you must go, I will walk a little way with you. I love to be out such nights as this. I often wish Pete would take me with him."

"He's out somewhere tonight, sure," replied the other, as they started. "We heard him a-singin' last night." Then he

149

stopped and asked, "Where's your gun, Dad? There's a panther somewhere on this range."

"I know," returned the shepherd. "I heard it scream last night; and I meant to go up to the house today for a gun. I broke the hammer of mine yesterday."

"That's bad," said Young Matt. "But come on, I'll leave mine with you until tomorrow. That fellow would sure make things lively, if he should come to see you, and catch you without a shootin' iron."

Together the two walked through the timber, until they came to where the trail that leads to the Matthews place begins to climb the low spur of the hill back of the house. Here Mr. Howitt stopped to say good-night, adding, as the young man gave him the rifle, "I don't like to take this, Grant. What if you should meet that panther between here and home?"

"Shucks!" returned the other, "you're the one that'll need it. You've got to take care of them sheep. I'll get home all right."

"Don't forget the other beast, lad. Remember what it is that makes the man."

25

Young Matt Remembers

After parting with his friend, Young Matt continued on his way until he reached the open ground below the point where the path from the ranch joins the Old Trail. Then he stopped and looked around.

Before him was the belt of timber, and beyond, the dark mass of the mountain ridge with the low gap where his home nestled among the trees. He could see the light from the cabin window shining like a star. Behind him lay the darker forest of the Hollow, and beyond, like a great sentinel, was the round, treeless form of Dewey Bald. From where he stood, he could even see clearly against the sky the profile of the mountain's shoulder, and the ledge at Sammy's Lookout. Another moment, and the young man had left the path that led to his home, and was making straight for the distant hill. He would climb to that spot where he had stood in the afternoon, and would look down once more upon the little cabin on the mountainside. Then he would go home along the ridge.

Three quarters of an hour later, he pushed up out of a ravine that he followed to its head below the Old Trail, near the place where, with Pete and the shepherd, he had watched Sammy reading her letter. He was climbing to the Lookout, for it was the easiest way to the ledge, and, as his eye came on a level with the bench along which the path runs, he saw clearly on the big rock above the figure of a

151

man. Instantly Young Matt stopped. The moon shone full upon the spot, and he easily recognized the figure. It was Ollie Stewart.

Young Stewart had been greatly puzzled by Sammy's attitude. It was so unexpected, and, to his mind, so unreasonable. He loved the girl as much as it was possible for one of his weak nature to love; and he had felt sure of his place in her affections. But the door that had once yielded so readily to his touch he had found fast shut. He was on the outside, and he seemed somehow to have lost the key. In this mood on his way home, he had reached the spot that was so closely associated with the girl, and, pausing to rest after the sharp climb, had fallen to brooding over his disappointment. So intent was he upon his gloomy thoughts that he had not heard Young Matt approaching, and was wholly unconscious of that big fellow's presence in the vicinity.

For a time the face at the edge of the path regarded the figure on the rock intently; then it dropped from sight. Young Matt slipped quietly down into the ravine, and a few moments later climbed again to the Old Trail at a point hidden from the Lookout. Here he stepped quickly across the narrow open space and into the bushes on the slope of the mountain above. Then with the skill of one born and reared in the woods, the mountaineer made his way toward the man on the shoulder of the hill.

What purpose lay under his strange movement Young Matt did not know. But certainly it was not in his mind to harm Ollie. He was acting upon the impulse of the moment; an impulse to get nearer and to study unobserved the person of his rival. So he stalked him with all the instinct of a creature of the woods. Not a twig snapped, nor a leaf rustled, as from bush to fallen log, from tree trunk to rock, he crept, always in the black shadows, or behind some object.

But there were still other eyes on Old Dewey that night, and sharp ears heard the big woodsman climbing out of the

ravine, if Ollie did not. When the young man in the clear
light of the moon crossed the Old Trail, a figure near the
clump of trees, where he had sat with his two friends that
day, dropped quietly behind a big rock, half hidden in the
bushes. As the giant crept toward the Lookout, this figure
followed, showing but little less skill than the mountaineer
himself. Once a loose stone rattled slightly, and the big fellow turned his head; but the figure was lying behind a log
that the other had just left. When Young Matt finally
reached the position as close to Ollie as he could go without certain discovery, the figure also came to a rest, not far
away.

The moments passed very slowly now to the man crouching in the shadows. Ollie looked at his watch. It was early
yet to one accustomed to late hours in the city. Young
Matt heard distinctly the snap of the case as the watch was
closed and returned to its owner's pocket. Then Stewart
lighted a cigar, and flipped the burned out match almost
into his unseen companion's face.

It seemed to Young Matt that he had been there for
hours. Years ago he left his home yonder on the ridge, to
look for stray stock. They must have forgotten him long
before this. The quiet cabin in the Hollow, and his friend,
the shepherd, too, were far away. In all that lonely mountain there was no one—no one but that man on the rock
there; that man, and himself. How bright the moon was!

Suddenly another form appeared upon the scene. It came
creeping around the hill from beyond the Lookout. It was a
long, low, lithe-bodied form that moved with the easy, glid-
ing movements of a big cat. Noiselessly the soft padded feet
fell upon the hard rock and loose gravel of the old pathway; the pathway along which so many things had gone for
their kill, or had gone to be killed.

Young Matt saw it the moment it appeared. He started in
his place. He recognized it instantly as the most feared of all
the wild things in the mountain wilderness—a panther. He
saw it sniff the footprints on the trail—Ollie's footprints.

153

He saw it pause and crouch as it caught sight of the man on the rock.

Instantly wild and unwelcome thoughts burned within the strong man's brain. The woodsman knew why that thing had come. Against such a foe the unconscious weakling on the rock there, calmly puffing his cigar, would have no chance whatever. He would not even know of its presence, until it had made its spring, and its fangs were in his neck. The man of the wildnerness knew just how it would be done. It would be over in a minute.

The giant clenched his teeth. Why had he not gone on to his home after leaving the shepherd? Why had he followed that impulse to stand again where he had stood that afternoon? Above all, what had possessed him—what had led him to creep to his present position? He shot a quick glance around. How bright—how bright the moon was!

The panther turned aside from the trail and with silent grace leaped to the ledge, gaining a position on a level with Ollie—still unconscious of its presence. A cold sweat broke out on the big man's forehead. The great hands worked. His breath came in quick gasps. It could not be laid to his door. He had only to withdraw, to stop his ears and run, as he had fled that afternoon. God! How slowly that thing crept forward, crouching low upon its belly, its tail twitching from side to side, nearer, nearer. Young Matt felt smothered. He loosened the collar of his shirt. The moon—the moon was so bright! He could even see the muscles in the beast's heavy neck and shoulders working under the sleek skin.

Suddenly the words of the shepherd came to him, as though shouted in his ears, *"Remember the other beast, lad. Don't you see it is this victory only that gives you the right to think of yourself as a man?"*

Ollie was almost brushed from his place as the big mountaineer sprang from the shadows, while the panther, startled by the appearance of another man upon the rock, paused. An exclamation of fright burst from young Stewart, as he

154

took in the situation. And the giant by his side reached forth a hand to push him back, as he growled, "Shut up and get out of the way! This here's my fight!"

At the movement the wild beast seemed to understand that the newcomer was there to rob him of his prey. With a snarl, it crouched low again, gathering its muscles for the spring. The giant waited. Suddenly the sharp crack of a rifle rang out on the still night, echoing, and re-echoing along the mountain. The panther leaped, but fell short. The startled men on the rock saw it threshing the ground in its death struggle.

"That was a lucky shot for you," said Ollie.

"Lucky for me," repeated Young Matt slowly, eyeing his well-dressed companion. "Well, yes, I reckon it was."

"Who fired it?"

The big fellow shook his head in a puzzled way.

Stewart looked surprised. "Wasn't it someone hunting with you?"

"With me? Huntin'? Not tonight," muttered the other, still searching the hillside.

"Well, I'd like to know what you were doing here alone, then," said Ollie suspiciously.

At his tone, Young Matt turned upon him savagely. " 'Tain't none of your business, what I was a-doin' here, that I can see. I reckon these hills are free yet. But it's mighty lucky for us both that someone was 'round, whoever he is. Maybe you ain't thankful that that critter ain't fastened on your neck. But I am. An' I'm goin' to find out who fired that shot if I can."

He started forward, but Ollie called imperiously, "Hold on there a minute, I want to say something to you first." The other paused, and young Stewart continued, "I don't know what you mean by prowling around this time of night. But it looks as though you were watching me. I warn you fairly, don't try it again. I know how you feel toward Miss Lane, and I know how you have been with her while I was away. I tell you it's got to stop. She is to be my wife,

155

and I shall protect her. You may just as well—"

He got no further. The big man sprang forward to face him with a look that made the dandy shrink with fear. "Protect Sammy Lane from me! Protect her, you! You know what I feel toward her? You!" He fairly choked with his wild rage.

The frightened Ollie drew a weapon from his pocket but, with a snarling laugh, the big fellow reached out his great hand and the shining toy went whirling through the air. "Go home," said the giant. "Damn you, go home! Don't you hear? For God's sake get out o' my sight 'fore I forget again.!"

Ollie went.

26

Ollie's Dilemma

As "Preachin' Bill" used to say, "Every hound has hits strong pints, but some has more of 'em."

Young Stewart was not without graces pleasing to the girl whom he hoped to make his wife. He seemed to know instinctively all those little attentions in which women so delight, and he could talk, too, very entertainingly of the things he had seen. To the simple girl of the backwoods, he succeeded in making the life in the city appear very wonderful, indeed. Neither was Sammy insensible to the influence of his position, and his prospective wealth, with the advantages that these things offered. Then, with all this, he loved her dearly; and when, if you please, was ever a woman wholly unmoved by the knowledge that she held first place in a man's heart?

For two weeks they were together nearly every day, sometimes spending the afternoon at the girl's home on the side of Dewey, or roving over the nearby hills; sometimes going for long rides through the great woods to pass the day with friends, returning in the evening to find Jim smoking in the doorway of the darkened cabin.

When Mr. Lane, at the end of the first week, asked his daughter, in his point blank fashion, what she was going to do with young Stewart, the girl answered, "He must have his chance, Daddy. He must have a good fair chance. I—I don't know what it is, but there is—I—I don't know,

157

Daddy. I am sure I loved him when he went away, that is,
I think I am sure." And Jim, looking into her eyes, agreed
heartily; then he took down his violin to make joyful music
far into the night.

Ollie did not see Young Matt after their meeting on the
Lookout. The big fellow, too, avoided the couple, and
Sammy, for some reason, carefully planned their rides so
that they would not be likely to meet their neighbor on the
ridge. Once, indeed, they called at the Matthews place,
walking over in the evening, but that was when Sammy
knew that Young Matt was not at home.

Day after day as they talked together, the girl tried honestly to enter into the life of the man she had promised to
marry. But always there was that feeling of something lacking. Just what that something was, or why she could not
feel completely satisfied, Sammy did not understand. But
the day was soon to come when she would know the real
impulses of her heart.

Since that first afternoon, Ollie had not tried to force his
suit. While, in a hundred little ways, he had not failed to
make her feel his love, he had never openly attempted the
role of lover. He was conscious that to put the girl constantly upon the defensive would be disastrous to his hopes;
and in this, he was wise. But the time had come when he
must speak, for it was the last day of his visit. He felt that
he could not go back to the city without a definite understanding.

Sammy, too, realized this, but still she was not ready to
give an answer to the question he would ask. They had
been to the Forks, and were on their way home. As they
rode slowly under the trees, the man pleaded his cause, but
the woman could only shake her head and answer quite
truthfully, "Ollie, I don't know."

"But tell me, Sammy, is there anyone in the way?"

Again she shook her head. "I—I think not."

"You think not! Don't you know?" The young man reined
his horse closer to the brown pony. "Let me help you

decide, dear. You are troubled because of the change you see in me, and because the life that I have tried to tell you about is so strange, so different from this. You need not fear. With me, you will very soon be at home there; as much at home as you are here. Come, dear, let me answer for you."

The girl lifted her face to his. "Oh, if you only could!" But, even as she spoke, there came to her the memory of that ride home from the party at Ford's when her pony had crowded close to the big white-faced sorrel. It was Brownie this time who was pulled sharply aside. The almost involuntary act brought a quick flush to the young man's cheek, and he promptly reined his own horse to the right, thus placing the full width of the road between them. So they went down the hill into the valley, where Fall Creek tumbled and laughed on its rocky way.

A thread of blue smoke, curling lazily up from the old stack, and the sound of a hammer, told them that someone was at the mill. Sammy was caught by a sudden impulse. "Why, that must be Young Matt!" she exclaimed. "Let us stop. I do believe you haven't seen him since you came home."

"I don't want to see him, nor anyone else, now," returned Ollie. "This is our last evening together, Sammy, and I want you all to myself. Let us go up the old Roark trail, around Cox's Bald, and home through the big, low gap." He checked his horse as he spoke, for they had already passed the point where the Roark trail leaves Fall Creek.

But the girl was determined to follow her impulse. "You can stop just a minute," she urged. "You really ought to see Matt, you know. We can ride back this way if you like. It's early yet."

But the man held his place, and replied shortly, "I tell you I don't want to see anybody, and I am very sure that Young Matt doesn't want to see me, not with you, anyway."

Sammy flushed at this, and answered with some warmth, "There is no reason in the world why you should refuse to meet an old friend; but you may do as you please, of course. Only I am going to the mill." So saying, she started down the valley, and as there was really nothing else for him to do, the man followed.

As they approached the mill, Sammy called for Young Matt, who immediately left his work, and came to them. The big fellow wore no coat, and his great arms were bare, while his old shirt, patched and faded and patched again, was soiled by engine grease and perspiration. His trousers, too, held in place by suspenders repaired with belt lacing and fastened with a nail, were covered with sawdust and dirt. His hands and arms and even his face were treated liberally with the same mixture that stained his clothing; and the shaggy red brown hair, uncovered, was sadly tumbled. In his hand he held a wrench. The morrow was grinding day, and he had been making some repairs about the engine.

Altogether, as the backwoodsman came forward, he presented a marked contrast to the freshly-clad, well-groomed gentleman from the city. And to the woman, the contrast was not without advantages to the man in the good clothes. The thought flashed through her mind that the men who would work for Ollie in the shops would look like this. It was the same old advantage; the advantage that the captain has over the private; the advantage of rank, regardless of worth.

Sammy greeted Young Matt warmly. "I just told Ollie that it was too bad he had not seen you. You were away the night we called at your house, you know, and he is going home tomorrow."

The giant looked from one to the other. Evidently Sammy had not heard of that meeting at the Lookout, and Stewart's face grew red as he saw what was in the big fellow's mind. "I'm mighty glad to see you again," he said lamely. "I told Sammy that I had seen you, but she has forgotten."

"Oh, no, I haven't," replied the girl. "You said that you saw him in the field as you passed the first day you came, but that you were in such a hurry you didn't stop."

At this Ollie forced a loud laugh, and remarked that he was in something of a hurry that day. He hoped that in the girl's confusion the point might be overlooked.

But the mountaineer was not to be sidetracked so easily. Ollie's poor attempt only showed more clearly that he had purposely refrained from telling Sammy of the night when Young Matt had interfered to save his life. To the simple, straightforward lad of the woods, such a course revealed a spirit most contemptible. Raising his soiled hands and looking straight at Ollie, he said, deliberately, "I'm sorry, seein' as this is the first time we've met, that I can't shake hands with you. This here's *clean* dirt, though."

Sammy was puzzled. Ollie's objection to their calling at the mill, his evident embarrassment at the meeting, and something in Young Matt's voice that hinted at a double meaning in his simple words, all told her that there was something beneath the surface which she did not understand.

After his one remark to her escort, the woodsman turned to the girl, and, in spite of Sammy's persistent attempts to bring the now sullen Ollie into the conversation, ignored the man completely. When they had talked for a few moments, Young Matt said, "I reckon you'll have to excuse me a minute, Sammy; I left the engine in such a hurry when you called that I'll have to look at it again. It won't take more'n a minute."

As he disappeared in the mill shed, the young lady turned to her companion, "What's the matter with you two? Have you met and quarreled since you came home?"

Fate was being very unkind to Ollie. He replied gruffly, "You'll have to ask your friend. I told you how it would be. The greasy hobo doesn't like to see me with you, and hasn't manners enough even to hide his feelings. Come, let us go on."

"I can't shake hands with you. This here's clean dirt, though."

A look that was really worth seeing came into the girl's fine eyes, but she only said calmly, "Matt will be back in a minute."

"All the more reason why we should go. I should think you have had enough. I am sure I have."

The young woman was determined now to know what lay at the bottom of all this. She said quietly, but with a great deal of decision, "You may go on home if you wish. I am going to wait here until Young Matt comes back."

Ollie was angry now in good earnest. He had not told Sammy of the incident at the Lookout because he felt that the story would bring the backwoodsman into a light altogether too favorable. He thought to have the girl safely won before he left the hills; then it would not matter. That Young Matt would have really saved Ollie's life at the risk of his own there was no doubt. And Stewart realized that his silence under such circumstances would look decidedly small and ungrateful to the girl. To have the story told at this critical moment was altogether worse than if he had generously told of the incident at once. He saw, too, that Sammy guessed at something beneath the surface, and he felt uneasy in remaining until Young Matt came back to renew the conversation. And yet he feared to leave. At this stage of his dilemma, he was relieved from his plight in a very unexpected manner.

27

The Champion

A big wagon, with two men on the seat, appeared coming up the valley road. It was Wash Gibbs and a crony from the river. They had stopped at the distillery on their way, and were just enough under the influence of drink to be funny and reckless.

When they caught sight of Ollie Stewart and Miss Lane, Wash said something to his companion, at which both laughed uproariously. Upon reaching the couple, the wagon came to a stop, and after looking at Ollie for some moments, with the silent gravity of an owl, Gibbs turned to the young lady. "Howdy, honey. Where did you git that there? Did your paw give hit to you fer a doll baby?"

Young Stewart's face grew scarlet, but he said nothing.

"Can't hit talk?" continued Gibbs with mock interest.

Glancing at her frightened escort, the girl replied, "You drive on, Wash Gibbs. You're in no condition to talk to anyone."

An ugly leer came over the brutal face of the giant. "Oh, I ain't, ain't I? You think I'm drunk. But I ain't, not so mighty much. Jest enough t' perten me up a pepper grain." Then, turning to his companion, who was grinning in appreciation of the scene, he continued, "Here, Bill; you hold th' ribbens, an' watch me tend t' that little job I told you I laid out t' do first chance I got." At this, Ollie grew as pale as death. Once he started as if to escape, but he could not under Sammy's eyes.

As Wash was climbing down from the wagon, he caught sight of Young Matt standing in the door of the mill shed. "Hello, Matt," he called cheerfully. "I ain't a-lookin' fer you t'day; 'tend t' you some other time. Got more important business jest now."

Young Matt made no reply, nor did he move to interfere. In the backwoods every man must fight his own battles, so long as he fights with men. When Stewart was in danger from the panther, it was different. This was man to man. Sammy, too, reared in the mountains, and knowing the code, waited quietly to see what her lover would do.

Coming to Ollie's side, Gibbs said, "Git down, young feller, an' look at yer saddle."

"You go on, and let me alone, Wash Gibbs. I've never hurt you." Ollie's naturally high-pitched voice was shrill with fear.

Wash paused, looked back at his companion in the wagon, then to Young Matt, and then to the girl on the horse. "That's right," he said, shaking his head with ponderous gravity. "You all hear him. He ain't never hurted me, nary a bit. Nary a bit, ladies an' gentlemen. But, good Lord! Look at him! Hain't it awful?" Suddenly he reached out one great arm, and jerked the young man from his horse, catching him with the other hand as he fell, and setting him on his feet in the middle of the road.

Ollie was like a child in the grasp of his huge tormentor, and, in spite of her indignation, a look of admiration flashed over Sammy's face at the exhibition of the bully's wonderful physical strength; an admiration that only heightened the feeling of shame for her lover's weakness.

Gibbs addressed his victim, "Now, dolly, you an' me's goin' t' play a little. Come on, let's see you dance." The other struggled feebly a moment and attempted to draw a pistol, whereupon Wash promptly captured the weapon, remarking in a sad tone as he did so, "You hadn't ought t' tote such a gun as that, sonny; hit might go off. Hit's a

165

right pretty little thing, ain't hit?" he continued, holding his victim with one hand, and examining the pearl-handled, nickel-plated weapon with great interest. "Hit sure is. But say, dolly, if you was ever t' shoot me with that there, an' I found hit out, I'd sure be powerful mad. You hear me, now, an' don't you pack that gun no more; not in these mountains. Hit ain't safe."

The fellow in the wagon roared with delight at these witticisms, and looked from Young Matt to Sammy to see if they also appreciated the joke.

"Got any more pretties?" asked Gibbs of his victim. "No? Let's see." Catching the young man by the waist, he lifted him bodily, and, holding him head downward, shook him roughly. Again Sammy felt her blood tingle at the feat of strength.

Next holding Ollie with one huge hand at the back of his neck, Wash said, "See that feller in th' wagon there?" He's a mighty fine gentleman; friend o' mine. Make a bow t' him." As he finished, with his free hand he struck the young man a sharp blow in the stomach, with the result that Stewart did make a bow, very low, but rather too suddenly to be graceful.

The fellow in the wagon jumped up and bowed again and again. "Howdy, Mr. City Man, howdy. Mighty proud t' meet up with you; mighty proud, you bet!"

The giant whirled his captive toward the mill. "See that feller yonder? I'm goin' t' lick him some day. Make a face at him." Catching Ollie by the nose and chin, he tried to force his bidding, while the man in the wagon made the valley ring with his laughter. Then Wash suddenly faced the helpless young man toward Sammy. "Now ladies and gentlemen," he said in the tones of a showman addressing an audience, "This here pretty little feller from th' city's goin' t' show us hillbillies how t' spark a gal."

The bully's friend applauded loudly, roaring at the top of his voice, "Marry 'em, Wash. Marry 'em. You can do hit as good as a parson! You'd make a good parson. Let's see how'd you go at hit."

The notion tickled the fancy of the giant, for it offered a way to make Sammy share the humiliation more fully. "Git down an' come here t' yer honey," he said to the girl. "Git down, I say," he repeated, when the young woman made no motion to obey.

"Indeed, I will not," replied Sammy shortly.

Her tone and manner angered Gibbs, and dropping Ollie he started toward the girl to take her from the horse by force. As he reached the pony's side, Sammy raised her whip and with all her strength struck him full across the face. The big ruffian drew back with a bellow of pain and anger. Then he started toward her again. "I'll tame you, you wildcat," he yelled. And Sammy raised her whip again.

But before Gibbs could touch the girl, a powerful hand caught him by the shoulder. "I reckon you've had fun enough, Wash Gibbs," remarked Young Matt in his slow way. "I ain't interfering between man and man, but you'd best keep your dirty hands off that lady."

The young woman's heart leaped at the sound of that deep calm voice that carried such a suggestion of power. And she saw that the blue eyes under the tumbled red-brown locks were shining now like points of polished steel. The strong man's soul was rejoicing with the fierce joy of battle.

The big bully drew back a step, and glared at the man who had come between him and his victim; the man whom, for every reason, he hated. Lifting his huge paws, he said in a voice hoarse with deadly menace, "Dirty, be they? By hell, I'll wash 'em. An' hit won't be water that'll clean 'em, neither. Don't you know that no man ever crosses my trail and lives?"

The other returned easily, "Oh, shucks! Get into your wagon and drive on. You ain't on Roark now. You're on Fall Creek, and over here you ain't no bigger'n anybody else."

While Young Matt was speaking, Gibbs backed slowly

167

away, and, as the young man finished, suddenly drew the pistol he had taken from Ollie. With a quickness and lightness astonishing in one of his bulk and usually slow movements, the mountaineer leaped upon his big enemy. There was a short, sharp struggle, and Wash staggered backward, leaving the shining weapon in Young Matt's hand. "It might go off, you know," said the young fellow quietly, as he tossed the gun on the ground at Ollie's feet.

With a mad roar, Gibbs recovered himself and rushed at his antagonist. It was a terrific struggle, not the skillful sparring of trained fighters, but the rough-and-tumble battling of primitive giants. It was the climax of long months of hatred; the meeting of two who were by every instinct mortal enemies. Ollie shrank back in terror, but Sammy leaned forward in the saddle, her beautiful figure tense, her lips parted, and her face flushed with excitement.

It was soon evident that the big champion of the hills had at last met his match. As he realized this, a look of devilish cunning crept into the animal face of Gibbs, and he maneuvered carefully to bring his enemy's back toward the wagon.

Catching a look from his friend, over Young Matt's shoulder, the man in the wagon slipped quickly to the ground, and Sammy saw with horror a naked knife in his hand. She glanced toward Ollie appealingly, but that gentleman was helpless. The man with the knife began creeping cautiously toward the fighting men, keeping always behind Young Matt. The young woman felt as though an iron band held her fast. She could not move. She could not speak. Then Gibbs went down, and the girl's scream rang out, "*Behind you, Matt! Look quick!*"

As he recovered his balance from the effort that had thrown Wash, Young Matt heard her cry, saw the girl's look of horror, and her outstretched hand pointing. Like a flash he whirled just as the knife was lifted high for the murderous blow. It was over in an instant. Sammy saw him catch the wrist of the uplifted arm, heard a dull snap and a

"Behind you, Matt! Look quick!"

groan, saw the knife fall from the helpless hand, and then saw the man lifted bodily and thrown clear over the wagon, to fall helpless on the rocky ground. The woman gave a low cry. "Oh, *what a man!*"

Wash Gibbs, too, opened his eyes, just in time to witness the unheard-of feat, and to see the bare-armed young giant who performed it turn again, breathing heavily with his great exertion, but still ready to meet his big antagonist.

The defeated bully rose from the ground. The other stepped forward to meet him. But without a word, Gibbs climbed into the wagon and took up the reins. Before they could move, Young Matt had the mules by their heads. "You have forgotten something," he said quietly, pointing to the man on the ground, who was still unconscious from his terrible fall. "That there's your property. Take it along. We ain't got no use for such as that on Fall Creek."

Sullenly Wash climbed down and lifted his companion into the wagon. As Young Matt stood aside to let him go, the bully said, 'I'll see you agin fer this."

The strong man only answered, "I reckon you'd better stay on Roark, Wash Gibbs. You got more room there."

28

What Pete Told Sammy

No word was spoken by either Sammy or her lover, while their horses were climbing the mill road, and both were glad when they reached the top of the ridge, and turned into the narrow path where they would need to ride one before the other. It was not easy to ride side by side, when each was busy with thoughts not to be spoken.

At the gate, Ollie dismounted to help the girl from her horse. But before he could reach the pony's side, Sammy sprang lightly to the ground, unassisted. Opening the big gate, she turned Brownie loose in the yard, while the man stood watching her, a baffled look upon his face. He had always done these little things for her. To be refused at this time was not pleasant. The feeling that he was on the outside grew stronger.

Turning to his own horse, Ollie placed his foot in the stirrup to mount, when Sammy spoke—perhaps she felt that she had been a little unkind—"You were going to stay to supper," she said.

"Not tonight," he answered, gaining his seat in the saddle, and picking up the reins.

"But you are going to leave in the morning, are you not? You—you must not go like this."

He dropped the reins to the horse's neck again. "Look here, Sammy, do you blame me because I did not fight that big bully?"

171

Sammy did not reply.

"What could I do? You know there is not another man in the mountains beside Young Matt who could have done it. Surely you cannot blame me."

The young woman moved uneasily. "No, certainly not. I do not blame you in the least. I—but it was very fortunate that Young Matt was there, wasn't it?" The last sentence slipped out before she knew.

Ollie retorted angrily, "It seems to be very fortunate for him. He will be a greater hero than ever now, I suppose. If he is wise, he will stay in the backwoods to be worshipped for he'll find that his size won't count for much in the world. He's a great man here, where he can fight like a beast, but his style wouldn't go far where brains are of value. It would be interesting to see him in town; a man who never saw a railroad."

Sammy lifted her head quickly at this, and fixed her eyes on the man's face with that wide, questioning gaze that reminded one so of her father. "I never saw a railroad, either; not that I can remember; though, I suppose we must have crossed one or two on our way to Texas when I was a baby. Is it the railroads then that makes one so-so superior?"

The man turned impatiently in the saddle, "You know what I mean."

"Yes," she answered slowly. "I think I do know what you mean."

Ollie lifted the reins again from his horse's neck, and fingered them nervously. "I'd better go now; there's no use talking about this tonight. I won't leave in the morning, as I had planned. I—I can't go like this." There was a little catch in his voice. "May I come again tomorrow afternoon, Sammy?"

"Yes, you had better go now, and come back tomorrow."

"And Sammy, won't you try to think that I am not altogether worthless, even if I am not big enough to fight Wash Gibbs? You are sure that you do not blame me for what happened at the mill?"

"No," she said, "of course not. You could not help it. Why should I blame anyone for that which he cannot help?"

Then Ollie rode away, and Sammy, going to her pony, stood petting the little horse, while she watched her lover up the Old Trail, and still there was that wide, questioning look in her eyes. As Ollie passed from sight around the hill above, the girl slipped out of the gate, and a few minutes later stood at the Lookout, where she could watch her lover riding along the ridge. She saw him pass from the open into the fringe of timber near the big gap; and, a few minutes later, saw him reappear beyond the deer lick. Still she watched as he moved along the rim of the Hollow, looking in the distance like a toy man on a toy horse; watched until he passed from sight into the timber again, and was gone. And all the time that questioning look was in her eyes.

Did she blame Ollie that he had played so poorly his part in the scene at the mill? No, she told herself over and over again, as though repeating a lesson; no, Ollie was not to blame, and yet—

She knew that he had spoken truly when he said that there were things that counted for more than brute strength. But was there not something more than brute strength in the incident? Was there not that which lay deeper? Something of which the brute strength, after all, was only an expression? The girl stamped her foot impatiently, as she exclaimed aloud, "Oh, why did he not try to do something? He should have forced Wash Gibbs to beat him into insensibility rather than to have submitted so tamely to being played with."

In the distance she saw the shepherd following his flock down the mountain, and the old scholar, who always watched the Lookout, when in the vicinity, for a glimpse of his pupil, waved his hand in greeting as he moved slowly on after his charges. It was growing late. Her father, too,

173

would be coming home for his supper. But as she rose to go, a step on the mountainside above caught her attention, and, looking up, she saw Pete coming toward the big rock. Sammy greeted the youth kindly. "I haven't seen Pete for days and days; where has he been?"

"Pete's been everywhere; an' course I've been with him," replied the lad with his wide, sweeping gesture. Then throwing himself at full length at the girl's feet, he said abruptly, "Pete was here that night, and God, he was here, too. Couldn't nobody else but God o'done it. The gun went bang, and a lot more guns went bang, bang, all along the mountains. And the moonlight things that was a-dancin' quit 'cause they was scared; and that panther it just doubled up and died. Matt and Ollie wasn't hurted nary a bit. Pete says it was God done that; He was sure in the hills that night."

Sammy was startled. "Matt and Ollie, a panther? What do you mean, boy?"

The troubled look shadowed the delicate face, as the lad shook his head. "Don't mean nothin', Sammy, not me. Nobody can't mean nothin', can they?"

"But what does Pete mean? Does Pete know about it?"

"Oh, yes, course Pete knows everything. Don't Sammy know 'bout that night when God was in the hills?" He was eager now, with eyes wide and face aglow.

"No," said Sammy, "I do not know. Will Pete tell me all about it?"

The strange youth seated himself on the rock, facing the valley below, saying in a low tone, "Ollie was a-settin' like this, all still; just a-smokin' and a-watchin' the moonlight things that was dancin' over the tops of the trees down there." Then leaping to his feet the boy ran a short way along the ledge, to come stealing back, crouching low, as he whispered, "It come a-creepin' and a-creepin' towards Ollie, and he never knowed nothin' about it. But Matt he knowed, and God he knowed too." Wonderingly, the girl watched his movement. Suddenly he sprang to the rock

174

again, and facing the imaginary beast, cried in childish imita-
tion of a man's deep voice, "Get out of the way. This
here's my fight." Then in his own tones, "It was sure
scared when Young Matt jumped on that rock. Everything's
scared of Matt when he talks like that. It was mad, too,
'cause Matt he wouldn't let it get Ollie. And it got ready to
jump at Matt, and Matt he got ready for a tussle, and Ollie
he got out of the way. And all the moonlight things stopped
dancin', and the shadow things come out to see the fight."
He had lowered his voice again almost to a whisper. Sammy
was breathless. "Bang!" cried the lad, clapping his hands
and shouting the words. "Bang! Bang! God, he fired and all
the guns in the hills went off, and that panther it just
doubled up and died. It would sure got Ollie, though, if
Matt hadn't a-jumped on the rock when he did. But do
you reckon it could o' got Matt, if God hadn't been there
that night?"

It was all too clearly portrayed to be mistaken. "Sammy
needn't be afeared," continued Pete, seeing the look on the
girl's face. "It can't come back no more. It just naturally
can't, you know, Sammy, 'cause God he killed it plumb
dead. And Pete dragged it way over on yon side of the
ridge and the buzzards got it."

29

Jim Lane Makes a Promise

Sammy went home to find her father getting supper. Rushing into the cabin, the girl gave him a hug that caused Jim to nearly drop the coffeepot. "You poor abused Daddy, to come home from work, all tired and find no supper, no girl, no nothing. Sit right down there now, and rest, while I finish things."

Jim obeyed with a grin of appreciation. "I didn't fix no taters; thought you wasn't comin'."

"Going to starve yourself, were you? Just because I was gone," replied the girl with a pan of potatoes in her hand. "I see right now that I will have to take care of you always—always, Daddy Jim."

The smile suddenly left the man's face. "Where's Ollie Stewart? Didn't he come home with you?"

"Ollie's at home, I suppose, I have been up to the Lookout talking to Pete."

"Ain't Ollie goin' back to the city tomorrow?"

"No, not tomorrow; the next day. He's coming over here tomorrow afternoon. Then he's going away." Then, before Jim could ask another question, she held up the half of a ham. "Daddy, Daddy! How many times have I told you that you must not—you must not slice the ham with your pocketknife? Just look there! What would Aunt Mollie say if she saw that, so haggled and one-sided?"

All during the evening meal, the girl kept up a ceaseless

merry chatter, changing the subject abruptly every time it approached the question that her father was most anxious to ask. And the man, delighted with her gay mood responded to it as he answered to all her moods, until they were like two school children in their fun. But, when supper was over and the work done, and Jim, taking down his violin, would have made music, Sammy promptly relieved him of his instrument, and seated herself on his knee. "Not tonight, Daddy. I want to talk tonight, real serious."

She told him then of the encounter with Wash Gibbs and his friend at the mill, together with the story that Pete had illustrated so vividly at the Lookout. "And so, Daddy," she finished, "I know now what I shall do. He will come tomorrow afternoon to say good-bye, and then he will go away again back to the city and his fine friends for good. And I'll stay and take care of my Daddy Jim. It isn't that he is a bad man like Wash Gibbs. He couldn't be a bad man like that; he isn't big enough. And that's just it. He is too little—body, soul and spirit—he is too little. He will do well in the world; perhaps he will even do big things. But I heard dear old Preachin' Bill say once, that 'some fellers can do mighty big things in a durned little way.' So he is going back to the city, and I am going to stay in the hills."

Jim took no pains to hide his delight. "I knowed it, girl. I knowed it. Bank on the old blood every time. There ain't a drop of yeller in it; not a drop, Sammy. Ollie ain't to say bad, but he ain't just our kind. Lord! But I'd like to o' seen Young Matt a givin' it to Wash Gibbs!" He threw back his head and roared with delight. "Just wait 'til I see Wash. I'll ask him if he thinks Young Matt would need a pry for to lift that mill engine with, now." Then all of a sudden the laugh died out, and the man's dark face was serious, as he said slowly. "The boy'll have to watch him, though. It'll sure be war from this on; the worst kind of war."

"Daddy, what do you think Wash would have done to me, if Young Matt had not been there?"

177

That metallic ring was in Jim's voice, now, as he replied, "Wash Gibbs ought to knowed better than to done that. But it was a blessin' Young Matt was there, wasn't it? He'd take care of you anywhere. I wouldn't never be afraid for you with him."

The girl hid her face on her father's shoulder, as she said, "Daddy, will Wash Gibbs come here any more now? It seems to me he wouldn't dare meet you after this."

Jim answered uneasily, "I don't know, girl, I reckon he'll be around again after a time."

There was a pause for a little while. Then Sammy, with her arms still about his neck, said, "Daddy, I'm going to stay in the hills with you now. I am going to send Ollie away tomorrow, because as you say, he isn't our kind. Daddy, Wash Gibbs is not our kind either, is he?"

"You don't understand, girl, and I can't tell you now. It all started way back when you was a little trick."

The young woman answered very gently, "Yes, I know. You have told me that often. But, Daddy, what will—what will our friends think, if you keep on with Wash Gibbs now, after what happened at the mill today? Young Matt fought Gibbs because he insulted me and was going to hurt me. You say yourself that it will be war between them now. Will you side with Wash? And if you do, won't it look like there was just a little, tiny streak of yellow in us?"

This side of the situation had not struck Jim at first. He got up and walked the floor, while the girl, standing quietly by the fireplace, watched him, a proud, fond light in her eyes. Sammy did not know what the bond between her father and the big ruffian was, but she knew that it was not a light one. Now that the issue was fairly defined, she felt confident that, whatever the cost, the break would be made.

But at this time it was well that she did not know how great the cost of breaking the bond between the two men would be.

Jim stopped before his daughter, and, placing a hand upon each shoulder, said, "Tell me, girl; are you so power-

178

ful anxious to have me and Young Matt stay good friends like we've always been?"

"I—I am afraid I am, Daddy."

And then, a rare smile came into the dark face of Jim Lane. He kissed the girl and said, "I'll do it, honey. I ain't afraid to, now."

30

Sammy Graduates

The next day when young Stewart came, the books were all back on the shelf in the main room of the cabin, and Sammy, dressed in a fresh gown of simple goods and fashion, with her hair arranged carefully, as she had worn it the last two months before Ollie's coming, sat at the window reading.

The man was surprised and a little embarrassed. "Why, what have you been doing to yourself?" he exclaimed.

"I have not been doing anything to myself. I have only done some things to my clothes and hair," returned the girl.

Then he saw the books. "Why, where did these come from?" He crossed the room to examine the volumes. "Do you—do you read all these?"

"The shepherd has been helping me," she explained.

"Oh, yes. I understood that you were studying with him." He looked at her curiously, as though they were meeting for the first time. Then as she talked of her studies, his embarrassment deepened, for he found himself floundering hopelessly before this clear-eyed, clear-brained backwoods girl.

"Come," said Sammy at last. "Let us go for a walk." She led the way to her favorite spot, high up on the shoulder of Dewey, and there, with Mutton Hollow at their feet and the big hills about them, with the long blue ridges in the distance beyond which lay Ollie's world, she told him what he feared to learn. The man refused to believe that he heard her right. "You do not understand," he protested, and he tried to tell her of the place in life that would be hers as his wife. In his shallowness, he talked even of jewels, and dresses, and such things.

"But can all this add one thing to life itself?" she asked. "Is not life really independent of all these things? Do they not indeed cover up the real life, and rob one of freedom? It seems to me that it must be so."

He could only answer, "But you know nothing about it. How can you? You have never been out of these woods."

"No," she returned, "that is true; I have never been out of these woods, and you can never, now, get away from the world into which you have gone." She pointed to the distant hills. "It is very, very far over there to where you live. I might, indeed, find many things in your world that would be delightful, but I fear that I should lose the things that after all are, to me, the really big things. I do not feel that the things that are greatest in your life could bring happiness without that which I find here. And there is something here that can bring happiness without what you call the advantages of the world to which you belong."

"What do you know of the world?" he said roughly.

"Nothing," she said. "But I know a little of life. And I have learned some things that I fear you have not. Beside, I know now that I do not love you. I have been slow to find the truth, but I have found it. And this is the one thing that matters, that I found it in time."

"Did you reach this conclusion at the mill yesterday?" he asked with a sneer.

"No. It came to me here on the rock last evening after you were gone. I heard a strange story; the story of a weak man, a strong man, and a God who was very kind."

Ollie saw that further persuasion was of no avail, and as he left her, she watched him out of sight for the last time—along the trail that is nobody knows how old. When he was gone, in obedience to an impulse she did not try to understand, she ran down the mountain to the cabin in the Hollow—Young Matt's cabin. And when the shepherd came in from the hills

181

with his flock he found the house in such order as only a woman's hand can bring. The table was set, and his supper cooking on the stove.

"Dad," she asked, "Do you think I know enough now to live in the city?"

The old man's heart sank. It had come then. Bravely he concealed his feelings, as he assured her in the strongest terms, that she knew enough, and was good enough to live anywhere.

"Then," said Sammy, "I know enough, even if I am not good enough, to live in the hills."

The brown eyes, deep under their shaggy brows, were aglow with gladness, and there was a note of triumph in the scholar's voice as he said, "Then you do not regret learning things I have tried to teach you? You are sure you have no sorrow for the things you are losing."

"Regret? Dad. Regret?" The young woman drew herself up and lifted her arms. "Oh, Dad, I see it all, now; all that you have been trying in a thousand ways to teach me. You have led me into a new world, the real world, the world that has always been and must always be, and in that world man is king; king because he is a man. And the treasure of his kingdom is the wealth of his manhood."

"And the woman, Sammy, the woman?"

" 'And they twain shall be one flesh.' "

Then the master knew that his teaching had not been in vain. "I can lead you no farther, my child," he said with a smile. "You have passed the final test."

She came close to him. "Then I want my diploma," she said, for he had told her about the schools.

Reverently the old scholar kissed her brow. "This is the only diploma I am authorized to give—the love and homage of your teacher."

"And my degree?" She waited with that wide, questioning look in her eyes.

"The most honorable in all the world—a sure enough lady."

31

Castle Building

The corn was big enough to cultivate the first time, and Young Matt with Old Kate was hard at work in the field west of the house.

It was nearly three weeks since the incident at the mill, since which time the young fellow had not met Sammy Lane to talk with her. He had seen her, though, at a distance nearly every day, for the girl had taken up her studies again, and spent most of her time out on the hills with the shepherd. That day he saw her as she turned into the mill road at the lower corner of the field, on her way to the Forks. And he was still thinking of her three hours later, as he sat on a stump in the shade of the forest's edge, while his horse was resting.

Young Matt recalled the fight at the mill with a wild joy in his heart. Under any circumstances it was no small thing to have defeated the champion strong man and terror of the hills. It was a glorious thing to have done the deed for the girl he loved, and under her eyes. Sammy might give herself to Ollie, now, and go far away to the great world, but she could never forget the man who had saved her from insult, when her lover was far too weak to save even himself. And Young Matt would stay in the hills alone, but always he would have the knowledge and the triumph of this thing that he had done. Yes, it would be easier now, but still—still the days would be years when there was no longer each morning the hope that somewhere before the day was gone he would see her.

The sun fell hot and glaring on the hillside field, and in the air was the smell of the freshly turned earth. High up in the blue a hawk circled and circled again. A puff of air came sighing through the forest, touched lightly the green blades in the open, slipped over the ridge, and was lost in the sky beyond. Old Kate, with head down, was dreaming of cool springs in shady dells, and a little shiny brown lizard with a bright blue tail crept from under the bottom rail of the fence to see why the man was so still.

The man turned his head quickly; the lizard dodged under the rail; and Old Kate awoke with a start. Someone was coming along the road below. Young Matt knew the step of that horse, as well as he knew the sound of Old Kate's bell, or the neigh of his own sorrel.

The brown pony stopped at the lower corner of the field, and a voice, called, "You'd better be at work. I don't believe you have plowed three rows since I passed."

The big fellow went eagerly down the hill to the fence. "I sure ought to o' done better'n that, for it's been long enough since you went by. I always notice, though, that it gets a heap farther to the other side of the field and back about this time o' day. What's new over to the Forks?"

Sammy laughed. "Couldn't hear a thing but how the champion strong man was beaten at his own game. Uncle Ike says, 'Ba Thundas! You tell Young Matt that he'd better come over. A man what can ride Wash Gibbs a bug huntin' is too blamed good a man t' stay at home all th' time. We want him t' tell us how he done it. Ba thundas! He'll be gittin' a job with th' gov'ment next. What!' "

The man crossed his arms on the top rail of the worm fence, and laughed. It was good to have Sammy deliver her message in just that way. "I reckon Uncle Ike thinks I ought to go dancin' all over the hills now, with a chip on my shoulder," he said.

"I don't think you'll do that," she returned. "Dad How-

184

itt wouldn't, would he? But I must hurry on now, or Daddy's supper won't be ready when he comes in. I stopped to give you these papers for your father." She handed him the package. "And—and I want to thank you, Matt, for what you did at the mill. All my life you have been fighting for me, and—and I have never done anything for you. I wish I could do something—something that would show you how— how I care."

Her voice faltered. He was so big and strong, and there was such a look of hopeless love and pain on his rugged face—a face that was as frank and open as a child's. Here was a man who had no need for the shallow cunning of little fox-like men. This one would go open and bold on his way, and that which he could not take by his strength he would not have. Had she not seen him in battle? Had she not seen his eyes like polished steel points? Deep down in her heart, the woman felt a thrill of triumph that such a man should stand so before her. She must go quickly.

Young Matt climbed slowly up the hill again to his seat on the stump. Here he watched until across the Hollow he saw the pony and his rider come out of the timber and move swiftly along the ridge; watched until they faded into a tiny spot, rounded the mountain and disappeared from sight. Then, lifting his eyes, he looked away beyond the long blue line that marked the distant horizon. Someday he would watch Sammy ride away and she would go on, and on, and on, beyond that blue line, out of his life forever.

Ollie had gone over there to live, and the shepherd had come from there. What was that world like, he wondered. Between the young man of the mountains and that big world yonder there had always been a closely shut door. He had seen the door open to Ollie, and now Sammy stood on the threshold. Would it ever open for him? And, if it did, what? Then came a thought that made his blood leap. Might he not force it open? The shepherd had told him of others who had done so.

Young Matt felt a strong man's contempt for the things

Ollie had gotten out of the world, but he stood in awe before Mr. Howitt. He told himself, now, that he would look for and find the things yonder that made Dad the man he was. He would carry to the task his splendid strength. Nothing should stop him. And Sammy, when she understood that he was going away to be like the shepherd, would wait awhile to give him his chance. Surely, she would wait when he told her that. But how should he begin?

Looking up again, his eye caught a slow, shifting patch of white on the bench above Lost Creek, where the little stream begins its underground course. The faint bark of a dog came to him through the thin, still air, and the patch of white turned off into the trail that leads to the ranch. "Dad!" exclaimed the young man in triumph. Dad should tell him how. He had taught Sammy.

And so while the sunlight danced on the green field, and Old Kate slept in the lengthening shadows of the timber, the lad gave himself to his dreams and built his castles—as we all have builded.

His dreaming was interrupted as the supper bell rang, and, with the familiar sound, a multitude of other thoughts came crowding in; the father and mother—they were growing old. Would it do to leave them alone with the graves on the hill yonder, and the mystery of the Hollow? And there was the place to care for, and the mill. Who but Young Matt could get work from the old engine?

It was like the strong man that the fight did not last long. Young Matt's fights never lasted very long. By the time he had unhitched Old Kate from the cultivator, it was finished. The lad went down the hill, his bright castles in ruin—even as we all have gone, or must sometime go down the hill with our brightest castles in ruin.

32

Preparation

That same night, Mr. Lane told his daughter that he would leave home early the next morning to be gone two days. Jim was cleaning his big forty-five when he made the announcement.

Sammy paused with one hand on the cupboard door to ask, "With Wash Gibbs, Daddy?"

"No, I ain't goin' with Wash; but I'll likely meet up with him before I get back." There was a hint of that metallic ring in the man's voice.

The girl placed her armful of dishes carefully on the cupboard shelf. "You're—you're not going to forget your promise, are you, Daddy Jim?"

The mountaineer was carefully dropping a bit of oil into the lock of his big revolver. "No, girl, I ain't forgettin' nothin'. This here's the last ride I aim to take with Wash. I'm goin' to see him to"—he paused and listened carefully to the click, click, click, as he tested the action of his weapon—"to keep my promise."

"Oh, Daddy, Daddy, I'm so glad! I wanted this more than I ever wanted anything in all my life before. You're such a good daddy to me, I never could bear to see you with that bad, bad man." She was behind his chair now, and, stooping, laid her fresh young cheek against the swarthy, furrowed face.

The man sat like a grim, stone image, his eyes fixed on

187

"I'm goin' to see him to keep my promise."

the gun resting on his knees. Not until she lifted her head to stand erect behind his chair, with a hand on each shoulder, did he find words. "Girl, there's just one thing I've got to know for sure before I go tomorrow. I reckon I'm right, but somehow a man can't never tell about a woman in such things. Will you tell your daddy, Sammy?"

"Tell what, Daddy Jim?" the girl asked, her hands stealing up to caress her father's face.

"What answer will you give to Young Matt when he asks you what Ollie did?"

"But why must you know that before you go tomorrow?"

" 'Cause I want to be plumb sure I ain't makin' no mistake in sidin' with the boy in this here trouble."

"You couldn't make a mistake in doing that, Daddy, no matter whether I—no matter what—but perhaps Matt will not ask me what Ollie did."

Just a ray of humor touched the dark face. "I ain't makin' no mistake there. I know what the man will do." He laid the gun upon the table, and reaching up caught the girl's hand. "But I want to know what you'll say when he asks you. Tell me, honey, so I'll be plumb certain I'm doin' right."

Sammy lowered her head and whispered in his ear.

"Are you sure this time, girl, dead sure?"

"Oh, I'm so sure that it seems as if I—I couldn't wait for him to come to me. I never felt this way before, never."

The mountaineer drew his daughter into his arms, and held her close, as he said, "I ain't afraid to do it, now, girl."

The young woman was so occupied with her own thoughts and the emotions aroused by her father's question, that she failed to note the ominous suggestion that lay under his words. So she entered gaily into his plans for her during his two days' absence.

Jim would leave early in the morning, and Sammy was to stay with her friend, Mandy Ford, over on Jake Creek. Mr.

189

Lane had arranged with Jed Holland to do the milking, so there would be no reason for the girl's return until the following evening, and she must promise that she would not come home before that time. Sammy promised laughingly. He need not worry; she and Mandy had not had a good visit alone for weeks.

When his daughter had said good-night, Jim extinguished the light, and slipping the big gun inside his shirt went to sit outside the cabin door with his pipe. An hour passed. Sammy was fast asleep. And still the man sat smoking. A half hour more went by. Suddenly the pipe was laid aside, and Jim's hand crept inside his shirt to find the butt of the revolver. His quick ear had caught the sound of a swiftly moving horse coming down the mountain.

The horse stopped at the gate and a low whistle came out of the darkness. Leaving his seat, Sammy's father crossed the yard, and, a moment later, the horse with its rider was going on again down the trail toward the valley below and the distant river.

Jim waited at the gate until the sound of the horse's feet had died away in the night. Then he returned to the cabin. But even as he walked toward the house, a dark figure arose from a clump of bushes within a few feet of the spot where Jim and the horseman had met. The figure slipped noiselessly away into the forest.

The next morning Jim carefully groomed and saddled the brown pony for Sammy, then, leading his own horse ready for the road, he came to the cabin door. "Going now, Daddy?" said the girl, coming for the good-by kiss.

"My girl, my girl," whispered the man, as he took her in his arms.

Sammy was frightened at the sight of his face, so strange and white. "Why Daddy, Daddy Jim, what is the matter?"

"Nothin', girl, nothin'. Only—only you're so like your mother, girl. She—she used to come just this way when I'd be leavin'. You're sure like her, and—and I'm glad. I'm glad you're like the old folks, too. Remember now, stay at

Mandy's until tomorrow evenin'. Kiss me again, honey. Good-by."

He mounted hurriedly and rode away at a brisk gallop. Pulling up a moment at the edge of the timber, he turned in the saddle to wave his hand to the girl in the cabin door.

33

A Ride in the Night

Sammy arrived at the Ford homestead in time for dinner, and was joyfully received by her friend Mandy. But early in the afternoon, their pleasure was marred by a messenger from Long Creek on the other side of the river. Mrs. Ford's sister was very ill, and Mrs. Ford and Mandy must go at once.

"But Sammy can't stay here alone," protested the good woman. "Mandy, you'll just have to stay."

"Indeed, she shall not," declared their guest. "I can ride up Jake Creek to the Forks and stay all night at Uncle Ike's. Brownie will make it easily in time for supper. You just get your things on and start right away."

"You'd better hurry, too," put in Mr. Ford. "There's a storm comin' 'fore long, an' we got t' git across th' river 'fore hit strikes. I'll be here with th' horses by the time you get your bonnets on." He hurried away to the barn for his team, while the women with Sammy's assistance made their simple preparation.

As mother Ford climbed into the big wagon, she said to Sammy, "Hit's an awful lonely ol' trip fer you, child; an' you must start right away, so's t' be sure t' get there 'fore hit gets plumb dark," while Mr. Ford added, as he started the team, "Your pony's ready saddled, an' if you'll hurry along, you can jest 'bout make hit. Don't get catched on Jakey in a big rain whatever you do."

"Don't you worry about me," returned the girl. "Brownie

and I could find the way in the dark."

But when her friends had gone, Sammy, womanlike, busied herself with setting the disordered house aright before she started on her journey. Watching the clouds, she told herself that there was a plenty of time for her to reach the Post Office before the storm. It might not come that way at all, in fact.

But the way up Jake Creek was wild and rough, and along the faint trail, that twisted and wound like a slim serpent through the lonely wilderness, Brownie could make but slow time. As they followed the little path, the walls of the narrow valley grew steeper, more rocky, and barren; and the road became more and more rough and difficult, until at last the valley narrowed to a mere rocky gorge, through which the creek ran, tumbling and foaming on its way.

It was quite late when Sammy reached the point near the head of the stream where the trail leads out of the canyon to the road on the ridge above. It was still a good two miles to the Forks. As she passed the spring, a few big drops of rain came pattering down, and, looking up, she saw, swaying and tossing in the wind, the trees that fringed the ledges above, and she heard the roar of the oncoming storm.

A short way up the side of the mountain at the foot of a great overhanging cliff there is a narrow bench, and less than a hundred feet from where the trail finds its way through a break in the rocky wall, there is a deep cavelike hollow. Sammy knew the spot well. It would afford excellent shelter.

Pushing Brownie up the steep path, she had reached this bench, when the rushing storm cloud shut out the last of the light, and the hills shook with a deafening crash of thunder. Instinctively the girl turned her pony's head from the trail, and, following the cliff, reached the sheltered nook, just as the storm burst in all its wild fury.

The rain came down in torrents; the forest roared; and against the black sky, in an almost continuous glare of lightning, the big trees tugged and strained in their wild wrestle with the wind; while peal after peal of thunder, rolling, crashing, reverberating through the hills, added to the uproar.

It was over in a little while. The wind passed; the thunder rumbled and growled in the distance; and the rain fell gently; but the sky was still lighted by the red glare. Though it was so dark that Sammy could see the trees and rocks only by the lightning's flash, she was not frightened. She knew that Brownie would find the way easily, and, as for the wetting, she would soon be laughing at that with her friends at the Post Office.

But, as the girl was on the point of moving, a voice said, "It's mighty good thing for us this old ledge happened to be here, ain't it?" It was a man's voice, and another replied, "Right you are. And it's a good thing, too, that this blow came early in the evening."

The speakers were between Sammy and the trail. They had evidently sought shelter from the storm a few seconds after the girl had gained her position. In the wild uproar she had not heard them, and they crouched under the cliff, they were hidden by a projection of the rock, though now and then, when the lightning flashed, she could see a part of one of the horses. They might be neighbors and friends. They might be strangers, outlaws even. The young woman was too wise to move until she was sure.

The first voice spoke again. "Jack got off in good time, did he?"

"Got a good start," replied the other. "He ought to be back with the posse by ten at latest. I told him we would meet them at nine where this trail comes into the big road."

"And how far do you say it is to Jim Lane's place, by the road and the Old Trail?" asked the first voice.

At the man's words a terrible fear gripped Sammy's heart. *"Posse,"* that could mean only one thing—officers of the law. But her father's name and her home—in an instant Jim's strange companionship with Wash Gibbs, their long mysterious rides together, her father's agitation that morning, when he said good-by, with a thousand other things rushed through her mind. What terrible thing was this that she had happened upon in the night? What horrible trap had they set for her daddy, her Daddy Jim? For trap it was. It could be nothing else. At any risk she must hear more. She had already lost the other man's reply. Calming herself, the girl listened eagerly for the next word.

A match cracked. The light flared out, and a whiff of tobacco smoke came curling around the rock, as one of the men said: "Are you sure there is no mistake about their meeting at Lane's tonight?"

"Can't possibly be," came the answer. "I was lying in the brush, right by the gate when the messenger got there, and I heard Jim give the order myself. Take it all the way through, unless we make a slip tonight, it will be one of the prettiest cases I ever saw."

"Yes," said the other, "but you mustn't forget that it all hinges on whether or not that bank watchman was right in thinking he recognized Wash Gibbs."

"The man couldn't be mistaken there," returned the other. "There is not another man in the country the size of Gibbs, except the two Matthews, and of course they're out of the question. Then, look! Jim Lane was ready to move out because of the drought, when all at once, after being away several days, the very time of the robbery, he changes his mind, and stays with plenty of money to carry him through. And now, here we are tonight, with that same old Bald Knobber gang, what's left of them, called together in the same old way by Jim himself, to meet in his cabin. Take my word for it, we'll bag the whole outfit, with the rest of the swag before morning. It's as sure as fate. I'm glad that girl is away from home, though."

Sammy had heard enough. As the full meaning of the officers' words came to her, she felt herself swaying dizzily in the saddle and clung blindly to the pony's mane for support. Then something in her brain kept beating out the words, "Ride, ride, ride."

Never for an instant did Sammy doubt her father. It was all some horrible mistake. Her Daddy Jim would explain it all. Of course he would, if—if she could only get home first. But the men were between her and the path that led to the road.

Then all at once she remembered that Young Matt had told her how Jake Creek hollow headed in the pinery below the ridge along which they went from Fall Creek to the Forks. It might be that this bench at the foot of the ledge would lead to a way out.

As quick as thought the girl slipped to the ground, and taking Brownie by the head began feeling her way along the narrow shelf. Dead leaves, tangled grass and ferns, all wet and sodden, made a soft carpet, so that the men behind the rock heard no sound. Now and then the lightning revealed a glimpse of the way for a short distance, but mostly she trusted blindly to her pony's instinct. Several times she stumbled over jagged fragments of rock that had fallen from above, cutting her hand and bruising her limbs cruelly. Once, she was saved from falling over the cliff by the little horse's refusal to move. A moment she stood still in the darkness; then the lightning showed a way past the dangerous point.

After a time that seemed hours, she noticed that the ledge had become no higher than her head, and that a little farther on the bench was lost in the general slope of the hill. She had reached the head of the hollow. A short climb up the side of the mountain, and, pushing through the wet bushes, she found herself in the road. She had saved about three miles. It was still nearly five to her home. An instant later the girl was in her saddle, and the brown pony was running his best.

Sammy always looked back upon that ride in the darkness, and, indeed, upon all that happened that night, as to a dream of horror. As she rode, that other night came back to her, the night she had ridden to save the shepherd, and she lived over again that evening in the beautiful woods with Young Matt. Oh, if he were only with her now! Unconsciously, at times, she called his name aloud again and again, keeping time to the beat of her pony's feet. At other times she urged Brownie on, and the little horse, feeling the spirit of his mistress, answered with the best he had to give. With eager, outstretched head, and wide nostrils, he ran as though he understood the need.

How dark it was! At every bound they seemed plunging into a black wall. What if there should be a tree blown across the road? At the thought she grew faint. She saw herself lying senseless, and her father carried away to prison. Then rallying, she held her seat carefully. She must make it as easy as possible for Brownie, dear little Brownie. How she strained her eyes to see into the black night! How she prayed God to keep the little horse!

Only once in a lifetime, it seemed to her, did the pony's iron shoe strike sparks of fire from the rocks, or the lightning give her a quick glimpse of the road ahead. They must go faster, faster, faster. Those men should not—they should not have her Daddy Jim; not unless Brownie stumbled.

Where the road leaves the ride for Fall Creek Valley, Sammy never tightened the slack rein, and the pony never shortened his stride by so much as an inch. It was well that he was hill bred, for none but a mountain horse could have kept his feet at such a terrific pace down the rocky slope. Down the valley road, past the mill, and over the creek they flew; then up the first rise of the ridge beyond. The pony was breathing hard now, and the girl encouraged him with loving words and endearing terms; pleading with him to go on, go on, go on.

At last they reached the top of the ridge. The way was easier now. Here and there, where the clouds were breaking, the stars looked through; but over the distant hills, the lightning still played, showing which way the storm had gone; and against the sky, now showing but dimly under ragged clouds and peeping stars, now outlined clearly against the flashing light, she saw the round treeless form of Old Dewey above her home.

197

34

Jim Lane Keeps His Promise

Sammy, on her tired pony, approached the Lookout on the shoulder of Dewey. As they drew near a figure rose quickly from its place on the rock, and, running swiftly along the ledge, concealed itself in the clump of cedars above the trail on the southern side of the mountain. A moment later the almost exhausted horse and his rider passed, and the figure, slipping from the ledge, followed them unobserved down the mountain.

Nearing the house Sammy began to wonder what she should do next. With all her heart the girl believed in her father's innocence. She did not know why those men were at her home. But she did know that the money that helped her father over the drought had come through the shepherd; the Matthew's family, too, had been helped the same way. Surely Dad Howitt was incapable of any crime. It was all some terrible mistake; some trap from which her father must be saved. But Sammy knew, too, that Wash Gibbs and his companions were bad men, who might easily be guilty of the robbery. To help them escape the officers was quite a different matter.

Leaving the trembling Brownie in a clump of bushes a little way from the clearing, the girl went forward on foot, and behind her still crept the figure that had followed from the Lookout. Once the figure paused as if undecided which course to pursue. Close by, two saddle horses that had carried their riders on many a long ride were tied to a tree a few feet from the corner of the barn. Sammy would have recognized these, but in her excitement she had failed to notice them.

At first the girl saw no light. Could it be that the officers were wrong, that there was no one at the cabin after all? Then a little penciled gleam set her heart throbbing wildly. Blankets were fastened over the windows.

Sammy remembered that a few days before, a bit of chinking had fallen from between the logs in the rear of the cabin. She had spoken to her father about it, but it was not likely that he had remembered to fix it. Cautiously she passed around the house, and, creeping up to the building, through the crevice between the logs, gained a clear view of the interior.

Seated or lounging on chairs and on the floor about the room were eleven men; one, the man who had been with Wash Gibbs at the mill, carried his arm in a sling. The girl outside could hear distinctly every word that was spoken. Wash himself was speaking. "Well, boys, we're all here. Let's get through and get away. Bring out the stuff, Jim."

Mr. Lane went to one corner of the cabin, and pulling up a loose board of the flooring, drew out two heavy sacks. As he placed the bags on the table, the men all rose to their feet. "There it is just as you give it to me," said Jim. "But before you go any further, men, I've got something to say."

The company stirred uneasily, and all eyes turned from Jim to their big leader, while Sammy noticed for the first time that the table had been moved from its usual place, and that her father had taken such a position that the corner of the cabin was directly behind him, with the table in front. For her life the girl could not have moved.

Slowly Jim swept the group of scowling, wondering faces on the other side of the table. Then, in his slow drawling speech, he said, "Most of you here was in the old organization. Tom and Ed and me knows how it started away back,

199

for we was in it at the beginnin'. Wash, here, was the last man to join, 'fore we was busted, and he was the youngest member, too; bein' only a boy, but big for his age. You remember how he was taken in on account of his daddy's bein' killed by the gov'ment.

"Didn't ary one of us fellers that started it ever think the Bald Knobbers would get to be what they did. We begun it as a kind of protection, times bein' wild then. But first we knowed some was a-usin' the order to protect themselves in all kinds of devilment, and things went on that way, 'cause nobody didn't dare say anything; for if they did they was tried as traitors, and sentenced to the death.

"I ain't a-sayin, boys, that I was any better than lots of others, for I reckon I done my share. But when my girl's mother died, away down there in Texas, I promised her that I'd be a good daddy to my little one, and since then I done the best I know.

"After things quieted down, and I come back with my girl, Wash here got the old crowd, what was left of us, together, and wanted to reorganize again. I told you then that I'd go in with you and stand by the old oath, so long as it was necessary to protect ourselves from them that might be tryin' to get even for what had been done, but that I wouldn't go no farther. I don't mind tellin' you now, boys—though I reckon you know it—that I went in because I knowed what you'd do for me if I didn't. And I didn't dare risk leaving my girl all alone then. I've 'tended every meetin', and done everything I agreed, and there ain't a man here can say I ain't."

Some of the men nodded, and "That's so," and "You're right, Jim," came from two or three.

Jim went on, "You know that I voted against it, and tried to stop you when you hung old man Lewis. I thought then, and I think yet, that it was spite work and not protection; and you know how I was against goin' for the shepherd, and you went when I didn't know it. As for this here bank business, I didn't even know of it, 'til you give me this stuff to keep for you. I had to take it 'count of the oath.

"It's got to be just like it was before. We come together first to keep each other posted, and save ourselves if there was any call to, and little by little you've been led into first one thing and then another, 'til you're every bit as bad as the old crowd was, only there ain't so many of you, and you've kept me in it 'cause I didn' dare leave my girl." Jim paused. There was an ominous silence in the room.

With his eyes covering every scolwing face in the company, Jim spoke again, "But things has changed for me right smart, since our last meetin', when you give me this stuff to hold. You boys all know how I've kept Wash Gibbs away from my girl, and there ain't one of you that don't know I'm right, knowin, him as we do. More'n two week ago, when I wasn't around, he insulted her, and would have done worse, if Young Matt hadn't been there to take care of her. I called you here tonight, because I knowed that after what happened at the mill, Wash and Bill would be havin' a meetin' as soon as they could get around, and votin' you all to go against Young Matt and his people. But I'm goin' to have my say first."

Wash Gibbs reached stealthily for his weapon, but hesitated when he saw that the dark-faced man noted his movement.

Jim continued, in his drawling tones, but his voice rang cold and clear, "I ain't never been mealy-mouthed with no man, and I'm too old to begin now. I know the law of the order, and I reckon Gibbs there will try to have you keep it. You boys have got to say whether you'll stand by him or me. It looks like you was goin' to go with him all right. But whether you do or don't, I don't aim to stay with nobody that stands by such as Wash Gibbs. I'm goin' to side with decent folks, who have stood by my girl, and you can do your damnedest. You take this stuff away from here. And as for you, Wash Gibbs, if you ever set foot on my place again, if you ever cross my path after tonight I'll kill you like the measly yeller hound you are." As he finished, Jim stood with his back to the corner of the room, his hand inside of the hickory shirt where the button was missing.

While her father was speaking, Sammy forgot everything, in the wild joy and pride of her heart. He was her daddy, her Daddy Jim; that man standing so calmly there before the wild company of men. Whatever the past had been, he had wiped it clean tonight. He belonged to her now, all to her. She looked toward Wash Gibbs. Then she remembered the posse, the officers of the law. They could not know what she knew. If her father was taken with the others and with the stolen gold, he would be compelled to suffer with the rest. Yet if she called out to save him, she would save Wash Gibbs and his companions also, and they would menace her father's life day and night.

The girl drew back from the window. She must think. What should she do? Even as she hesitated, a score of dark forms crept swiftly, silently toward the cabin. At the same moment a figure left the side of the house near the girl, and, crouching low, ran to the two horses that were tied near the barn.

Sammy was so dazed that for a moment she did not grasp the meaning of those swiftly moving forms. Then a figure riding one horse and leading another dashed away from the barn and across a corner of the clearing. The silence was broken by a pistol shot in the cabin. Like an echo came a shot from the yard, and a voice rang out sharply, "Halt!" The figure reeled in the saddle, as if to fall, but recovered, and disappeared in the timber. The same instant there was a rush toward the house—a loud call to surrender—a woman's scream—and then, came to Sammy, blessed, kindly darkness.

*"If you ever cross my path after tonight,
I'll kill you like the measly yeller hound you are."*

35

"I Will Lift Up Mine Eyes

Unto the Hills"

When Sammy opened her eyes, she was on the bed in her own room. In the other room someone was moving about, and the light from a lamp shone through the door.

At first the girl thought that she had awakened from a night's sleep, and that it was her father whom she heard, building the fire before calling her, as his custom was. But no, he was not building the fire, he was scrubbing the floor. How strange. She would call presently and ask what he meant by getting up before daylight, and whether he thought to keep her from scolding him by trying to clean up what he had spilled before she should see it.

She had had a bad dream of some kind, but she could not remember just what it was. It was very strange that something seemed to keep her from calling to her father just then. She would call presently. She must remember first what that dream was. She felt that she ought to get up and dress, but she did not somehow wish to move. She was strangely tired. It was her dream, she supposed. Then she discovered that she was already fully dressed, and that her clothing was wet, muddy and torn. And with this discovery every incident of the night came vividly before her. She hid her face.

After awhile, she tried to rise to her feet, but fell back

weak and dizzy. Who was that in the other room? Could it be her father? Would he never finish scrubbing the floor in that corner? When she could bear the suspense no longer, she called in a voice that sounded weak and far away, "Daddy, oh, Daddy."

Instantly the noice ceased. A step crossed the room, and the shepherd appeared in the doorway. Placing the lamp on a little stand, the old man drew a chair to the side of the bed, and laid his hand upon her forehead, smoothing back the tangled hair. He spoke no word, but in his touch there was a world of tenderness.

Sammy looked at him in wonder. Where had he come from? Why was he there at all? And in her room? She glanced uneasily about the apartment, and then back to the kind face of her old teacher. "I—don't think I understand."

"Never mind now, dear. Don't try to understand just yet. Aunt Mollie will be here in a few minutes. Matt has gone for her. When she comes and you are a little stronger, we shall talk."

The girl caught his hand. "You—you won't leave me, Dad? You won't leave me alone? I'm afraid, Dad. I never was before."

"No, no, my child, I shall not leave you. But you must have something warm to drink. I have been preparing it." He stepped into the other room, soon returning with a steaming cup. When she had finished the strengthening draft, Young Matt, with his mother and father, arrived.

While helping the girl into clean, dry clothing, Aunt Mollie spoke soothingly to her, as one would reassure a frightened child. But Sammy could hear only the three men, moving about in the other room, doing something and talking always in low tones. She did not speak, but in her brown eyes, that never left the older woman's face, was that wide, questioning look.

When Mrs. Matthews had done what she could for the comfort of the girl, and the men had finished whatever they were doing in the other room, Sammy said, "Aunt Mollie,

I want to know. I must know. Won't you tell Dad to come, please?" Instinctively she had turned to her teacher.

When the shepherd came, she met him with the old familiar demand, "Tell me everything, Dad, everything. I want to be told all about it."

"You will be brave and strong, Sammy?"

Instantly, as ever, her quick mind grasped the meaning that lay back of the words and her face grew deathly white. Then she answered, "I will be brave and strong. But first, please open the window, Dad." He threw up the sash. It was morning, and the mists were over the valley, but the mountaintops were bathed in light.

Sammy arose, and walked steadily to a chair by the open window. Looking out upon the beautiful scene, her face caught the light that was on the higher ground, and she said softly, " 'I will lift up mine eyes unto the hills' That's our word, now, isn't it, Dad? I can share it with you, now." Then the shepherd told her. Young Matt had been at the ranch with Mr. Howitt since early in the evening, and was taking his leave for the night when they heard horses stopping at the corral, and a voice calling. Upon their answering, the voice said, "There is trouble at Jim Lane's. Take these horses and go quick." And then as they had run from the house, the messenger had retreated into the shadow of the bluff, saying, "Never mind me. If you love Sammy, hurry." At this they mounted and had ridden as fast as possible.

The old man did not tell the girl that he had found his saddle wet and slippery, and that when he reached the light his hands were red.

They had found the officers ready to leave with their prisoners. All but two of the men were captured with their booty—Wash Gibbs alone escaping badly hurt, they thought, after killing one of the posse.

When they had asked for Sammy, one of the officers told them that she was at Ford's over on Jake Creek, but another declared that he had heard a woman scream as they

were making the attack. Young Matt had found her unconscious on the ground behind the cabin.

When the shepherd finished his brief account, the girl
said, "Tell me all, Dad. I want to know all. Did—did they
take Daddy away?"

The old man's eyes were dim as he answered gently,
"No, dear girl; *they* did not take him away." Then Sammy
knew why Dad had scrubbed the cabin floor, and what the
three men who talked so low had been doing in the other
room.

She made no outcry, only a moan, as she looked away
across the silent hills and the valley, where the mists were
slowly lifting; lifting slowly like the pale ghost of the star-
light that was. "Oh, Daddy, Daddy Jim. You *sure* kept your
promise. You sure did. I'm glad—glad they didn't get you,
Daddy. They never *would* have believed what I know; never—
never."

But there were no tears, and the shepherd, seeing, after a
little touched her hand. "Everything is ready, dear; would
you like to go now?"

"Not just yet, Dad. I must tell you first how I came to
be at home, and why I am glad—oh, so glad, that I was
here. But call the others, please; I want them all to know."

When the three, who with her teacher loved her best,
had come, Sammy told her story; repeating almost word for
word what she had heard her father say to the men. When
she had finished, she turned her face again to the open
window. The mists were gone. The landscape lay bright in
the sun. But Sammy could not see.

"It is much better, so much better, as it is, my child,"
said the old scholar. "You see, dear, they would have taken
him away. Nothing could have saved him. It would have
been a living death behind prison walls away from you."

"Yes, I know, Dad. I understand. It is better as it is.
Now, we will go to him, please." They led her into the
other room. The floor in the corner of the cabin where the
shepherd had washed it was still damp.

Through it all, Sammy kept her old friend constantly by her side. "It is easier, Dad, when you are near." Nor would she leave the house until it was all over, save to walk a little way with her teacher.

Young Matt and his father made the coffin of rough boards, sawed at the mill; and from the country round about, the woods-people came to the funeral, or, as they called it in their simple way, the "burying." The grave was made in a little glen not far from the house. When some of the neighbors would have brought a minister from the settlement, Sammy said, "No." Dad would say all that was necessary. So the shepherd, standing under the big trees, talked a little in his simple kindly way, and spoke the words, "Earth to earth, dust to dust, ashes to ashes." "As good," declared some, "as any preacher on earth could o' done hit"; though one or two held "it warn't jest right to put a body in th' ground 'thout a regular parson t' preach th' sermon."

When the last word was spoken, and the neighbors had gone away over the mountains and through the woods to their homes, Aunt Mollie with her motherly arm about the girl, said, "Come, honey, you're our girl now. As long as you stay in the hills, you shall stay with us." And Old Matt added, "You're the only daughter we've got, Sammy; and we want you a heap worse than you know."

When Sammy told them that she was not going to the city to live, they cried in answer, "Then you shall be our girl always," and they took her home with them to the big log house on the ridge.

For a week after that night at the Lane cabin, Pete was not seen. When at last, he did appear, it was to the shepherd on the hill, and his voice and manner alarmed Dad. But the boy's only reply to Mr. Howitt's question was, "Pete knows; Pete knows." Then in his own way he told something that sent the shepherd to Young Matt, and the two followed the lad to a spot where the buzzards were flying low through the trees.

By the shreds of clothing and the weapon lying near, they knew that the horrid thing, from which as they approached, carrion birds flapped their wings in heavy flight, was all that remained of the giant, Wash Gibbs.

Many facts were brought out at the trial of the outlaws and it was made clear that Jim Lane had met his death at the hands of Wash Gibbs, just at the beginning of the attack, and that Gibbs himself had been wounded a moment later by one of the attacking posse.

Thus does justice live even in the hills.

36

Another Stranger

Mr. Matthews and his son first heard of the stranger through Lou Gordon, the mail carrier, who stopped at the mill on his way to Flag with the week's mail.

The native rode close to the shed, and waited until the saw had shrieked its way through the log of oak, and the carriage had rattled back to first position. Then with the dignity belonging to one of his station, as a government officer, he relieved his overcharged mouth of an astonishing quantity of tobacco, and drawled, "Howdy, men."

"Howdy, Lou," returned Young Matt from the engine, and Old Matt from the saw.

"Reckon them boards is fer a floor in Joe Gardner's new cabin?"

"Yes," returned Old Matt. "We ought to got 'em out last week, but seems like we couldn't get at it with the buryin' an' all."

" 'Pears like you all 'r gettin' mighty proud in this neighborhood. *Puncheon* floors *used* t' be good enough fer anybody t' dance on. Be a-buildin' board houses next, I reckon."

Mr. Matthews laughed, "Bring your logs over to Fall Creek when you get ready to build, Lou; we'll sure do you right."

The representative of the government recharged his mouth. " 'Lowed as how I would," he returned. "I ain't one o' this here kind that don't want t' see no changes. Gov'ment's all

th' time makin' 'provements. Inspector 'lowed last trip we'd
sure be a-gettin' mail twice a week at Flag next summer.
This here's sure bound t' be a big country some day.

"Talkin' 'bout new-fangled things, though, men! I seed
the blamedest sight las' night that ever was in these woods,
I reckon. I gonies! Hit was a plumb wonder!" Kicking one
foot from the wooden stirrup and hitching sideways in the
saddle, he prepared for an effort.

"Little feller, he is. Ain't as tall as Preachin' Bill even, an'
fat! I gonies! He's fat as a possum 'n 'simmon time. He
don't walk, can't; just naturally waddles on them little duck
legs o' hisn. An' he's got th' prettiest little ol' face; all red
an' white, an' as round's a walnut; an' a fringe of th' whit-
est hair you ever seed. An' clothes! Say, men." In the pause
the speaker deliberately relieved his overcharged mouth. The
two in the mill waited breathlessly. "Long-tailed coat, stove-
pipe hat, an' cane with a gold head as big as a 'tater. 'Fo'
God, men, there ain't been ary such a sight within a thousand miles of these here hills ever. An' doin's! My Lord,
a'mighty!"

The thin form of the native doubled up as he broke into
a laugh that echoed and re-echoed through the little valley,
ending in a wild "Whoop-e-e-e! Say! When he got out of
th' hack last night at th' Forks, Uncle Ike he catched sight
o' him an' says, says he t' me, 'Ba thundas! Lou, looky
there! Talk 'bout prosperity. I'm dummed if there ain't ol'
Santa Claus a-comin' t' th' Forks in th' summa time. Ba
thundas! What!'

"An' when Santa come in, he—he wanted—now what d'
you reckon he wanted? A *bath!* Yes, sir-e-e. Dad burn me,
'f he didn't. A bath! Whoop-e-e, you ought t' seen Uncle
Ike! He told him, 'Ba thundas!' He could give him a bite to
eat an' a place to sleep, but he'd be pisined, bit by rattlers,
clawed by wildcats, chawed by the hogs, et by buzzards, an'
everlastin'ly damned 'fore he'd tote water 'nough fer anybody t' swim in. 'Ba thundas! What!' "

"What's he doin' here?" asked Mr. Matthews, when the

mountaineer had recovered from another explosion.

Lou shook his head, as he straightened himself in the saddle. "Blame me 'f I kin tell. Jest wouldn't tell 't all last night. Wanted a *bath*. Called Uncle Ike some new-fangled kind of a savage, an' th' old man 'lowed he'd show him. He'd sure have him persecuted fer 'sultin' a gov'ment servant when th' inspector come around. Yes he did. Oh, thar was doin's at the Forks last night!"

Again the mail carrier's laugh echoed through the woods.

"Well, I must mosey along. He warn't up this mornin' when I left. Reckon he'll show up round here sometime 'fore sundown. Him an' Uncle Ike won't hitch worth a cent an' he'll be huntin' prouder folks. I done told th' old man he'd better herd him fer a spell, fer if he was t' get loose in these woods, there wouldn't be nary deer er bear left come Thanksgivin' time. Uncle Ike said, 'Ba thundas!' He'd let me know that he warn't runnin' no dummed asylum. He 'lowed he was postmaster, 'Ba thundas!' an' had all he could do t' keep th' dad-burned gov'ment straight."

Late that afternoon Lou's prophecy was fulfilled. A wagon going down the Creek with a load of supplies for the distillery stopped at the mill shed and the stranger began climbing carefully down over the wheels. Budd Wilson on his high seat winked and nodded at Mr. Matthews and his son, as though it was the greatest joke of the season.

"Hold those horses, driver. Hold them tight, tight, sir."

"Got 'em, mister," responded Budd promptly. The mules stood with their drooping heads and sleepy eyes, the lines under their feet.

The gentleman was feeling carefully about the hub of the wheel with a foot that, stretch as he might, could not touch it by a good six inches.

"That's right, man, right," he puffed. "Hold them tight, tight. Start now, break a leg sure, sure. Then what would Sarah and the girls do? Oh, blast it all, where is that step? Can't stay here all day. Bring a ladder. Bring a high chair, a table, a box, a big box, a—heh—heh—Look out, I say, look out! Blast it all, what do you mean?" This last was called forth by Young Matt lifting the little man bodily to the ground, as an ordinary man would lift a child.

To look up at the young giant, the stranger tipped back his head, until his shining silk hat was in danger of falling in the dirt. "Bless my soul, what a specimen! What a specimen!" Then with a twinkle in his eye, "Which one of the boys are you, anyway?"

At this the three mountaineers roared with laughter. With his dumpy figure in the long coat, and his round face under the tall hat, the little man was irresistible. He fairly shone with good humor; his cheeks were polished like big red apples; his white hair had the luster of silver; his blue eyes twinkled; his silk hat glistened; his gold watch guard sparkled; his patent leathers glistened; and the cane with the big gold head gleamed in the sunlight.

"That's him, Doc," called the driver. "That's the feller what wallered Wash Gibbs like I was a-tellin' ye. Strongest man in the hills he is. Dad burn me if I believe he knows how strong he is."

"Doc—Doc—Dad burned—Doc," muttered the stranger. "What would Sarah and the girls say!" He waddled to the wagon, and reached up one fat hand with a half dollar to Budd, "Here, driver, here. Get cigars with that; cigars, mind you, or candy. I stay here. Mind you don't get anything to drink, nothing to drink, I say."

Budd gathered up the reins and woke the sleepy mules with a vigorous jerk. "Nary a drink, Doc, nary a drink. Thank you kindly all the same. Got t'mosey 'long t' th' still now; ought t' o' been there hour ago. 'f I can do anything fer you, jest le' me know. I live over on Sow Coon Gap, when I'm t' home. Come over an' visit with me. Young Matt there'll guide you."

As he watched the wagon down the valley, the stranger mused. "Doc—Doc—huh. Quite sure that fellow will buy a drink; quite sure."

When the wagon had disappeared, he turned to Mr.

Matthews and his son. "According to that fellow, I am not far from a sheep ranch kept by a Mr. Howitt. That's it, Mr. Daniel Howitt; fine-looking man, fine; brown eyes; great voice; gentleman, sir, gentleman, if he is keeping sheep in this wilderness. Blast it all, just like him, just like him; always keeping somebody's sheep; born to be a shepherd; born to be. Know him?"

At mention of Mr. Howitt's name, Young Matt had looked at his father quickly. When the stranger paused, he answered, "Yes, sir. We know Dad Howitt. Is he a friend on yourn?"

"Dad—Dad Howitt. Doc and Dad. Well, what would Sarah and the girls say? Friend of mine? Young man, Daniel and David. I am David; Daniel and David lay on the same blanket when they were babies; played in the same alley; school together same classes; colleged together; next door neighbors. Know him! Blast it all, where *is* this sheep place?"

Again the two woodsmen exchanged glances. The elder Matthews spoke. "It ain't so far from here, sir. The ranch belongs to me and my son. But Mr. Howitt will be out on the hills somewhere with the sheep now. You'd better go home with us and have supper, and the boy will take you down this evenin'."

"Well, now, that's kind, sir, very kind, indeed. Man at the Post Office is a savage, sir; blasted, old incorrigible savage. My name is Coughlan, Dr. David Coughlan, of Chicago; practicing physician for forty years; don't do anything now; not much, that is. Sarah and the girls won't let me. Your name, sir?"

"Grant Matthews. My boy there has the same. We're mighty glad to meet any friend of Dad's, I can tell you. He's sure been a God's blessin' to this neighborhood."

Soon they started homeward, Young Matt going ahead to do the chores, and to tell his mother of their coming guest, while Mr. Matthews followed more slowly with the doctor. Shortening his stride to conform to the slow pace of the smaller man, the mountaineer told his guest about the shep-

"Yes, sir. We know Dad Howitt. Is he a friend of yourn?

herd; how he had come to them; of his life; and how he had won the hearts of the people. When he told how Mr. Howitt had educated Sammy, buying her books himself from his meager wages, the doctor interrupted in his quick way, "Just like him! Just like him. Always giving away everything he earned. Made others give, too. Blast it all, he's cost me thousands of dollars, thousands of dollars, treating patients of his that never paid a cent; not a cent, sir. Proud, though; proud as Lucifer. Fine old family; finest in the country, sir. Right to be proud, right to be."

Old Matt scowled as he returned coldly, "He sure don't seem that way to us, Mister. He's as common as an old shoe." And then the mountaineer told how his son loved the shepherd, and tried to explain what the old scholar's friendship had meant to them.

The stranger ejaculated, "Same old thing; same old trick. Did me that way; does everybody that way. Same old Daniel. Proud, though; can't help it; can't help it."

The big man answered with still more warmth, "You ought to hear how he talks to us folks when we have meetin's at the Cove schoolhouse. He's as good as any preacher you ever heard; except that he don't put on as much, maybe. Why, sir, when we buried Jim Lane week before last, everybody 'lowed he done as well as a regular parson."

At this Dr. Coughlan stopped short and leaned against a convenient tree for support, looking up at his big host, with merriment he could not hide. "Parson, parson! Daniel Howitt talked as good as a parson! Blast it all! Dan is one of the biggest D. D.'s in the United States; as good as a parson, I should think so! Why, man, he's my pastor; my pastor. Biggest church, greatest crowds in the city. Well, what would Sarah and the girls say!" He stood there gasping and shaking with laughter, until Old Matt, finding the ridiculous side of the situation, joined in with a guffaw that fairly drowned the sound of the little man's merriment.

When they finally moved on again, the Doctor said, "And you never knew? The papers were always full, always. His real name is—"

"Stop!" Old Matt spoke so suddenly and in such a tone that the other jumped in alarm. "I ain't a meanin' no harm, Doc; but you oughtn't to tell his name, and—anyway I don't want to know. Preacher or no preacher, he's a man, he is, and that's what counts in this here country. If Dad had wanted us to know about himself, I reckon he'd a-told us, and I don't want to hear it until he's ready."

The doctor stopped short again. "Right, sir, right. Daniel has his reasons, of course, I forgot. That savage at the Post Office tried to interrogate me; tried to draw me. I was close; on guard, you see. Fellow in the wagon tried; still on guard. You caught me. Blast it all, I like you! Fine specimen, that boy of yours, fine!"

When they reached the top of the ridge the stranger looked over the hills with exclamations of delight. "Grand, sir, grand! Wish Sarah and the girls could see. Don't wonder Daniel stayed. That Hollow down there you say, way down there? Mutton—Mutton Hollow? Daniel lives there? Blast it all; come on, man, come on."

As they drew near the house, Pete came slowly up the Old Trail and met them at the gate.

217

37

Old Friends

After supper Young Matt guided the stranger down the trail
to the sheep ranch in Mutton Hollow.

When they reached the edge of the clearing, the mountaineer stopped. "Yonder's the cabin, sir, an' Dad is there,
as you can see by the smoke. I don't reckon you'll need
me any more now, an' I'll go back. We'll be mighty glad to
see you on the ridge any time, sir. Any friend of Dad's is
mighty welcome in this neighborhood."

"Thank you; thank you; very thoughtful; very thoughtful,
indeed; fine spirit, fine. I shall see you again when Daniel
and I have had it out. Blast it all, what is he doing here?
Good-night, young man, good-night." He started forward
impetuously. Matt turned back toward home.

The dog barked as Dr. Coughlan approached the cabin,
and the shepherd came to the open door. He had been
washing the supper dishes. His coat was off, his shirt open
at the throat, and his sleeves rolled above his elbows. "Here,
Brave." The deep voice rolled across the little clearing, and
the dog ran to stand by the master's side. Then, as Mr.
Howitt took in the unmistakable figure of the little physician, he put out a hand to steady himself.

"Oh, it's me, Daniel, it's me. Caught you, didn't I? Blast
it all; might have known I would. Bound to; bound to,
Daniel; been at it ever since I lost you. Visiting in Kansas
City last week with my old friends, the Stewarts; young fel-

low there, Ollie, put me right. First part of your name, description, voice and all that; knew it was you; knew it. Didn't tell them, though; blasted reporters go wild. Didn't tell a soul, not a soul. Sarah and the girls think I am in Kansas City or Denver. Didn't tell old man Matthews, either; came near, though, very near. Blast it all; what does it mean? What does it all mean?"

In his excitement the little man spoke rapidly as he hurried toward the shepherd. When he reached the cabin, the two friends, so different, yet so alike, clasped hands.

As soon as the old scholar could speak, he said, "David, David! To think that this is really you. You of all men; you, whom I most needed."

"Huh!" grunted the other. "Look like you never needed me less. Look fit for anything; ten years younger; every bit of ten years. Blast it all, what have you done to yourself? What have you done?" He looked curiously at the tanned face and rude dress of his friend. "Bless my soul, what a change! What a change! Told Matthews you were an aristocrat. He wouldn't believe it. Don't wonder. Doubt it myself, now."

The other smiled at the doctor's amazement. "I suppose I have changed some, David. The hills have done it. Look at them!" He pointed to the encircling mountains. "See how calm and strong they are; how they lift their heads above the gloom. They are my friends and companions, David. And they have given me of their calmness and strength a little. But come in, come in; you must be very tired. How did you come?"

The doctor followed him into the cabin. "Railroad, hack, wagon, walked. Post Office last night. Man there is a savage, blasted incorrigible savage. Mill this afternoon. Home with your friends on the ridge. Old man is a gentleman, a gentleman, sir, if God ever made one. His boy's like him. The mother, she's a real mother; made to be a mother couldn't help it. And that young woman, with the boy's name, bless my soul, I never saw such a creature before, Daniel, never! If I had, I—I—blast it all, I wouldn't be

219

bossed by Sarah and the girls, I wouldn't. See in that young man and woman what God meant men and women to be. Told them they ought to marry, that they owed it to the race. You know my ideas, Daniel. Think they will?"

The shepherd laughed, a laugh that was good to hear.

"What's the matter now, Daniel? What is the matter? Have I said anything wrong again? Blast it all; you know how I always do the wrong thing. Have I?"

"No, indeed, David, you are exactly right," returned Mr. Howitt. "But tell me, did you see no one else at the house? There is another member of the family."

The doctor nodded. "I saw him; Pete, you mean. Looked him over. Mr. Matthews asked me to. Sad case, very sad. Hopeless, absolutely hopeless, Daniel."

"Pete has not seemed as well as usual lately. I fear so much night roaming is not good for the boy," returned the other slowly. "But tell me, how are Sarah and the girls? Still looking after Dr. Davie, I suppose."

"Just the same; haven't changed a bit; not a bit. Jennie looks after my socks and handkerchiefs; Mary looks after my shirts and linen; Anna looks after my ties and shoes; Sue looks after my hats and coats; and Kate looks after the things I eat; and Sarah, Sarah looks after everything and everybody, same as always. Blast it all! If they'd give me a show, I'd be as good as ever; good as ever, Daniel. What can a man do; what can a man do, with an only sister and her five old maid daughters looking after him from morning until night, from morning until night, Daniel? Tell them I am a full grown man; don't do no good; no good at all. Blast it all; poor old things, just got to mother something; got to, Daniel."

While he was speaking, his eyes were dancing from one object to another in the shepherd's rude dwelling, turning for frequent quick glances to Dad himself. "You live here, you? You ought not, Daniel, you ought not. What would Sarah and the girls say? Blast it all; what do you mean by it? I ordered you away on a vacation. You disappear. Think you dead; row in the papers, mystery! I hate mystery. Blast it all; what does it mean, what does it all mean? Not fair to me, Daniel; not fair."

By this time the little man had worked himself up to an astonishing pitch of excitement. His eyes snapped. His words came like pistol shots. His ejaculations were genuine explosions. He tapped with his feet, rapped with his cane, shook his finger, and fidgeted in his chair. "We want you back, Daniel. I want you. Church will want you when they know; looking for a preacher right now. I come after you, Daniel. Blast it all, I'll tell Sarah and the girls, and they'll come after you, too. Chicago will go wild when they know that Daniel Howitt Cha—"

"Stop!" The doctor bounced out of his chair. The shepherd was trembling, and his voice shook with emotion. "Forgive me, David. But that name must never be spoken again, never. My son is dead, and that name died with him. It must be forgotten."

The physician noted his friend's agitation in amazement. "There, there, Daniel. I didn't mean to. Thought it didn't matter when we were alone. I—I—blast it all! Tell me Daniel, what do you mean by this strange business, this very strange business?"

A look of mingled affection, regret and pain came into the shepherd's face, as he replied, "Let me tell you the story, David, and you will understand."

When he had finished, Mr. Howitt asked gently, "Have I not done right, David? The boy is gone. It was hard, going as he did. But I am glad, now, for Old Matt would have killed him, as he would kill me yet, if he knew. Thank God, we have not also made the father a murderer. Did I not say rightly, that the old name died with Howard? Have I not done well to stay on this spot and to give my life to this people?"

"Quite right, Daniel, quite right. You always are. It's me that goes wrong; blundering, bumping, smashing into things. Blast it all! I—I don't know what to say. B—B—Blast it all!"

221

The hour was late when the two men finally retired for the night. Long after his heavy, regular breathing announced that the doctor was sleeping soundly, the shepherd lay wide awake, keenly sensitive to every sound that stirred in the forest. Once he arose from his bed, and stepping softly left the cabin, to stand under the stars, his face lifted to the dark summit of Old Dewey and the hills that rimmed the Hollow. And once, when the first light of day came over the ridges, he went to the bunk where his friend lay, to look thoughfully down upon the sleeping man.

Breakfast was nearly ready when Dr. Coughlan awoke. The physician saw at once by the worn and haggard look on his friend's face that his had been a sleepless night. It was as though all the pain and trouble of the old days had returned. The little doctor muttered angrily to himself while the shepherd was gone to the spring for water. "Blast it all, I'm a fool, a meddlesome old fool. Ought to have let well enough alone. No need to drag him back into it all again; no need. Do no good; no good at all."

When the morning meal was finished, Mr. Howitt said, "David, will you think me rude, if I leave you alone today? The city pavements fit one but poorly to walk these hills of mine, and you are too tired after your trip and the loss of your regular sleep to go with me this morning. Stay at the ranch and rest. If you care to read, here are a few of your favorites. Will you mind very much? I should like to be alone today, David."

"Right, Daniel, right. I understand. Don't say another word; not a word. Go ahead. I'm stiff and sore anyway; just suit me."

The shepherd arranged everything for his friend's comfort, putting things in readiness for his noonday meal, and showing him the spring. Then, taking his own lunch, as his custom was, he went to the corral and released the sheep. The doctor watched until the last of the flock was gone, and he could no longer hear the tinkle of the bells and the bark of a dog.

38

"I Ain't Nobody No More"

With the coming of the evening, the shepherd returned to his guest. Dr. Coughlan heard first the bells on the leaders of the flock, and the barking of the dog coming nearer and nearer through the woods. Soon the sheep appeared trooping out of the twilight shadows into the clearing; then came Brave followed by his master.

The countenance of the old scholar wore again that look of calm strength and peace that had marked it before the coming of his friend. "Have you had a good rest, David? Or has your day been long and tiresome? I fear it was not kind of me to leave you alone in this wilderness."

The doctor told how he had passed the time, reading, sleeping and roaming about the clearing and the nearby woods. "And you," he said, looking the other over with a professional eye, "you look like new man; a new man, Daniel. How do you do it? Some secret spring of youth in the wilderness? Blast it all, wish you would show me. Fool Sarah and the girls, fool them, sure."

"David, have you forgotten the prescription you gave me when you ordered me from the city? You took it, you remember, from one of our favorite volumes." The shepherd bared his head and repeated,

" 'If thou art worn and hard beset,
With sorrows, that thou wouldst forget;
If thou wouldst read a lesson, that will keep

Thy heart from fainting and thy soul from sleep,
Go to the woods and hills! No tears
Dim the sweet look that Nature wears.'

"David, I never understood until the past months why the Master so often withdrew alone into the wilderness. There is not only food and medicine for one's body; there is also healing for the heart and strength for the soul in nature. One gets very close to God, David, in these temples of God's own building."

Dr. Coughlan studied his old friend curiously. "Change; remarkable change in you! Remarkable! Never said a thing like that in all your life before, never."

The shepherd smiled. "It's your prescription, Doctor," he said.

They retired early that evening, for the physician declared that his friend must need the rest. "Talk tomorrow," he said. "All day; nothing else to do." He promptly enforced his decision by retiring to his own bunk, leaving the shepherd to follow his example. But not until the doctor was sure that his friend was sleeping soundly did he permit himself to sink into unconsciousness.

It was just past midnight, when the shepherd was aroused by the doctor striking a match to light the lamp. As he awoke, he heard Pete's voice, "Where is Dad? Pete wants Dad."

Dr. Coughlan, thinking it some strange freak of the boy's disordered brain, and not wishing to break his friend's much needed rest, was trying in low tones to persuade the boy to wait until morning.

"What does Pete want?" asked the shepherd, entering the room.

"Pete wants Dad, Dad and the other man. They must sure go with Pete right quick."

"Go where with Pete? Who told Pete to come for Dad?" asked Mr. Howitt.

"*He* told Pete. Right now, he said. And Pete he come. Course I come with him. Dad must go, an' the other man too, 'cause he said so."

In sickness or in trouble of any kind the people for miles around had long since come to depend upon the shepherd of Mutton Hollow. The old man turned now to the doctor. "Someone needs me, David. We must go with the boy."

"But, Daniel, Daniel! Blast it all! The boy's not responsible. Where will he take us? Where do you want us to go, boy?"

"Not me; not me; nobody can't go nowhere, can they? You go with Pete, Mister."

"Yes, yes, we'll go with Pete; but where will Pete take us?" persisted the doctor.

"Pete knows."

"Now, look at that, Daniel! Look at that. Blast it all, we ought not go; not in the night this way. What would Sarah and the girls say?" Notwithstanding his protests, the doctor was ready even before the shepherd. "Take a gun, Daniel, take a gun, at least," he said.

The other hesitated, then asked, "Does Pete want Dad to take a gun?"

The youth, who stood in the doorway waiting impatiently, shook his head and laughed. "No, no; nothing can't get Dad where Pete goes. God he's there just like Dad says."

"It's all right, David," said the shepherd with conviction. "Pete knows. It is safe to trust him tonight."

And the boy echoed, as he started forward, "It's all right, mister. Pete knows."

"I wish you had your medicine case, though, David," added Mr. Howitt, as they followed the boy out into the night.

"Got one, Daniel; got one. Always have a pocket case; habit."

Pete led the way down the road, and straight to the old cabin ruin below the corral. Though the stars were hidden behind clouds, it was a little light in the clearing; but, in the timber under the shadow of the bluff, it was very dark. The two men were soon bewildered and stood still. "Which

"Come on, Dad. Come, other man. Don't be scared."

way, Pete?" said the shepherd. There was no answer. "Where's Pete? Tell Pete to come here," said Mr. Howitt again. Still there was no reply. Their guide seemed to have been swallowed up in the blackness. They listened for a sound. "This is strange," mused the shepherd.

A grunt of disgust came from the doctor, "Crazy, man, crazy. There's three of us. Which way is the house? Blast it all, what would—" A spot of light gleamed under the bushes not fifty feet away.

"Come, Dad. Come on, Pete's ready."

They were standing close to the old cabin under the bluff. In a narrow space between the log wall of the house and the cliff, Pete stood with a lighted lantern. The farther end of the passage was completely hidden by a projection of the rock; the overhanging roof touched the ledge above; while the opening near the men was concealed by the heavy growth of ferns and vines and the thick branches of a low cedar. Even in daylight the place would have escaped anything but a most careful search.

Dropping to his knees and to one hand, the shepherd pushed aside the screen of vines and branches with the other, and then on all fours crawled into the narrow passage. The doctor followed. They found their guide crouching in a small opening in the wall of rock. Mr. Howitt uttered an exclamation. "The lost cave! Old man Dewey!"

The boy laughed. "Pete knows. Come, Dad. Come, other man. Ain't nothin' can get you here." He scrambled ahead of them into the low tunnel. Some twenty feet from the entrance, the passage turned sharply to the left and opened sudenly into a hallway along which the shepherd could easily walk erect. Pete went briskly forward as one on very familiar ground, his lantern lighting up the way clearly for his two companions.

For some distance their course dipped downward at a gentle angle, while the ceilings and sides dripped with moisture. Soon they heard the sound of running water, and entering a wider room saw sparkling in the lantern's light a

227

stream that came from under the rocky wall, crossed their path, and disappeared under the other wall of the chamber. "Lost Creek!" ejaculated the shepherd, as he picked his way over the stream on the big stones. And the boy answered, "Pete knows. Pete knows."

From the bank of the creek the path climbed strongly upward, the footing grew firmer, and the wall and ceiling drier. As they went on, the passage, too, grew wider and higher, until they found themselves in a large underground hallway that echoed loudly as they walked. Overhead, pure white stalactites and frost-like formations glittered in the light, and the walls were broken by dark nooks and shelf-like ledges with here and there openings leading who could tell where?"

At the farther end of this hallway where the ceiling was highest, the guide paused at the foot of a ledge against which rested a rude ladder. The shepherd spoke again. "Dewey Bald?" he asked. Pete nodded, and began to climb the ladder.

Another room, and another ledge; then a long narrow passage, the ceiling of which was so high that it was beyond the lantern light; then a series of ledges, and they saw that they were climbing from shelf to shelf on one side of an underground canyon. Following along the edge of the chasm, the doctor pushed a stone over the brink, and they heard it go bounding from ledge to ledge into the dark heart of the mountain. "No bottom, Daniel. Blast it all, no bottom to it! What would Sarah and the girls say?"

They climbed one more ladder and then turned from the canyon into another great chamber, the largest they had entered. The floor was perfectly dry. The air, too, was dry and pure, and, from what seemed to be the opposite side of the huge cavern, a light gleamed like a red eye in the darkness. They were evidently nearing the end of their journey. Drawing closer, they found that the light came from the window of a small cabin built partly of rock and partly of logs.

Instinctively the two men stopped. Pete said in a low tone, as one would speak in a sacred presence, "*He* is there. Come on, Dad. Come, other man. Don't be scared."

Still the boy's companions hesitated. Mr. Howitt asked, "Who, boy? Who is there? Do you know who it is?"

"No, no, not me. Nobody can't know nothin', can they?"

"Hopeless case, Daniel; hopeless. Too bad, too bad," muttered the physician, laying his hand upon his friend's shoulder.

The shepherd tried again. "Who does Pete say it is?"

"Oh, Pete says it's him, just him."

"But who does Pete say he is?" suggested Dr. Coughlan.

Again the boy's voice lowered to a whisper. "Sometimes Pete says it must be God, 'cause he's so good. Dad says God is good an' that he takes care of folks, an' *he* sure does that. 'Twas him that scared Wash Gibbs an' his crowd that night. An' he sent the gold to you, Dad. God's gold it was. He's got heaps of it. He killed that panther, too, when it was a goin' to fight Young Matt. Pete knows. You see, Dad, when Pete is with him, I ain't nobody no more. I'm just Pete then, an' Pete is me. Funny, ain't it? But he says that's the way it is, an' he sure knows."

The two friends listened with breathless interest. "And what does Pete call him?" asked the doctor.

"Pete calls him father, like Dad calls God. He talks to God, too, like Dad does. Do you reckon God would talk to God, mister?"

With a cry the shepherd reeled. The doctor caught him. "Strong, Daniel, strong." Pete drew away from the two men in alarm.

The old scholar's agitation was pitiful. "David, David, tell me, what is this thing? Can it be—my boy—Howard, my son—can it be? My God, David, what am I saying? He is dead. Dead, I tell you. Can the dead come back from the grave, David?" He broke from his friend and ran staggering toward the cabin; but at the door he stopped again. It was as if he longed yet feared to enter, and the doctor and the

229

boy came to his side. Without ceremony, Pete pushed open the door.

The room was furnished with a cupboard, table and small cookstove. It was evidently a living room. Through a curtained opening at the right, a light showed from another apartment, and a voice called, "Is that you, Pete?"

A look of pride came into the face of the lad. "That's me," he whispered. "I'm Pete here, an' Pete is me. It's always that way with him." Aloud, he said, "Yes, Father, it's Pete. Pete an' Dad an' the other man." As he spoke he drew aside the curtain.

For an instant the two men paused on the threshold. The room was small, and nearly bare of furniture. In the full glare of the lamp, so shaded as to throw the rest of the room in deep shadow, hung a painting that seemed to fill the rude chamber with its beauty. It was the picture of a young woman, standing by a spring of water, a cup brimming full in her outstretched hand.

On a bed in the shadow, facing the picture, lay a man. A voice faltered, "Father. Dr. Coughlan."

39

A Matter of Hours

Father—Father. Can—you—can—you—forgive me?"

The man on his knees raised his head. "Forgive you, my son? Forgive you? My dear boy, there has never been in my heart a thought but of love and sympathy. Pain there has been, I can't deny, but it has helped me to know what you have suffered. I understand it now, my boy. I understand it all, for I, too, have felt it. But when I first knew, even beneath all the hurt, I was glad—glad to know, I mean. It is a father's right to suffer with his child, my son. It hurt most, when the secret stood between us, and I could not enter into your life, but I understand that, too. I understand why you could not tell me. I, too, came away because I was not strong enough."

"I—I thought it would be easier for you never to know," said the son as he lay on the bed. "I am—sorry, now. And I am glad that you know. But I must tell you all about it just the same. I must tell you myself, you see, so that it will be all clear and straight when I—when I go." He turned his eyes to the picture on the wall.

"When you go?"

Howard laid a hand upon the gray head. "Poor father; yes, I am going. It was an accident, but it was a kindness. It will be much better this way—only—only I am sorry for you, father. I thought I could save you all this. I intended to slip quietly away without your ever knowing, but when

Pete said that Dr. Coughlan was here, I could not go without—without—"

The little doctor came forward. "I am a fool, Howard, an old fool. Blast it all; no business to go poking into this; no business at all! Daniel would have sent if he had wanted me. Ought to have known. Old native can give me lessons on being a gentleman every time. Blast it all! What's wrong, Howard? Get hurt? Now I am here, might as well be useful."

"Indeed, Doctor, you did right to come. You will be such a help to father. You will help us both, just as you have always done. Will you excuse us, father, while Dr. Coughlan looks at this thing here in my side?"

The physician arranged the light so that it shone full upon the man on the bed, then carefully removed the bandages from an ugly wound in the artist's side. Dr. Coughlan looked very grave. "When did this happen, Howard?"

"I—I can't tell exactly. You see, I thought at first I could get along with Pete to help, and I did, for a week, I guess. Then things—didn't go so well. Some fever, I think, for she—she came." He turned his eyes toward the picture again. "And I—I lost all track of time. It was the night of the eighteenth. Father will know."

"Two weeks," muttered the physician.

A low exclamation came from the shepherd. "It was you—you who brought the horses to the ranch that night?"

The artist smiled grimly. "The officers saw me, and thought that I was one of the men they wanted. It's all right, though." The old scholar instinctively lifted his hands and looked at them. He remembered the saddle, wet with blood.

Making a careful examination, the doctor asked more questions. When he had finished and had skillfully replaced the bandages, the wounded man asked, "What about it, Dr. Coughlan?" The kind-hearted physician jerked out a volley of scientific words and phrases that meant nothing, and busied himself with his medicine case.

When his patient had taken the medicine, the doctor

watched him for a few minutes, and then asked, "Feel stronger, Howard?"

The artist nodded. "Tell me the truth, now, Doctor. I know that I am going. But how long have I? Wait a minute first. Where's Pete? Come here, my boy." The lad drew near. "Father." Mr. Howitt seated himself on the bedside. "You'll be strong, father? We are ready now, Dr. Coughlan."

"Yes, tell us, David," said the shepherd, and his voice was steady.

The physician spoke, "Matter of hours, I would say. Twenty-four, perhaps; not more; not more."

"There is no possible chance, David?" asked the shepherd.

Again the little doctor took refuge behind a broadside of scientific terms before replying, "No, no possible chance."

A groan slipped from the gray-bearded lips of the father. The artist turned to the picture and smiled. Pete looked wonderingly from face to face.

"Poor father," said the artist. "One thing more, Doctor. Can you keep up my strength for awhile?"

"Reasonably well, reasonably well, Howard."

"I am so glad of that because there is much to do before I go. There is so much that must be done first, and I want you both to help me."

233

40

The Shepherd's Mission

During the latter part of that night and most of the day, it rained; a fine, slow, quiet rain, with no wind to shake the wet from burdened leaf or blade. But when the old shepherd left the cave by a narrow opening on the side of the mountain, near Sammy's Lookout the sky was clear. The mists rolled heavily over the valley, but the last of the sunlight was warm on the knobs and ridges.

The old man paused behind the rock and bushes that concealed the mouth of the underground passage. Not a hundred feet below was the Old Trail. He followed the little path with his eye until it vanished around the shoulder of Dewey. Along that way he had come into the hills. Then lifting his eyes to the faraway lines of darker blue, his mind looked over the ridge to the world that is on the other side, the world from which he had fled. It all seemed very small and meaningless now; it was so far—so far away.

He started as the sharp ring of a horse's iron shoes on the flint rocks came from beyond the Lookout, and, safely hidden, he saw a neighbor round the hill and pass on his way to the store on Roark. He watched, as horse and rider followed the Old Trail around the rim of the Hollow; watched, until they passed from sight in the belt of timber. Then his eyes were fixed on a fine thread of smoke that curled above the trees on the Matthews place; and, leaving the shelter of rock and bush, he walked along the Old Trail toward the big log house on the distant ridge.

Below him, on his left, Mutton Hollow lay submerged in the drifting mists, with only a faint line of light breaking now and then where Lost Creek made its way; and on the other side Compton Ridge lifted like a wooded shore from the sea. A black spot in the red west shaped itself into a crow, making his way on easy wing toward a dead tree on the top of Boulder Bald. The old shepherd walked wearily; the now familiar objects wore a strange look. It was as though he saw them for the first time, yet had seen them somewhere before, perhaps in another world. As he went his face was the face of one crushed by shame and grief, made desperate by his suffering.

Supper was just over and Young Matt was on the porch when Mr. Howitt entered the gate. The young fellow greeted his old friend, and called back into the house, "Here's Dad, Father." As Mr. Matthews came out, Aunt Mollie and Sammy appeared in the doorway. How like it all was to that other evening!

The mountaineer and the shepherd sat on the front porch, while Young Matt brought the big sorrel and the brown pony to the gate, and with Sammy rode away. They were going to the Post Office at the Forks. "Ain't had no news for a week," said Aunt Mollie, as she brought her chair to join the two men. "And besides, Sammy needs the ride. There's goin' to be a moon, so it'll be light by the time they start home."

The sound of the horses' feet and the voices of the young people died away in the gray woods. The dusk thickened in the valley below, and, as the light in the west went out, the three friends saw the clump of pines etched black and sharp against the blood red background of the sky.

Old Matt spoke. "Reckon everything's all right at the ranch, Dad. How's the little doctor? You ought to brung him up with you." He watched the shepherd's face curiously from under his heavy brows, as he pulled at his cob pipe.

"Tired out trampin' over these hills, I reckon," ventured

Aunt Mollie. Mr. Howitt tried to answer with some commonplace, but his friends could not but note his confusion. Mrs. Matthews continued, "I guess you'll be a-leavin' us pretty soon, now. Well, I ain't a-blamin' you; and you've sure been a God's blessin' to us here in the woods. I don't reckon we're much 'longside the fine friends you've got back where you come from in the city; and we—we can't do nothin' for you, but—but—" The good soul could say no more.

"We've often wondered, sir," added Old Matt, "how you've stood it here, an educated man like you. I reckon, though, there's somethin' deep under it all, keepin' you up; somethin' that ignorant folks, without no education, like us, can't understand."

The old scholar could have cried aloud, but he was forced to sit dumb while the other continued, "You're goin' won't make no difference, though, with what you've done. This neighborhood won't never go back to what it was before you come. It can't with all you've taught us, and with Sammy stayin' here to keep it up. It'll be mighty hard, though, to have you go; it sure will, Mr. Howitt."

Looking up, the shepherd said quietly, "I expect to live here until the end if you will let me. But I fear you will not want me to stay when you know what I've come to tell you this evening."

The mountaineer straightened his huge form as he returned, "Dad, there ain't nothin' on earth or in hell could change what we think of you, and we don't want to hear nothin' about you that you don't like to tell us. We ain't a-carin' what sent you to the hills. We're takin' you for what you are. And there ain't nothin' can change that."

"Not even if it should be the grave under the pine yonder?" asked the other in a low voice.

Old Matt looked at him in a half-frightened way, as though, without knowing why, he feared what the shepherd would say next. Mr. Howitt felt the look and hesitated. He was like one on a desperate mission in the heart of an

"Tonight I know the other side of the story. I've come to tell you."

enemy's country, feeling his way. Was the strong man's passion really tame? Or was his fury only sleeping, waiting to destroy the one who should wake it? Who could tell?

The old scholar looked away to Dewey Bald for strength. "Mr. Matthews," he said, "you once told me a story. It was here on this porch when I first came to you. It was a sad tale of a great crime. Tonight I know the other side of that story. I've come to tell you."

At the strange words, Aunt Mollie's face turned as white as her apron. Old Matt grasped the arms of his chair, as though he would crush the wood, as he said shortly, "go on."

At the tone of his voice, the old shepherd's heart sank.

41

The Other Side of the Story

With a prayer in his heart for the boy who lay dying in that strange underground chamber, the artist's father began.

"It is the story, Mr. Matthews, of a man and his only son, the last of their family. With them will perish—has perished one of the oldest and proudest names in our country.

"From his childhood this man was taught the honored traditions of his people, and, thus trained in pride of ancestry, grew up to believe that the supreme things of life are what his kind call education, refinement, and culture. In his shallow egotism, he came to measure all life by the standards of his people.

"It was in keeping with this that the man should enter the pulpit of the church of his ancestors, and it was due very largely, no doubt, to the same ancestral influence that he became what the world calls a successful minister of the gospel. But Christianity to him was but little more than culture, and his place in the church merely an opportunity to add to the honor of his name. Soon after leaving the seminary, he married. The crowning moment of his life was when his firstborn—a boy—was laid in his arms. The second child was a girl. There were no more.

"For ten years before her death the wife was an invalid. The little girl, too, was never strong, and six months after they buried the mother the daughter was laid beside her.

"You, sir, can understand how the father lavished every care upon his son. The first offspring of the parents' love, the sole survivor of his home, and the last to bear the name of a family centuries old, he was the only hope of a proud man's ambition.

"The boy was a beautiful child, a delicate, sensitive soul in a body of uncommon physical grace and strength, and the proud father loved to think of him as the flower of long ages of culture and refinement. The minister himself jealously educated his son, and the two grew to be friends, sir, constant companions. This, also, *you* will understand— you and your boy. But with all this the young man did not follow his father in choosing his profession. He—he became an artist."

Old Matt started from his seat. Aunt Mollie uttered an exclamation. But the shepherd, without pausing, continued: "When his schooling was completed the boy came into the Ozarks one summer to spend the season painting. The man had expected to go with his son. For months they had planned the trip together, but at last something prevented, and the father could not go—no, he could not go—" The speaker's voice broke. The big mountaineer was breathing hard; Aunt Mollie was crying.

Presently Mr. Howitt went on. "When the young artist returned to his father, among many sketches of the mountains, he brought one painting that received instant recognition. The people stood before it in crowds when it was exhibited in the art gallery; the papers were extravagant in their praise; the artist became famous; and wealthy patrons came to his studio to sit for their portraits. The picture was of a beautiful girl, standing by a spring, holding out a dripping cup of water."

At this a wild oath burst from the giant. Springing to his feet, he started toward the speaker. Aunt Mollie screamed, "Grant, oh, Grant! Think what Dad has done for us." The mountaineer paused.

"Mr. Matthews," said the shepherd, in trembling tones,

240

"for my sake, will you not hear me to the end?"

The big man dropped back heavily into his chair. "Go on," he said. But his voice was as the growl of a beast.

"The boy loved your girl, Mr. Matthews. It was as though he had left his soul in the hills. Night and day he heard her calling. The more his work was praised, the more his friends talked of honors and planned his future, the keener was his suffering, and most of all there was the shadow that had come between him and his father, breaking the old comradeship, and causing them to shun each other, though the father never knew why. The poor boy grew morose and despondent, giving way at times to spells of the deepest depression. He tried to lose himself in his work. He fled abroad and lived alone. It seemed a blight had fallen on his soul. The world called him mad. Many times he planned to take his life, but always the hope of meeting her again stopped him.

"At last he returned to this country determined to see her at any cost, and, if possible, gain her forgiveness and his father's consent to their marriage. He came into the hills only to find that the mother of his child had died of a broken heart.

"Then came the end. The artist disappeared, leaving a long, pitiful letter, saying that before the word reached his father, he would be dead. The most careful investigation brought nothing but convincing evidence that the unhappy boy had taken his own life. The artist knew that it would be a thousand times easier for the proud man to think his son dead than for him to know the truth, and he was right. Mr. Matthews, he was right. I cannot tell you of the man's suffering, but he found a little comfort in the reflection that such extravagant praise of his son's work had added to the honor of the family, for the lad's death was held by all to be the result of a disordered mind. There was not a whisper of wrongdoing. His life, they said, was without reproach, and even his sad mental condition was held to be evidence of his great genius.

"The minister was weak, sir. He knew something of the intellectual side of his religion and the history of his church, but he knew little, very little, of the God that could sustain him in such a trial. He was shamefully weak. He tried to run away from his trouble, and, because the papers had made so much of his work as a preacher, and because of his son's fame, he gave only the first part of his name thinking thus to get away from it all for a season.

"But God was to teach the proud man of culture and religious forms a great lesson, and to that end directed his steps. He was led here, here, sir, to your home, and you—you told him the story of his son's crime."

The shepherd paused. A hoarse whisper came from the giant in the chair. "You—you, Dad, your—name is—"

The other threw out his hand, as if to guard himself, and shrank back. "Hush, oh, hush! I have no name but the name by which you know me. The man who bore that name is dead. In all his pride of intellect and position he died. Your prayers for vengeance were answered, sir. You—you killed him, killed him as truly as if you had plunged a knife into his heart. And you—did—well."

Aunt Mollie moaned.

"Is that all?" growled the mountaineer.

"All! God, no! I—I must go on. I must tell you how the man you killed stayed in the hills and was born again. There was nothing else for him to do but stay in the hills. With the shame and horror of his boy's disgrace on his heart, he could not go back—back to the city, his friends and his church—to the old life. He knew that he could not hope to deceive them. He was not skilled in hiding things. Every kind word in praise of himself, or in praise of his son, would have been keenest torture. He was a coward; he dared not go back. His secret would have driven him mad, and he would have ended it all as his son had done. His only hope for peace was to stay here; here on the very spot where the wrong was done, and to do what little he could to atone for the crime.

"At first it was terrible; the long, lonely nights with no human friend near; the weight of shame; the memories; and the lonely wind—always the wind—in the trees—her voice, Pete said, calling for him to come. God, sir, I wonder the man did not die under his punishment!

"But God is good, Mr. Matthews. God is good and merciful. Every day out on the range with the sheep, the man felt the spirit of the hills, and little by little their strength and their peace entered into his life. The minister learned here, sir, what he had not learned in all his theological studies. He learned to know God, the God of these mountains. The hills taught him, and they came at last to stand between him and the trouble from which he had fled. The nights were no longer weary and long. He was never alone. The voices in the wilderness became friendly voices, for he learned their speech, and the poor girl ceased to call in the wailing wind. Then Dr. Coughlan came, and—"

Again the shepherd stopped. He could not go on. The light was gone from the sky and he felt the blackness of the night. But against the stars he could still see the crown of the mountain where his son lay. When he had gathered strength, he continued, saying simply, "Dr. Coughlan came, and—last night we learned that my son was not dead but living."

Again that growl like the growl of a wild beast came from the mountaineer. Silently Mr. Howitt prayed. "Go on," came the command in hoarse tones.

In halting, broken words, the shepherd faltered through the rest of his story as he told how, while using the cabin under the cliff as a studio, the artist had discovered the passage to the old Dewey cave; how, since his supposed death, he had spent the summers at the scene of his former happiness; how he had met his son roaming the hills at night, and had been able to have the boy with him much of the time; how he had been wounded the night Jim Lane was killed; and finally how Pete had led them to his bedside.

"He is dying yonder. Dr. Coughlan is with him—and

243

Pete—Pete is there, too. I—I came for you. He is calling for you. I came to tell you. All that a man may suffer here, he has suffered, sir. Your prayer has been doubly answered, Mr. Matthews. Both father and son are dead. The name— the old name is perished from the face of the earth. For Christ's dear sake, forgive my boy, and let him go. For my sake, sir, I—I can bear no more."

Who but He that looketh upon the heart of man could know the battle that was fought in the soul of that giant of the hills? He uttered no sound. He sat in his seat as if made of stone; save once, when he walked to the end of the porch to stand with clenched hands and passion-shaken frame, facing the dark clump of pines on the hill.

Slowly the moon climbed over the ridge and lighted the scene. The mountaineer returned to his chair. All at once he raised his head, and, leaning forward, looked long and earnestly at the old shepherd, where he sat crouching like a convict awaiting sentence.

From down the mill road came voices and the sound of horses' feet. Old Matt started, turning his head a moment to listen. The horses stopped at the lower gate.

"The children," said Aunt Mollie softly. "The children. Grant, oh, Grant! Sammy and our boy."

Then the shepherd felt a heavy hand on his shoulder, and a voice that had in it something new and strange said, "Dad—my brother—Daniel, I—I ain't got no education, an' I—don't know rightly how to say it—but, Daniel, what these hills have been to you, you—you have been to me. It's sure God's way, Daniel. Let's—let's go to the boy."

42

The Way of the Lower Trail

Fix—the—light, as it was—please? That's—it. Thank you, Doctor. How beautiful she is—how beautiful!" He seemed to gather strength, and looked carefully into the face of each member of the little group about the bed; the shepherd, Old Matt, Aunt Mollie, Pete, and the physician. Then he turned his eyes back to the painting. To the watchers, the girl in the picture, holding her brimming cup, seemed to smile back again.

"I loved her—I loved—her. She was my natural mate—my other self. I belonged to her—she to me. I—I can't tell you of that summer—when we were together—alone in the hills—the beautiful hills—away from the sham and the ugliness of the world that men have made. The beauty and inspiration of it all I put into my pictures, and I knew because of that they were good—I knew they would win a place for me—and—they did. Most of all—I put it there," he pointed to the painting on the wall, "and the crowd saw it and felt it, and did not know what it was. But I knew—I knew—all the time, I knew. Oh!—if that short summer could have been lengthened—into years, what might I not have done? Oh, God! That men—can be—so blind—so blind!"

For a time he lay exhausted, his face still turned toward the picture, but with eyes closed as though he dreamed. Then suddenly, he started up again, raising himself on his elbows, his eyes opened wide, and on his face a look of wondering gladness. They drew near.

"Do—do—you—hear? She is calling—she is calling again. Yes—sweetheart—yes, dear. I—I am—com—"

Old Matt and Aunt Mollie led the shepherd from the room.

And this way runs the trail that follows the lower level, where those who travel, as they go, look always over their shoulders with eyes of dread, and the gloomy shadows gather long before the day is done.

43

Poor Pete

They buried the artist in the cave as he had directed, close under the wall on the ledge above the canyon with no stone or mark of any sort to fix the place. The old mine which he had discovered was reached by one of the side passages far below in the depth of the mountain. the grave would never be disturbed.

For two weeks longer, Dr. Coughlan stayed with his friend; out on the hills with him all day, helping to cook their meals at the ranch, or sitting on the porch at the Matthews place when the day was gone. When the time finally came that he must go, the little physician said, as he grasped the shepherd's hand, "You're doing just right, Daniel; just right. Always did; always did. Blast it all! I would stay, too, but what would Sarah and the girls do? I'll come again next spring, Daniel, sure, sure, if I'm alive. Dont' worry, no one will ever know. Blast it all! I don't like to leave you, Daniel. Don't like it at all. But you are right, right, Daniel."

The old scholar stood in the doorway of his cabin to watch the wagon as it disappeared in the forest. He heard it rattle across the creek bottom below the ruined cabin under the bluff. He waited until from away up on Compton Ridge the sound of wheels came to him on the breeze that slipped down the mountainside. Still he waited, listening, listening, until there were only the voices of the forest and the bleating of the sheep in the corral. Slipping a book in his pocket

"There, where he went, up there in them white hills."

and taking a luncheon for himself and Pete, he opened the corral gate and followed his flock to the hills.

All that summer Pete was the shepherd's constant companion. At first he seemed not to understand. Frequently he would start off suddenly for the cave, only to return after a time, with that look of trouble upon his delicate face. Mr. Howitt tried to help the boy, and he appeared gradually to realize in part. Once he startled his old friend by saying quietly, "When are you goin', Dad?"

"Going where? Where does Pete think Dad is going?"

The boy was lying on his back on the grassy hillside watching the clouds. He pointed upward. "There, where *he* went, up there in the white hills. Pete knows."

The other looked long at the lad before answering quietly, "Dad does not know when he will go. But he is ready any time, now."

"Pete says better not wait long, Dad, 'cause Pete he's a-goin' an' course when he goes I've got to go 'long. Do you reckon Dad can see Pete when he is up there in them white hills? Some folks used to laugh at Pete when he told about the white hills, the flower things, the sky things, an' the moonlight things that play in the mists. An' once a fellow called Pete a fool, an' Young Matt whipped him awful. But folks wasn't really to blame, 'cause they couldn't see 'em. That's what *he* said. An' *he* knew, 'cause he could see 'em too. But Aunt Mollie, an' Uncle Matt, an' you all, they don't never laugh. They just say, 'Pete knows.' But they couldn't see the flower things, or the tree things neither. Only *he* could see."

The summer passed, and, when the blue gray haze took on the purple touch and all the woods and hills were dressed with cloth of gold, Pete went from the world in which he had never really belonged, nor had been at home. Mr. Howitt, writing to Dr. Coughlan of the boy's death, said:

"Here and there among men, there are those who pause in the hurried rush to listen to the call of a life that is more real. How often have we seen them, David, jostled and ridiculed by their fellows, pushed aside and forgotten, as incompetent or unworthy. He who sees and hears too much is cursed for a dreamer, a fanatic, or a fool, by the mad mob, who, having eyes, see not, ears and hear not, and refuse to understand.

"We build temples and churches, but will not worship in them; we hire spiritual advisers, but refuse to heed them; we buy bibles, but will not read them; believing in God, we do not fear Him; acknowledging Christ, we neither follow nor obey Him. Only when we can no longer strive in the battle for earthly honors or material wealth, do we turn to the unseen but more enduring things of life; and, with ears deafened by the din of selfish war and cruel violence, and eyes blinded by the glare of passing pomp and folly, we strive to hear and see the things we have so long refused to consider.

"Pete knew a world unseen by us, and we, therefore, fancied ourselves wiser than he. The wind in the pines, the rustle of the leaves, the murmur of the brook, the growl of the thunder, and the voices of the night were all understood and answered by him. The flowers, the trees, the rocks, the hills, the clouds were to him, not lifeless things, but living friends, who laughed and wept with him as he was gay or sorrowful.

" 'Poor Pete,' we said. Was he in truth, David, poorer or richer than we?"

They laid the boy beside his mother under the pines on the hills; the pines that showed so dark against the sky when the sun was down behind the ridge. And over his bed the wild vines lovingly wove a coverlet of softest green, while all his woodland friends gathered about his couch. Forest and hill and flower and cloud sang the songs he loved. All day the sunlight laid its wealth in bars of gold at his feet, and at night the moonlight things and the shadow things came out to play.

Summer and autumn slipped away; the winter passed;

spring came, with all the wonder of the resurrection of flower and leaf and blade. So peace and quiet came again into the shepherd's life. When no answer to his letter was received, and the doctor did not return as he had promised, the old man knew that the last link connecting him with the world was broken.

44

The Trail on the Sunlit Hills

When Young Matt first knew that Sammy had sent Ollie back to the city with no promise to follow, he took to the woods, and returned only after miles of tramping over the wildest, roughest part of the country. The big fellow said no word, but on his face was a look that his father understood, and the old mountaineer felt his own blood move more quickly at the sight.

But when Sammy with her books was fully established in the Matthews home, and Young Matt seemed always, as the weeks went by, to find her reading things that he could not understand, he was made to realize more fully what her studies with the shepherd meant. He came to feel that she had already crossed the threshold into that world where Mr. Howitt lived. And, thinking that he himself could never enter, he grew lonely and afraid.

With the quickness that was so marked in her character, Sammy grasped the meaning of his trouble almost before Young Matt himself knew fully what it was. Then the girl, with much care and tact, set about helping him to see the truths which the shepherd had revealed to her.

All through summer and fall, when the day's work was done, or on a Sunday afternoon, they were together, and gradually the woods and the hills, with all the wild life that is in them, began to have for the young man a new meaning; or, rather, he learned little by little to read the message that lay on the open pages. First a word here and there, then sentences, then paragraphs, and soon he was reading alone, as he tramped the hills for stray stock, or worked in the mountain field. The idle days of winter and the long evenings were spent in reading aloud from the books that had come to mean most to her.

So she led him on slowly, along the way that her teacher had pointed out to her, but always as they went, he saw her going before, far ahead, and he knew that in the things that men call education, he could never hope to stand by her side. But he was beginning to ask, are there not after all things that lie still deeper in life than even these?

Often he would go to his old friend in the Hollow with some thought, and the shepherd, seeing how it was, would smile as he helped the lad on his way. The scholar looked forward with confidence to the time when Young Matt would discover for himself, as Sammy had found for herself, that the only common ground whereon men and women may meet in safety is the ground of their manhood and womanhood.

And so it was, on that spring morning when the young giant felt the red life throbbing strongly in his great limbs, as he followed his team to and fro across the field. And in his voice, as he shouted to his horses at the end of the furrow, there was something under the words, something of a longing, something also of a challenge.

Sammy was going to spend the day with her friends on Jake Creek. She had not been to see Mandy since the night of her father's death. As she went, she stopped at the lower end of the field to shout a merry word to the man with the plow, and it was sometime later when the big fellow again started his team. The challenge in his tone had grown bolder.

Sammy returned that afternoon in time for the evening meal, and Aunt Mollie thought, as the girl came up the walk, that the young woman had never looked so beautiful. "Why, honey," she said, "you're just a-bubblin' over with life. Your cheeks are as rosy, your eyes are as sparklin', you're fairly shinin' all over. Your ride sure done you good." The young woman replied with a hug that made her admirer gasp. "Law, child, you're strong as a young panther. You walk like one too, so kind of strong, easy like." The girl laughed. "I hope I don't impress everybody that way, Aunt Mollie. I don't believe I want to be like a panther. I'd rather be like—like—" "Like what, child?" "Like you, just like you; the best, the very best woman in the whole world, because you've got the best and biggest heart." She looked back over her shoulder laughing, as she ran into the house.

When Young Matt came in from the field, Sammy went out to the barn, while he unharnessed his team. "Are you very tired tonight?" she asked.

The big fellow smiled. "Tired? Me tired? Where do you want to go? Haven't you ridden enough today? I should think you'd be tired yourself."

"Tired? Me tired?" said the girl. "I don't want to ride. I want to walk. It's such a lovely evening, and there's going to be a moon. I have been thinking all day that I would like to walk over home after supper, if you cared to go."

That night the work within the house and the chores about the barn were finished in a remarkably short time. The young man and woman started down the Old Trail like two school children, while the father and mother sat on the porch and heard their voices die away on the mountainside below.

The girl went first along the little path, moving with that light, sure step that belongs only to perfect health, the health of the woods and hills. The man followed, walking with the same sure, easy step, strength and power revealed in every movement of his body. Two splendid creatures they were— masterpieces of the Creator's handiwork; made by Him who created man, male and female, and bade them have dominion "over every living thing that moveth upon the earth";

kings by divine right.

In the belt of timber, where the trail to the ranch branches off, they met the shepherd on his way to the house for an evening visit. The old man paused only long enough to greet them, and pushed on up the hill, for he saw by their faces that the time was come.

Sammy had grown very quiet when they rounded the shoulder of Dewey, and they went in silence down to the cabin on the southern slope of the mountain. The girl asked Young Matt to wait for her at the gate, and, going to the house, she entered alone.

A short time she remained in the familiar rooms, then, slipping out through the rear door, ran through the woods to the little glen back of the house. Dropping beside the mound, she buried her face in the cool grass, as she whispered, "Oh, Daddy, Daddy Jim! I wish you were here tonight, this night that means so much to me. Do you know how happy I am, Daddy? Do you know, I wonder?" The twilight deepened. "I must go now, Daddy, I must go to him. You told me you would trust me anywhere with him. He is waiting for me, now; but I wish—oh, I wish that you were here tonight, Daddy Jim!"

Quickly she made her way back to the cabin, passed through the house, and rejoined Young Matt. The two returned silently up the mountainside, to the higher levels, where the light still lingered, though the sun was down. At the Lookout they stopped.

"We'll wait for the moon, here," she said, and so seated on a big rock, they watched the last of the evening go out from the west. From forest depth and mountainside came the myriad voices of Nature's chorus, blending softly in the evening hymn. And, rising clear above the low-breathed tones, yet in perfect harmony, came a whip-poor-will's plaintive call floating up from the darkness below; the sweet cooing of a wood dove in a tree on the ridge, and the chirping of a cricket in a nearby crevice of the ledge. Like shadowy spirits, the bats flitted here and there in the gathering gloom. The two on the mountain's shoulder felt themselves alone above it all; above it all, yet still a part of all.

Then the moon looked over the mountain behind them, turning Mutton Hollow into a wondrous sea of misty light out of which the higher hills lifted their heads like fairy islands. The girl spoke. "Come, Matt, we must go now. Help me down."

He slipped from his seat and stood beside the rock with uplifted arms. Sammy leaned forward and placed her hands upon his shoulders. He felt her breath upon his forehead. The next instant he held her close.

So they went home along the trail that is nobody knows how old, and the narrow path that was made by those who walked one before the other, they found wide enough for two.

Dad Howitt, returning to the ranch, saw them coming so in the moonlight, and slipped aside from the path into the deeper shadows. As they passed, the old shepherd, scholar and poet stood with bowed, uncovered head. When they were gone and their low voices were no longer heard, he said aloud, "What God hath joined; what God hath joined."

And this way runs the trail that lies along the higher, sunlit hills where those who journey see afar and the light lingers even when the day is done.

The two on the mountain's shoulder felt themselves alone above it all.

45

Some Years Later

A wandering artist, searching for new field, found his way into the Ozark country. One day, as he painted in the hills, a flock of sheep came over the ridge through a low gap, and worked slowly along the mountainside. A few moments later, the worker at the easel lifted his eyes from the canvas to find himself regarded by an old man in the dress of a native.

"Hello, uncle. Fine day," said the artist shortly, his eyes again upon his picture.

"The God of these hills gives us many such, young sir, and all His days are good."

The painter's hand paused between palette and canvas, and his face was turned toward the speaker in wonder. Every word was perfect in accent of the highest culture, and the deep, musical tone of the voice was remarkable in one with the speaker's snowy hair and beard. The young man arose to his feet. "I beg your pardon, sir. I thought—" He hesitated, as he again took in the rude dress of the other. The brown eyes, under their white shaggy brows, lighted with good nature. "You mean, young sir, that you did not think. 'Tis the privilege of youth, make the most of it. Very soon old age will rob you of your freedom, and force you to think, whether you will or no. Your greeting under the circumstance is surely excusable. It is I who should beg pardon, for I have interrupted your study, and I have no excuse. Neither my youth nor my occupation will plead for me."

The charm of his voice and manner was irresistible. The painter stepped forward with outstretched hand. "Indeed, sir, I am delighted to meet you. I am here for the summer from Chicago. My camp is over there."

The other grasped the offered hand cordially. "I am Daniel Howitt, young sir, from the sheep ranch in Mutton Hollow. Dad Howitt, the people call me. So you see you were not far wrong when you hailed me 'Uncle.' Uncle and Dad are 'sure close kin,' as Preachin' Bill would say."

Both men laughed, and the painter offered his folding easel chair. "Thank you, no. Here is a couch to which I am more accustomed. I will rest here, if you please." The old man stretched himself upon the grassy slope. "Do you like my hills?" he asked. "But I am sure you do," he added, as his eye dwelt fondly upon the landscape.

"Ah, you are the owner of this land, then? I was wondering who—"

"No, no, young sir," the old man interrupted, laughing again. "Others pay the taxes. These hills belong to me only as they belong to all who have the grace to love them. They will give you great treasure, that you may give again to others, who have not your good strength to escape from the things that men make and do in the restless world over there. One of your noble craft could scarcely fail to find the good things God has written on this page of His great book. Your brothers need the truths that you will read here, unless the world has greatly changed."

"You are not then a native of this country?"

"I was a native of that world yonder, young sir. Before your day, they knew me, but long since, they have forgotten. When I died there, I was born again in these mountains. And so," he finished with a smile, "I am, as you see, a native. It is long now since I met one from beyond the ridges. I will not likely meet another."

"I wonder that others have not discovered the real beauty

of the Ozarks," remarked the painter.

The old shepherd answered softly, "One did." Then rising to his feet and pointing to Roark valley, he said, "Before many years a railroad will find its way yonder. Then many will come, and the beautiful hills that have been my strength and peace will become the haunt of careless idlers. and a place of revelry. I am glad that I shall not be here. but I must not keep you longer from your duties."

"I shall see you again, shall I not?" The painter was loath to let him go.

"More often than will be good for your picture, I fear. You must work hard, young sir, while the book of God is still open, and God's message is easily read. When the outside world comes, men will turn the page, and you may lose the place."

After that they met often, and one day the old man led the artist to where a big house looked down upon a ridge-encircled valley. Though built of logs without, the house within was finished and furnished in excellent taste. To his surprise, the painter found one room lined with shelves, and upon the shelves the best things that men have written for their fellows. In another room was a piano. The floors were covered with rugs. Draperies and hangings softened the atmosphere, and the walls were hung with pictures, not many, but good and true; pictures that had power over those who looked upon them. The largest painting hung in the library and was veiled.

"My daughter, Mrs. Matthews," said the old shepherd, as he presented the stranger to the mistress of the house. In all his search for beauty, never had the artist looked upon such a form and such a face. It was a marvelous blending of the physical with the intellectual and spiritual. A firm step was heard on the porch. "My husband," said the lady. And the stranger rose to greet—the woman's *mate*. The children of this father and mother were like them, or, as the visitor afterwards said in his extravagant way, "like young gods for beauty and strength."

The next summer the painter went again to the Ozarks. Even as he was greeted by the strong master of the hills and his charming wife, there fell upon his ears a dull report as of distant cannon; then another, and another. They led him across the yard, and there to the north on the other side of Roark, Men were tearing up the mountain to make way for the railroad. As they looked, another blast sent the rocks flying, while the sound rolled and echoed through the peaceful hills.

The artist turned to his friends with questioning eyes. "Mr. Howitt said it would come. Is he—is he well?"

Mrs. Matthews answered softly, "Dad left us while the surveyors were at work. He sleeps yonder." She pointed to Dewey Bald.

Then they went into the library, where the large picture was unveiled. When the artist saw it, he exclaimed, "Mad Howard's lost masterpiece! How—where did you find it?"

"It was Father Howitt's request that I tell you the story, Sammy replied.

And then she told the artist a part of that which I have set down here.